No Girl
Left
Behind

A JAMIE AUSTEN Thriller

TERRY TOLER

PRAISE FOR THE JAMIE AUSTEN AND ALEX HALEE BOOKS

"I enjoy all the Alex and Jamie books because I prefer to read clean stories that include mystery and intrigue."

"Love his stories! Suspense and romance combined! Kept me guessing until the end!"

"I would definitely recommend these fantastic books."

"I read it in one sitting even while eating my lunch. Well done Mr. Toler!"

"The perfect read that projects enough suspense action to keep you on the edge-of-your-seat."

"This is an exciting spy thriller with complex, interesting characters. You can't help but root for the main characters."

"The characters are great! Can't wait to read the next book."

"Wonderful story. It is full of action and suspense. It's also heartwarming, and I love its message. It kept me awake at night to finish it."

"Love Toler's stories! Suspense and romance combined! Kept me guessing until the end!"

"I would recommend this book to anyone who wants to read clean action."

"Love Jamie, the female Jack Reacher."

"Love that Jamie Austen is top notch take no prisoners kind of woman. Saving kidnapped young women with her other CIA counterparts."

"It kept me reading page after page not wanting to stop. Action after action and always a new twist to the story. I can't wait for the next story."

"I enjoyed the rapid pace of the story as well as the development of the characters. A thrilling story. Well done."

"Enthralling is my best description of this 'nine lives' epic case assignment for a government female agent. Constantly in action and never boring."

"This series gives insights to current issues in the world. I found it interesting and easy to understand. I would recommend it to anyone who loves thrills and action. It is clean and a little heartwarming."

"I've read all the books in this series and have more than enjoyed them!"

"The ending made me smile because that's Jamie in a nutshell."

"Oh man! This is tugging at my heartstrings."

"That Jamie isn't afraid of anything! Always true to herself. 😊 Let the intrigue begin! 😊"

BOOKS BY TERRY TOLER

Fiction

The Longest Day
The Reformation of Mars
The Great Wall of Ven-Us
Saturn: The Eden Experiment
The Late, Great Planet Jupiter
Save The Girls
The Ingenue
The Blue Rose
Saving Sara
Save The Queen
No Girl Left Behind
The Launch
Body Count

Non-Fiction

How to Make More Than a Million Dollars
The Heart Attacked
Seven Years of Promise
Mission Possible
Marriage Made in Heaven
21 Days to Physical Healing
21 Days to Spiritual Fitness
21 Days to Divine Health
21 Days to a Great Marriage
21 Days to Financial Freedom
21 Days to Sharing Your Faith
21 Days to Mission Possible
7 Days to Emotional Freedom
Uncommon Finances
Uncommon Marriage
Uncommon Health
Suddenly Free
Feeling Free

For more information on these books and other resources
visit TerryToler.com.

FROM THE AUTHOR
PARENTAL GUIDANCE SUGGESTED

The scenes and descriptions depicted in this book may not be suitable for children.
—Terry Toler

39,000 girls under the age of eighteen are forced into marriages every day around the world.

The UN estimates that more than 5,000 women and girls die in honor killings worldwide each year.

1

Abu Dhabi

"I'll give you thirty million American dollars for it," I said to the Sheikh.

"I must have thirty-five, Mrs. Steele," Sheikh Saad Cemal Shakir said to me. My actual name was Jamie Austen, but Jamie Steele was the name I used for my cover.

The object of our negotiation was a renaissance era painting by Halil Dereli called *Tranquility*. A famous Persian artist who depicted the moment in the Bible when the two sons of Abraham, Isaac, and Ishmael, finally made peace with each other. For me, the painting was a biblical story. For the Sheikh, he'd consider it a depiction of the Quran account, which was probably more accurate, considering the nationality of the artist.

I wouldn't normally be interested in such a work, but I already had a buyer at forty million. Five million was a nice profit, but ten million was better.

"Thirty-one is my best offer," I said.

"Thirty-four is my lowest price," he countered.

"I'll have to think about it."

The painting was located in a high-end art gallery in Abu Dhabi City off Zayed the Second Street. Actually, everything in Abu Dhabi was high-end. At least in the city. Including the Sheikh who was on the high-end of the proverbial food chain when it came to riches and power. A cousin to the Crown Prince, he and his family were considered royalty. Along with his title, he had considerable wealth estimated to be upward of fifty billion dollars. Which made me wonder why he was quibbling with me over pocket change.

"Then we must think about it over dinner," the Sheikh said. "At my home. I have to show you my other artwork."

I knew that was coming. The Sheikh had a reputation as a woman-izer. To this point, he'd been a gentleman. I was hoping to close the deal by only having to endure his mild flirtations.

"I never mix business and pleasure," I said.

"Mrs. Jamie Steele, nothing is more pleasurable than discussing money."

"I'm a happily married woman," I retorted.

"There are many happily married men, but no happily married women. A woman is impossible to keep happy." With that statement, he roared in laughter. I gave him an obligatory laugh, although that wasn't the first time he had disparaged women that day.

I was married. To Alex Halee. Had been for a little over a year. To-gether we owned a company called AJAX which bought and sold art. The company was actually a cover for covert operations for the CIA. Off the books. This trip was strictly related to the art business, and no mission objective was associated with it. The purchase of the painting would be a favor for one of our best customers, not to mention a nice profit for AJAX.

"I agree that business can be pleasurable," I said, "which is why I'm going to make you happy and give you thirty-two million dollars for the painting."

"If you really wanted to make me happy, you'd give me thirty-three million and have dinner with me. I promise we won't do anything that you don't want to do."

"Split the difference," I said, ignoring his comment.

"You drive a hard bargain, Mrs. Steele."

"You paid nine million for it only five years ago!"

"It was an investment. I don't particularly like the painting. But it has grown on me which is why I'm reluctant to let it go for such a low price. It has... what do you Americans say? Sentimental value."

The Sheikh was lying. He couldn't care less about the painting. This was strictly a business deal. That, and he wanted to get me back to his place which was why he was dragging out the negotiations. I'm trained to read people. He would've sold me the painting at twenty-nine million. The ruse was to see how far he could get with me. Which was no further than this gallery. I'd walk away from the deal if I had to before I'd go back to his house alone.

"My friend," I said. "I know all about you. Since we've begun this conversation, you've made about twenty million dollars from your oil interests."

He nodded his head but changed the subject. "Do you know what my name means?" he asked.

"Why don't you tell me?" I said sweetly. While I didn't want to cross the line of flirting, I was anxious to get the deal closed and get back on my plane headed home. I'd bat my eyelashes a couple of times if it'd get the negotiations over with sooner. The Bombardier Global 7000 luxury jet Alex and I stole from a Turkish oligarch, was sitting on the tarmac at Abu Dhabi International Airport, warming its jets. My pilot, A-Rad, nicknamed such because he was a radical when it came to risk taking, was no doubt seeing to all the preparations. He'd wanted to come with me, but I insisted I could handle it.

The Sheikh explained the meaning of his names. "Saad means happiness. Your term for it is bliss, I believe. My surname, Shakir, means fortunate and lucky. My middle name is Cemal. Are you aware of its origin?"

"I'm not." I wanted to look at my watch but didn't want to be rude. I was prepared to meet his price of thirty-three million, just to get this over with.

"Cemal means handsome. Would you agree that all these names fit me perfectly?"

"Of course," I said, with nothing more than a smile.

He was handsome. Fifty-eight years old. Fit. Everything about him exuded royalty. Soft hands. Confident manner. The only thing weathered was his face which had endured the constant onslaught of hot desert sun, stiff winds, and blowing sand through the years.

I wanted to keep our focus. We were making progress. "Back to the painting," I said, "Do we have a deal?"

"What was our last price?"

He knew full well what it was.

"You're a very beautiful lady, Mrs. Steele. I like your outfit."

I simply nodded a thank you. He continued to stall. I'd purposefully toned my dress down, hoping it would make him less interested. Normally, I'd be wearing a short, tight fitting dress for such a meeting. Not to be noticed. The short length was so my legs would be free in the event I ran into trouble. Over the years of running dangerous missions, my knees, heels, feet, and legs had become like lethal weapons and had gotten me out of more jams than I could remember.

I'd prefer what I was wearing now, which was a skirt that came below my knees. My shoulders were covered, and the blouse was up to my neckline. A scarf was around my neck in case I needed to cover my head. The skirt was a couple sizes too big, held up by a belt, but not too tight, so it wouldn't be considered form fitting. Modest, but not conducive for combat in close quarters. Not that I was concerned about any type of confrontation. This was an almost zero-risk adventure.

For the most part, Abu Dhabi City was safer than most big cities. As long as you didn't do anything to attract the attention of the authorities. Immodest dress was one way to get in trouble. Tourists could get arrested for any number of things, including public displays of affection. It's a good thing Alex wasn't there. Alex had a hard time keeping his hands off me. In Abu Dhabi, that was frowned upon. The most we could do in public was hold hands. Even that was scoffed at. Anything else could result in expulsion. Fortunately, he wasn't here or I'm sure he'd test the limits of their laws.

Of course, those rules didn't apply to the Sheikh. He had his own little harem with him at the art gallery. Four girls. All stunningly beautiful. Standing off to the side. Their dresses were considerably shorter than my skirt. I doubted any of them were his wife, and I was sure all were meant for more than eye candy. I knew the look on their faces. They were at his beck and call to provide whatever services he desired.

Clearly his ladies-in-waiting, which made me wonder why he wanted me so much. Probably because he couldn't have me. Powerful men like the Sheikh were often more interested in the pursuit than in the actual conquest.

The Sheikh had more girls than bodyguards. Two bulky men stood off in the corner looking bored. Armed, but not at all concerned by me. If I wanted, I could kill the Sheikh in seconds. They didn't even search me. If they had, they might've found a knife hidden in the hem of my dress.

"What about the price?" I said, growing impatient after nothing was said for nearly a minute. "You were at thirty-three million, I'm at thirty-two. Shall we split the difference and call it a day?"

"What about dinner?"

"Not going to happen."

"He let out a huge sigh. Okay. We have a deal."

"Excellent. I've already taken the liberty to draw up the paperwork. If you'll give me wiring instructions, I'll see that the money is in your account later today."

I pulled out a bill of sale, wrote down the purchase price, and the Sheikh signed it. "I'll give you a copy at closing."

"I only take cashier checks." He probably never gave out his bank account information as a precaution. I didn't either.

"I can arrange that, but it'll take more time. Shall we meet in the morning?"

"For breakfast? At my house?"

"How about right here? Do you have a restroom I can use?"

"Down the hall and to the right."

"I'll be right back."

While I hated the fact that I'd have to spend the night in Abu Dhabi, closing the deal was worth it. I could sleep on my plane.

The restroom was as luxurious as the rest of the art gallery. Gold and white decorative marble everywhere with gold plated fixtures. I went into one of the stalls and allowed myself a moment to relax. I'd barely sat down when a door opened.

For some reason, it startled me.

Someone entered.

Quiet footsteps. Stiletto heels.

I was suddenly holding my breath, though I didn't know why.

I heard shuffling around.

The woman didn't go into one of the stalls. Didn't turn on any water. I didn't hear the sound of ruffling paper towels or drying of hands.

Probably one of the Sheikh's girls. Maybe she was checking her makeup.

I heard a squeaking sound.

Completely out of place.

What's that?

I stood and reassembled my skirt. Then paused. While I was dying to know who was out there and what she was doing, I preferred to stay out of sight.

When I heard the door open and close, I still waited a good ten to twenty seconds to make sure the person was gone.

I cracked open the bathroom stall and peeked around it.

My heart skipped a beat.

On the bathroom mirror was writing.

In red lipstick.

Help Me.

I glanced at the door again. Then back at the words. Was it one of the Sheik's girls? Who else could it be? Was she in danger? Was she being held against her will?

My mind ran through the images of the girls in the art gallery. Only one was wearing red lipstick. A French woman. I noticed her because she seemed nervous. Strikingly beautiful. Model pretty. Too thin. Black hair cropped short. A bob just above her shoulders in a stylish cut.

What do I do?

I rested my hands on the bathroom counter and leaned into them, staring at the words on the mirror. My role with the CIA was to infiltrate sex trafficking rings and rescue girls. While I wasn't on a mission, I was always on the lookout for girls who needed rescuing. The thought never occurred to me that I'd find that in Abu Dhabi. Not that I was naïve enough to believe it didn't exist there. These girls were clearly prostituting. But I generally focused my energies on sex slaves and girls who had no choice in the matter.

I assumed these girls were there on their own volition and were well paid for their services. That didn't mean I wasn't sympathetic. It's just that I didn't normally risk my life for those types of girls. Why should I care about them more than they care about themselves?

The easy thing to do was close the deal on the painting and get out of town. None of my business.

I couldn't.

Now it was personal. The girl made it my business when she reached out to me for help.

Curly would tell me to step away. He was my trainer with the CIA. He's the one who made me who I was. A trained operative. A killer if necessary. Curly said I was the best he'd ever trained. But he'd say not to run a mission by the seat of my pants. Do reconnaissance. Surveillance. Have a planned-out strategy. Not that things don't often go off kilter once you're in the throes. You just don't go into it that way.

Alex would say for me to use my own judgment. Brad, my CIA handler, would say no way. A-Rad would be raring to go. A tie. Two for taking action; two against.

What would I do? That wasn't even a question. I always fell on the side of helping people. This woman needed help. She probably risked her own life to ask me for it. How could I walk away?

I got out several paper towels, dipped them in water, and scrubbed off the writing on the mirror. I didn't want to leave the message for anyone else to see. The Sheikh was a powerful man. If he were holding women against their will, then he was evil as well. Dangerous. Not someone to take lightly. He was even willing to bring these ladies out in public. That's how confident he was of his hold over them.

What were my options? I couldn't act there at the gallery. My cover would be blown, and I had no exit or extraction strategy. Curly was right. I needed a plan.

It's settled.

I knew what to do.

I walked out of the bathroom and right up to the Sheikh and said, "If the invitation is still open, I'd love to join you for dinner."

A broad smile came on his face.

I hoped I didn't regret it.

2

Amina

Amina Noorani's name in Arabic meant safe and protected. The seventeen-year-old felt anything but. Darkness had fallen on the desert, and she was walking alone on the road between her work and her home.

Her father was to blame. She'd just finished a twelve-hour work shift at a local hotel. Her seventh in eight days. The night before, her employer had kept her thirty minutes late. When he finally let her go, her al'ab—father, daddy, tribal patriarch, and elder—was outside in the parking lot, waiting on her. Furious that she had wasted so much of his time.

"How is it my fault, Daddy?" she'd asked with tears building up in her eyes. One of the few times in her life she dared talk back to him.

"You work too slow. You must've been slacking off."

"I wasn't Daddy, I promise. He had more work for me to do than usual."

Which was true. Normally she just cleaned the rooms. That day, she had to help out in the kitchen and clean dishes for hours. She'd worked so hard, every muscle in her body ached. Her hands had blisters from scrubbing bathrooms with inadequate supplies, harsh chemicals, and an exacting boss. Worse than her own father, if that were even possible.

"Tomorrow, you can walk home," her father said. "That'll teach you a lesson."

And that's where she found herself now. Walking on a mostly deserted road, forcing her aching feet to put one step in front of the other so she could complete the five mile walk as quickly as possible. Of course, when she got home, at least two hours of chores awaited her. Maybe sometime after midnight, she could fall into bed, cry herself to sleep, and start the same arduous routine all over again the next morning.

Car headlights suddenly appeared on the horizon, coming toward her. It passed by, stopped, changed directions, and began heading back in her direction. It pulled up next to her with the passenger side window down. She strained in the darkness to see who it was. If a woman, perhaps she could catch a ride.

"Can I give you a ride?" a familiar voice said.

"No thank you," she said, and kept walking. The voice belonged to Waseem Akbar. A man who lived in her community but was from a different tribe. In the United Arab Emirates, generally known as UAE, most people were identified by the tribe they belonged to. Arab Skulls was another name for the tribal system. Members didn't actually belong to tribes; they were born into them. Amina was part of Al Parsa tribe, a subtribe on the lower end of the powerful Ghazi tribe.

He pulled up next to her again and said, "Come on. Get in. It's a long walk."

The laws of her tribe stated that girls could not fraternize with boys of another tribe. Tribes in the UAE were segmented into four main social classes. Amina was part of the lowest class. While Akbar was in her same social class, he wasn't a boy her father would choose for her.

The car pulled up alongside, again interrupting her thoughts. This time she noticed three men in the back seat. She strained to see who they were. Since her face was partially covered to protect from the blowing sand, they probably didn't know who she was.

"It's too far to walk," Akbar said. "Get in. We won't tell anyone. I'll let you out before we get to the village."

Amina didn't respond and kept walking, even though every part of her being wanted to accept the offer. But even talking to Akbar was against the tribal laws. A woman wasn't allowed to converse with another man in public who was not a relative. Punishable by a hundred lashes. If she was lucky. Six months to a year in jail, if she wasn't.

More problematic was that one of the men in the back seat was married. Those laws were even stricter. If she were caught talking to a married man, she could be thrown out of her own tribe. Her father might disown her. With no tribe to provide or protect her, she'd become destitute.

If a member broke the law, the elders dealt out their own punishment after the legal system was done with the violator. They were especially harsh on women.

Many tribes had relaxed social norms, and women were given more participation in the workforce and education. Not so in her tribe. Marriages were arranged. She'd be forced to work these twelve-hour days until her eighteenth birthday to prove her worth to a potential husband.

At eighteen, she'd have to quit to concentrate on marriage and raising children. Once that happened, for all practical purposes, she was a slave. Every aspect of her life would be controlled by her husband.

The choice would be made soon. The quality of the rest of her life was based on that choice. If she was lucky enough to get a gentle and kind man, things might not be so bad. If she got someone like her father, she'd rather just shrivel up and die. Getting in the car with this man might ruin it all. Her future husband might consider her damaged goods even if nothing happened. Unfair, but how life was for women in her tribe.

Amina had long since accepted her fate. She had no delusions about crusading for women's rights. Some fought against the unfair treatment of women, and the consequences were swift and cruel. A number of women and young girls had been stoned to death in the village square. She and the other girls were forced to watch. The elders called it a deterrent. It worked on Amina. From an early age, she lived under the constant fear of doing something wrong, and she never once purposefully broke a rule.

Shy and soft-spoken, her goal was to keep her nose to the grindstone and stay out of trouble. The only reason she was more educated than most women in her tribe was because of her mother, Samitah, who had secretly taught her the ways of the world from an early age. She'd taught her how to read and write, and Amina devoured every book she could find. To this day, her father didn't even know the extent of Amina's learning. He'd be furious if he did know. Something she didn't understand.

Her mom also drilled in her the importance of keeping the tribal laws. The one warning that kept resonating in Amina's mind at that moment was, *a woman who is raped by a married man has committed adultery. The punishment is death.*

Why did that come to mind?

Amina kept walking.

She had a bad feeling about this.

For whatever reason, the car was still behind her. Following at a slow pace.

She glanced around to see if there was any place where she could hide.

The road was desolate. She could see the lights of her village ahead, but she was still a couple miles away. The fields to the right and left were flat, with not even a rock or tree big enough to hide behind.

She quickened her steps, even though her feet were crying out in protest. Her heartbeat pounded now. Tears escaped from her eyes, dampening the cloth of her hijab.

She crossed to the other side of the road, so she was walking into the traffic. Away from the car. At least there, she could see it out of the corner of her eye. If someone came, she could flag them down. Except, there was no traffic. What she'd give for a car to suddenly appear.

The car behind sped up. The racing engine startled her even though she expected it.

Then it came to a sudden stop. Just ahead of her. Thirty or forty paces ahead. The tires screeched as Akbar slammed on the brakes.

It suddenly accelerated backward. Toward her.

Amina let out a scream.

She jumped out of the way or the car would've hit her.

Instinctively, she took off running. Faster than she'd ever run before in her life. A glance back confirmed her worst nightmare. Two of the men were out of the car, running toward her. The car sped up and was in front of her in no time.

The other two men got out.

Amina stopped running.

The men behind stopped running as well but kept walking slowly toward her.

Amina sat down on the road and put herself into a ball and sobbed.

Resigned to what she knew would happen next.

3

Bianca

Sheikh Saad Shakir's house
Halfway between Abu Dhabi and Dubai

The drive to the Sheikh's house for dinner took less than a half hour, and I arrived an hour early to get a lay of the land. Spying, by definition, was gathering information. We in the industry called it "intel." Curly drilled in us the need to go into every mission with as much information as possible. Knowledge was power, he always said. At some point, information would save your life. It only had to save my life once to be worth the effort to gather it every time.

Making a move to rescue Saad Shakir's girl tonight wasn't in the plans. But if the opportunity did present itself or I ran into trouble for some reason, I wanted to be prepared. Curly's words echoed in my head. *Don't go into a situation blind. Know the exit points. The roads in and out. Assess the threats. Envision every possible scenario.*

Get the house floor plans if possible, I could hear him say in my head. Something which was possible.

Alex, my husband, was the best computer hacker in the world. Within a few minutes, he found the floor plans to the Sheikh's home through the internet. He didn't say how, and I didn't ask. More than likely he and his team hacked into the computer of Saad's architect. After dating for four years and a year of marriage, I'd begun to take Alex's skills for granted. AJAX now had more than a dozen hackers working for us back in Virginia. Combined with the resources of the CIA, we had the ability to reach anywhere in the world to execute a plan in short notice.

Brad, our CIA handler, sent me satellite images of the sprawling estate that covered ninety-two acres. They didn't show me much more than what I found by simply looking at the home on Google Earth. What he did send that I didn't have and couldn't get on my own was the Sheikh's CIA file which was noticeably shy of information. I particularly wanted to know if Saad had any terrorist ties. A man of that wealth often made his money from drug smuggling and arms dealing. The Sheikh seemed to be running an honest operation and made his money through oil production.

The worst that could be said about him was his obsession with partying and weakness for beautiful ladies. As I already knew, he always had to be surrounded by them.

The only thing my surveillance efforts showed was that I didn't have much to worry about on the outside. No guard gates. No local police presence. A couple of armed security guards walking around the outside was about it. One road in and out was well maintained and free of traffic.

The main concern driving over there were the camels that often crossed the roads. I was driving a Lamborghini that I'd rented from a luxury car dealership in Abu Dhabi City. Any collision with a camel, and my money was on the camel coming out of it better than me.

The car was something I never could've done while working for the CIA. With AJAX, it fit my cover perfectly. If I were going to play the part of a wealthy art dealer, then I could add the toys to make it look legitimate. Perks of the trade. I loved our new role with AJAX. Not just because of the car, but because it gave us the freedom to choose our own missions. Before, I'd never have gotten permission from Brad to have dinner with Saad and consider helping the French girl. Not with my flimsy amount of information. Brad would've argued that the risks were too great to operate a CIA mission in the United Arab Emirates to rescue a single girl.

Now I got to make the decision. Alex was the only one I really had to run it by. I could pursue it or abort at any time. At this point, I saw no reason not to pursue it further.

The main problem for me was on the inside of the house.

Saad was inappropriate from the moment I stepped through the door. He welcomed me with a huge smile on his face and a drink already in his hand. With his free hand, he pulled me close to him, so our bodies touched and then he kissed me on both cheeks, his lips trying to brush mine as he passed from one side of my cheek to the other.

I almost gagged from the excess aftershave.

Disgusting.

But I was prepared. This wasn't the first time I'd been hit on, and it wouldn't be the last. I'd endured worse. Although honestly, I preferred a combatant with a gun to one with grabby hands. Nevertheless, there was a purpose to the evening. A woman's life was presumably in danger, and I was her best hope. She had no doubt endured more than I ever would. Restraint was the only thing preventing me from kicking Saad between the legs so hard, he'd never be able to use it again. Something I might've done if I didn't want to protect my cover and also didn't want to close on the painting.

The French woman stood off to the side when I made my entrance which surprised me as soon as I saw her. I expected to see all four women from the art gallery. Perhaps even more. She was the only one. I sensed her nervousness from across the room.

"Who is the beautiful lady?" I asked the Sheikh, as I extricated myself from his hand that gripped my waist. "I remember you from the art gallery."

I walked toward her as I said it.

"Meet the lovely Bianca," the Sheikh said proudly, like he was showing me one of his possessions.

I kissed her on both of her cheeks. As I did, I whispered in her ear, "I can help you."

She nodded and looked away nervously, which told me all I needed to know. Bianca was the one who had written *help me* on the mirror in the bathroom at the art gallery. No doubt about it. I had a plan on how to communicate with her, but now wasn't the time.

The Sheikh's hand had already grabbed my arm and was ushering me out of the foyer and into the main living area.

"May I have a tour of the house?" I asked, pulling away slightly. My way of doing inside reconnaissance. While I had memorized the floor plan, no amount of planning beat seeing it with my own eyes. Mostly, I was interested in where the other girls were. Did they live there? If so, which part of the house? Looking at the floor plans, they could be any number of places.

"If I gave you a tour, we'd be here all night," the Sheikh said with a smug grin.

The house was massive. From the blueprints, the total square footage was over sixty-thousand feet. It had fifteen bedrooms, twenty bathrooms, and a thirty-car garage complete with gas pumps. Not surprising, considering the Sheikh's primary source of income was oil and refining it. It also had six pools, eleven kitchens, two tennis courts, and a breathtaking view of the Persian Gulf which I could see from the large picture windows strategically placed across the entire back of the main living area.

Under any other circumstances, I'd love to see the house just to see it, although the extravagance and wastefulness of it was as offensive as its owner. Considering the man was a part of a chorus who frequently condemned the excesses of the west. Pictures of the Sheikh's house and cars would fit nicely in Webster's dictionary next to the word *hypocrite* as examples of real excess.

"I would like to show you my bedroom," the Sheikh said next.

He must've seen the revolting look on my face because his next words were, "I just want to show you the artwork in my suite." He held his hands in the air in a surrender pose. "No other reason. I promise."

Truthfully, I did want to see it. From the blueprints, the master bedroom was more than eight thousand square feet. I was in no danger from the Sheikh. Even in his bedroom. I could break him in two like a toothpick if I wanted to. For now, I'd play along with the ruse long enough to close the deal on the painting tomorrow and figure out how to help the French girl. Especially since I had now committed myself by telling her I could help her. I honestly had no idea whether I could or not and wouldn't until I knew what she needed help from.

I had another thing to be concerned about. The Sheikh brought it up almost immediately.

"May I pour you a drink?" he asked.

I wouldn't put it past him to spike it. My premeditated response was on the tip of my tongue. "I don't drink," I said.

Not entirely true. I did have an occasional wine at dinner, and under normal business situations, I would have a drink with him. This wasn't a normal situation. I was a married woman, in the home of a man who clearly had untoward intentions. For all I knew, he might be trafficking in women. The last thing I wanted to do was dull my senses with alcohol or give him the chance to knock me out with it.

"Ah… Are you one of those Christians?" Saad asked.

Another point of concern. I had to be careful how I answered. In the UAE, Christians were allowed to practice their religion freely, but proselytizing or speaking disparaging words about Islam or the prophet Mohammad were criminal offenses. While I wasn't ashamed of my faith, I wasn't about to enter into a conversation with a man powerful enough to have me thrown in jail for saying the wrong thing.

"I am," I said. "But that's not why I don't drink. To be clear, though, I accepted your invitation to see your artwork and continue the goodwill we've established in our business relationship. If you're expecting anything more tonight than friendly conversation and discussion on art, you'll be sorely disappointed."

Out of the corner of my eye, I could see the French woman fight back a smirk.

"Honey," the Sheikh said, clearly undeterred, "I assure you that you'll have a good time tonight if you'll give me the chance to show you one."

And for the next hour, we did have a good time. The Sheikh showed me his master suite and I could barely keep my mouth from gaping open. I'd spent my "wedding night" in the Belgian Suite at Buckingham Palace, so I wasn't easily impressed. The Sheikh's bedroom would hold its own with any room, anywhere. The contrast couldn't have been more different, though.

The Belgian Suite was filled with historical artifacts dating back centuries. The rooms were gaudy and over-the-top lavish.

The Sheikh's bedroom was modern with curves and fancy decor and state-of-the art everything.

At Buckingham Palace, I felt like I was stepping back in time. Here, I felt like I was stepping into the future.

The Sheikh did have an impressive array of art, although most of it by lesser-known artists. I enjoyed looking at them anyway.

By the time we got to dinner, I was famished. The Sheikh introduced me to his personal chef who prepared us a delightful meal. He described it for me. The first course was a salad of endives, gorgonzola, and caramelized walnuts with thinly sliced pieces of octopus on top. The main course consisted of tartare of tuna and Oscietra caviar with green lentils. I didn't remember having a more unique and exquisite meal.

A glass of wine would've been nice to have with it, but I'd already played my hand. The wine came straight from an unopened bottle, so there were no concerns of him spiking it with a drug. At any rate, I stuck with water directly from a bottle.

After we were finished eating, I couldn't wait any longer. Time to execute my plan. I was dying to know why the French girl needed help. She had joined us for dinner but only spoke when spoken to.

"Where are the other girls?" I asked the Sheikh. "I remember four at the art gallery."

"They have the night off," the Sheikh answered.

I think I knew what he meant.

"The girls are extremely beautiful. But none of them are Arab. How did you find them?"

"I own a modeling agency. These girls are my models."

"Where are you from, Bianca?"

She looked at the Sheikh who nodded permission for her to answer.

"I'm from Paris, France."

"Est-ce qu'il français?" I asked. *Does he speak French?*

She shook her head no and then put her head down and shoveled some food back and forth on her plate. Fidgeting.

"So, you speak French," the Sheikh said. "You're full of surprises, Mrs. Steele. You are an extraordinary woman. Educated. Beautiful. Resourceful. Too bad you're married. You'd have a lot of fun spending my money."

"I have plenty of money to spend," I quipped. "I'm buying a thirty-two-million-dollar painting from you!" By the tone, he could tell I was joking.

"Thirty-three million," he said with a sly grin.

"I can't pull anything over on you," I said, returning the smile.

"Not when it comes to money. I believe the agreed upon price was thirty-two million five hundred thousand American dollars. I already regret selling it so cheaply. What time shall we meet in the morning to finalize our business?"

"Let's make it later. Say eleven o'clock."

I didn't need to sleep in, but a plan was formulating in my mind on how I was going to help the French girl. But I needed more information and time in the morning to figure it out. If my worst fears were true, and Bianca's life was in danger, I'd make my move tomorrow at the art gallery. In a way the Sheikh would never expect.

Since the Sheikh didn't know French, I could communicate freely with Bianca and he wouldn't know what we were saying. I wanted to ask her if she was in danger, but the French words were "êtes-vous en danger?" I couldn't use words the Sheikh would understand.

"Bianca, êtes-vous retenu contre votre volonté?" *Are you being held against your will?*

"Oui."

"Pouvez-vous être à la galerie d'art demain?" *Can you be at the art gallery tomorrow?*

"Oui." Bianca smiled sweetly.

"Est-ce qu'il vous fait avoir des relations avec lui?" *Does he make you have sex with him?*

"Oui."

I could almost see her blush. That's all I needed to know. The specifics didn't matter. Getting her out of the situation now became my priority. Bianca was a sex slave. The fact she was in one of the ten nicest houses in the middle east was irrelevant.

I was already planning on helping her, but before I put my life on the line, I needed to know why. Now I knew.

Tomorrow. At the art gallery.

That's where I'd execute my plan.

4

When the Sheikh unexpectedly excused himself from the table to take an important phone call, Bianca and I suddenly had the opportunity to talk more freely.

"Assume we're being listened to," I said to her in French. "Only speak in French, and don't use his name. I don't want him to know we're talking about him."

I wouldn't put it past Saad to have listening devices throughout the house. I didn't know how long we'd have to talk, so I got right to the point.

"Do you want me to get you out of here?" I asked.

"Yes."

"Why don't you just leave?"

"He took my passport when I first arrived and said he'd hold it for me. How far could I get? He's always watching us."

"How long have you been here?"

"Five months."

I stood and picked up my plate and silverware. "Let's take the dishes into the kitchen."

Bianca followed my lead. We took the dirty dishes into the kitchen and then walked out onto the back deck. Darkness had set in, and the moon glistened off the Persian Gulf. A massive yacht was anchored off the shoreline. I assumed it belonged to Saad. A large infinity pool was directly below us. We still spoke in French, just in case he had eyes and ears on the outside as well. An added benefit to speaking French with her was that it gave me a chance to practice a skill I hadn't used in a while.

"How did you get in this mess?" I asked.

A hurt look crossed her face as she grimaced.

"My family is from Paris. I was in a bar one night, and a man approached me. He asked me if I'd like to be a model. I was skeptical at first, but he gave me a card. He seemed legitimate."

Saad really did own a modeling agency and a fashion magazine. I wondered if they were a front for something else. Or maybe a business just to attract innocent, young girls for something more.

Bianca continued. "Of course, all young girls dream about being a model."

"You're very pretty. You could be a model."

"Thank you. The man said he'd like to take pictures of me. So, we set an appointment for the next day at an expensive hotel. Like I said, it seemed legit. My brother went with me, just in case. You know. To protect his little sister. Everything went well. They took a whole set of pictures with a professional photographer. Even printed some of them and let me take them home with me. The pictures were incredible. I began to believe I could be a model. He asked for my number, but I never expected him to call me. When he did, I was thrilled."

The whole thing sounded like a sophisticated con job to me. I wondered why a man of Saad's wealth would go to all that trouble. Spend incredible sums of money to track down girls in foreign countries when he could have his pick of girls for free. A long time ago, I learned not to question the motives of a sex trafficker. Their behaviors often didn't make sense. In some ways, it's more about power than sex. In this case, Saad was a narcissist. He clearly wanted beautiful girls around him all the time. It made him feel important. More than that, he wanted to feel like he could control their every move. I noticed that when Bianca asked permission at dinner just to answer a simple question.

"Obviously, they did get back in touch with you," I said.

"A couple weeks later another man called. I met him at my house. He had a contract with him. He met my family. Even gave us an advance of ten thousand euros if I signed the contract. Of course, I did it. That was a lot of money for our family at the time."

"What are the terms of the agreement?"

"I'm still not sure. I'm not a lawyer. I was just a young girl with stars in my eyes. The man told me where to sign, and I signed it. Then he gave us the money. He said they'd make me a model, and that I'd be in magazines. Maybe even in the movies. I believed him. He told me I had what it took to be famous."

Tears were welled up in her eyes and her voice cracked. Bianca's hands were shaking. I wanted to reach out and comfort her but didn't in case Saad was watching.

Bianca took a deep breath and seemed to regain her composure. "They told me they had a job for me in Abu Dhabi. With a rich Sheikh." Now she was speaking with more bitterness in her tone.

"Don't use his name or title."

Being overly cautious might not have been necessary, but I didn't want to take any chances. Also, I was riveted to her every word and didn't want the conversation to end. In my line of work, how women got trapped in these kinds of snares was fascinating to me. In this instance, even educational. The more I got into the mind of a predator, the better prepared I might be in the future to stop them and educate other girls on their tactics.

I faked a laugh, so if Saad were watching, he'd think we were having a pleasant conversation. Bianca seemed confused at first, but eventually joined in and laughed with me. The ruse might've been unnecessary. I didn't even know if he was watching. The Sheikh had no reason to consider me a threat, and I intended to use that to my advantage. While he might not want Bianca to engage in a conversation with me outside his presence, I doubt he was overly concerned, which was why he had left us for as long as he had. Hopefully, he'd be detained even longer.

"What happened when you got here?" I asked.

"At first, everything seemed on the up and up."

"How long is the contract for?"

"One year."

"Go ahead. What happened next?"

I didn't want to keep interrupting but needed to fill in the blanks as we went along.

"I'm supposed to make three hundred thousand euros if I fulfill my end of the agreement."

If Saad was watching, he would've seen my mouth gape open. He was willing to pay these girls a lot of money. Just for sex. And power, I reminded myself.

"What do you have to do for that money?"

"At first, all I did was modeling. You know photoshoots. In swim-suits. Formal wear. At various exotic locations. Accompany him to events. I realized that in some ways, I was a paid escort. But I loved all the glamor. I actually made the cover of his magazine. And never once did he mention having sex with him. All he did was flirt with me. And I played along and flirted back. Probably a big mistake."

I saw guilt written all over her face. Also, not surprising. I'd yet to meet a victim who didn't blame herself in some way.

Bianca continued. Speaking faster now. Barely breathing between sentences. "Then came the advances. I told him no. But you know how he is. He won't take no for an answer."

"I do know how he is." The smell of his aftershave was still in my nostrils from where he tried to kiss me. Against my will. I could imag-ine the pressure he could apply to a naïve young girl living in his house.

"One night he called me into his bedroom. He kissed me. I didn't stop him at first. I was so shocked. I didn't know what to do. I sorta liked it. Then he forced himself on me. I don't know. I tried to resist. Not really. For some reason I just froze. I didn't know what to do."

"I understand," I said sincerely. "It's not your fault."

Her lips trembled. Her whole body shook. I didn't want her to relive it, and I didn't need this much detail, so I changed the subject.

"Why don't you go to the police?" I asked and immediately regretted it.

I already knew the answer as soon as the question came out of my mouth.

Bianca answered the question anyway. "Saad is a member of the royal family. He's above the authorities. He told me that I was the one who would be arrested if I told anyone. He said fulfilling his needs was part of my contract. He paid me good money, and I was the one who should be grateful that he wanted me."

Powerful men put young women in vulnerable positions all the time. He said she said. I was under no illusions that the authorities would believe Bianca over the word of a powerful Sheikh. Bianca was probably smart not to notify them. She had to be desperate to leave me the message on the bathroom mirror.

I wanted to get my hands on the contract to look at it myself.

"He said I'd get a hundred lashes and I'd lose the three hundred thousand euros if I broke the contract."

Typical predatory tactic. Use fear to control their subjects. In this case, the Sheikh could probably make it happen. Anger rose up inside me at the thought of beautiful Bianca being beaten with a cane because she refused to have sex him. To the point I was almost unable to control myself. That only confirmed what I was already thinking. She was trapped in every sense of the word. Not like the girls in Thailand or Vietnam or Cambodia who were sold into slavery, but a slave, nonetheless.

This situation was tricky. Some might not sympathize with her plight and would blame her. Argue that she fell for the money and the promise of fame. Three hundred thousand euros was a lot of money for what she was giving in return. Maybe she wasn't even a victim at all. I could hear the counter arguments in my head.

I didn't buy it. My job was to rescue girls from sex trafficking and exploitation. Bianca was being exploited for her body just as much as a ten-dollar hooker in the seediest brothel in Thailand. My heart broke for her just as much.

Bianca was practically crying again. I wanted to reach out and take her in my arms and comfort her. I couldn't. I didn't want Saad to see her crying or me showing her any affection at all. That would only make things worse for her.

"What if you refused? What would happen?" I asked.

"One girl did," she said excitedly. "The next day, they took her out to the yacht. We never saw her again."

"Whisper her name to me," I said.

"Odille Coste. She's from Canada."

I made a mental note to look her up. I was curious to see if she was missing.

"What about the other girls? Do they want to leave too?"

"Not all of them. Some of them like it here. Saad can be very generous. He gives us gifts. Expensive jewelry and clothes. He can be a very kind man. Most of the time."

"Has he ever hit you?"

"No."

Complicated.

"Where are the other girls? Do they live here?"

"Yes. How come they didn't have dinner with us?"

"He gives us a schedule. He tells us when it's *our* night. If you know what I mean. Tonight wasn't supposed to be my night. Anya was scheduled to be with him. I switched with her because I knew you were coming. I had to talk to you. She told him it was her time of the month, so he let us switch. Anya wants to leave too."

"Okay. I can help you. But you need to be at the art gallery tomorrow morning."

"I'm sure we'll all be there. He takes us almost everywhere he goes."

"Listen to me carefully. Tomorrow, you be there. Whatever happens, just go with it. I'm going to get you out of here."

"How will you do that?"

I wasn't sure, but I still had a little over twelve hours to figure it out.

Saad suddenly appeared out of nowhere, startling me.

"What are you girls talking about?" he asked.

"About how your name means handsome," I said. "Bianca was commenting about how true it was."

Saad put his arm around Bianca's waist and pulled her into him. She made no effort to resist. Clearly, Saad had moved on from me, but now had turned his attention to the sure thing. A mixture of guilt, sadness, and anger flooded my emotions. It was all I could do to not let them show on my face. Thirty-plus million or not, I didn't care. I hated the man.

What I did care about was my cover. I couldn't act tonight, or my cover would be blown. We'd gone to incredible lengths to establish AJAX as a credible art acquisition company. I couldn't blow it all on saving Bianca whatever she had to face tonight.

It took all my strength, though. To see the look on her face as I walked out the door and left her there, almost broke my heart.

The only satisfaction was in my knowing one unmistakable fact—tonight, would be the last time.

I'd make sure of it.

5

Amina

Leaving Bianca alone at that house with that disgusting swine of a man was hard, even if only for one night. I was so mad, I wanted to hit something. To the point that I almost couldn't see straight. Which was why I suddenly found myself lost.

Somehow, coming out of the Sheikh's house I made a wrong turn. Instead of heading in the direction of my plane, I was on a backroad outside of Abu Dhabi, with my surroundings deteriorating at every turn. Clearly, I had wandered into the poorer tribal areas. Made worse by the fact that my phone GPS wasn't picking up a signal.

A phone call to A-Rad earlier had also distracted me.

"I need you for a mission tomorrow," I said to him.

I could hear his excitement through the phone as he let out a yell. A-Rad was a wild man. When I first met him, he was an Air Force pilot who flew planes into hurricanes for a living. He flew me into the eye of hurricane Delilah so I could parachute into Cuba and rescue four girls kidnapped on their senior high-class trips.

When I told him I needed a pilot to fly me on missions, he jumped at the chance. In three months, he became certified for our plane and then went to the Farm where he was trained by Curly. Now, not only was he the best pilot I knew, but he could hold his own in the field with the best of them.

He was particularly proficient when we needed muscle. A-Rad wasn't good when it came to the nuances of spying. Ask him to spot or lose a tail, and he was lost as a goose. When we needed a bull in the china shop to come in and shake things up, A-Rad was our man. If we didn't have a shoot-out on a mission, A-Rad felt cheated. If we had to storm a building or knock down a door, he wanted to be the first one in.

Flying me to Abu Dhabi was not his idea of a good time. Art was of no interest to him. He couldn't tell the difference between the Mona Lisa or Whistler's Mother and didn't care, even though he worked for one of the premier art distributors in the world as a cover. While he was willing to come and fly me here, the entire time had been the ultimate downer for him, and he let me know it on more than one occasion. Now that I had mentioned a mission, his spirits had done a complete one eighty.

"Is it dangerous?" he asked.

"Very," I said.

"Yes!"

I could almost picture him pumping his fist in the air. I probably overstated the danger, but he would have to confront two armed men. Although, they were no match for his skills. Still, anytime guns were involved, a slight element of danger existed. Especially considering the brazen plan I hoped to pull off in the middle of downtown Abu Dhabi City in broad daylight.

"I'm in," he said. "Just tell me what to do."

"You haven't heard the mission yet."

"I don't care. You had me at dangerous."

I couldn't help but laugh. Another reason I loved A-Rad. He was a follower more than a leader. All I had to do was point him in the right direction, and he'd run through the proverbial wall for me. Except for my husband Alex, A-Rad was my favorite on our highly skilled and capable AJAX team. I also enjoyed his company. He was funny and up for anything. Over the past six months, we'd been bungee jumping, rock climbing, paintballing, paragliding, parasailing, and ski jumping. We'd raced together—motorcycles, bicycles, race cars, and anything else that moved at a high rate of speed.

And been shot at a few times. Much to his delight.

I explained what he needed. "Write this down. You'll need a weapon—"

"Yes!" he said before I could get the rest of the words out.

"Small caliber. Something you can hide in your pants."

"Got it."

He probably wished it were a machine gun, but he didn't say anything more.

"You'll need a ski mask to cover your face," I said.

"Okay."

That's the other thing I liked about A-Rad. He never asked why. He just did it. Whatever I said. Never questioning me.

"The last thing you'll need is a blond wig, women's sunglasses, and a woman's burqa."

Well, most of the time he didn't ask why or question me.

"I hope you don't expect *me* to wear them," he said in a raised voice.

I laughed. "No. You'll be wearing the ski mask."

"Whew! For a second there, I thought you were going to ask me to dress up like a woman. That ain't happenin."

"You'd make an ugly woman, A-Rad."

"That's for sure."

"I'll be home soon," I told him. That was thirty minutes ago. Before I got lost. Now I wasn't sure when I was going to get back to the plane. When I got cell phone service, I'd call him and let him know I'd be late. If I could get service. Getting lost in Abu Dhabi wasn't that easy to do. All I had to do was head toward the Persian Gulf, and I'd hit the road that led right to the airport. I just didn't know which direction that was.

"I'll wait up for you," A-Rad said.

That's the other thing about him. He was highly protective of me. If I wasn't where I was supposed to be when I was supposed to be there, he was the first to voice concern. Probably a tie between Alex and him as to which one would get in front of me first to take a bullet.

My mind returned to my present problem.

Where am I?

I had no clue and didn't know if I was making things worse. Complicated by the fact no one was on the roads. I hadn't seen a car in ten miles. Or a gas station. Or even a village. My Lamborghini made good time: I just didn't know to where. I rounded a curve and saw car lights just ahead, which caused me to breathe a sigh of relief. Hopefully, they could give me directions.

As I neared, things seemed off. My CIA radar kicked in. The car was on the wrong side of the road. On the shoulder. The driver side door was open. No one was in the car. Was someone hurt?

I saw movement out of the corner of my eye. In a field, to my left. Just off the road. No more than twenty paces. It looked like four people were standing over something. Or at least it seemed that way as I strained to see what was happening in the dark. I couldn't make out what was happening. I rolled down my window and called out to them.

"Hill yemkenk an tatini alatiahat?" I asked in Arabic, the official language of the UAE. *Can you give me directions?*

The four figures turned toward me. They suddenly took off running toward the car. *What's happening?* It took a second to process things. For whatever reason, they were spooked. Something was on the ground. I did a double take as my mind processed that it might be a person.

My phone was still in my hand with the maps pulled up. I switched to camera mode and hit the record button just in case I was witnessing something nefarious. One of the men ran straight for the open driver side door. He jumped in and slammed the door shut. A second man got in the backseat on the same side of the car. A third went around the front of the car and got in the passenger side door. I couldn't see any of the men's faces. Hopefully, the video on my phone picked them up.

The fourth man had to go right in front of my car to get to the backseat of the passenger side. I got a good look at him.

Our eyes met.

I held my camera up to the dashboard, so he could see that I was either filming him or taking his picture. He had no way of knowing which. At least he'd know I was on to him. His face was clearly on my video. My headlights illuminated his entire body for the camera.

He abruptly stopped in his tracks. Reversed field and bolted to my open window. I made no attempt to shut it. He reached his hand through to try and grab my phone.

"Tatini an al-kalabah al-hatef," he said roughly. *Give me that phone.* At the end of the sentence, he added a five-letter word, normally used to describe female dogs. That didn't sit too well with me.

"That's no way to talk to a lady," I said to him in Arabic.

I grabbed his wrist, now inside the car and twisted it violently upward. Counterclockwise. In a direction it wasn't meant to turn. A move Curly had demonstrated to our CIA training class on the Farm using me as the victim. I knew how much it hurt. Only I stopped shorter than Curly did. Before I could do any real damage. The man would have trouble sleeping tonight, but the soreness would leave in a couple days.

He let out a yelp. Something like what a female dog would sound like if you stepped on her tail.

"Who's the bitch now, buddy?" I said in English.

He jerked his arm out of the car and ran crying like a baby back to his vehicle. The car sped away once he was safely inside, but not before I got a good video of the license plate.

If I'd known what was about to happen next, I'd have done a lot more damage to his arm and to other parts of his body as well.

* * *

A woman staggered out of the field.

Wearing a hijab. Or what was left of it.

She was bloodied, and her clothes sandy and torn. I put the car in park, jumped out, and ran to her side, barely catching her before she collapsed to the ground.

Not a woman.

A teenage girl.

Badly beaten.

Her right eye was swollen shut and her nose was out of place, hideously hanging to the side, clearly broken. Blood gushed from several wounds. Her jaw might've been broken as well, because when she tried to speak the words were slurred. Like she'd been to the dentist and had a shot that numbed her mouth and jaw.

I helped her around to the passenger side of the car. Sat her down with her feet on the ground and facing me so I could assess her injuries in the light. A bottle of water in the center console helped me to clean some of the wounds. I tore off pieces of her hijab to use as tourniquets to stop the bleeding.

Even then, she was in bad shape. Probably had a concussion. Maybe a broken eye socket. The men had inflicted a tremendous beating on her. Probably done more than that.

"Agtisboni," she said several times confirming what I already suspected. *They raped me.*

"I know, honey," I said. "But you're safe now. I'm taking you to a hospital."

"No. Take me home."

"You need medical attention. You may have internal bleeding. You probably have a concussion." I didn't want to tell her about the facial injuries that might require surgery.

"Please take me home," she pleaded.

Five hours later, I wished I'd listened to her. Right after the tribal police showed up, took a look at my video, and arrested her.

6

Amina

Sheikh Zimraan Jaber General Hospital
Thirty minutes outside Abu Dhabi City

I had to be careful. I was coming perilously close to being arrested myself.

"Why is Amina being arrested?" I asked the man roughly after he tried to handcuff Amina and take her out of the hospital bed and down to the police station. My arguing with him provided the distraction that kept him from doing so. The man wasn't really a policeman. A tribal elder was how he introduced himself. From Amina's village. I didn't even know if he had the authority to arrest her.

"She has violated the law," he argued.

"What law did she violate?"

"The law of adultery."

I couldn't believe the words coming out of his mouth.

We were in Amina Noorani's hospital room. The girl had been brutally raped by four men, multiple times. Then savagely beaten. Had I not come along when I did, she probably would've died. As it was, she lay in the bed in critical but stable condition. Expected to live but with severe head injuries. Not to mention, the emotional scars that would be with her forever.

"Adultery? What are you talking about?" the conversation was getting more heated with each exchange. I wasn't sure if the man had the authority to arrest me as well. Something I didn't want to happen. Not only did I need to secure the painting, but I also promised Bianca I'd help get her out of her predicament. She was counting on me.

"The man on the video on your phone is married. Amina had sex with him."

I was almost beside myself.

The first thing I did when the man arrived was show him the video on my phone. Now, I realized how big a mistake that had been. This was why Amina had pleaded with me to take her home and not to the hospital. She knew how much trouble she was in.

"You call that sex!" I said, just barely below shouting. "He forced himself on her!"

"Our tribal laws make no distinction," he retorted. "They had relations."

I paced the room now. Trying to control my anger which was about to erupt like a volcano on steroids.

"That's not sexual relations. It's called rape! Do you not understand the difference?"

"She's already admitted her guilt. I have no choice but to arrest her."

"How did she admit her guilt?"

The man pulled out a little black book and began reading from it.

"She told the nurse she was walking on the highway. The men stopped and offered her a ride. She said no and kept walking. That's her first offense. She admitted talking to the men. It's against the tribal laws for a woman or girl to talk in public to a man who's not a relative."

I noticed he kept saying tribal laws. I couldn't believe that a sophisticated country like the UAE would still have such archaic laws.

"Oh, for heaven's sakes. All she did was answer the man. She told him no. That she didn't want a ride. Sounds to me like she did the right thing."

"What was she doing away from her home that late at night, walking on the highway? Alone. She was asking for trouble."

"I don't know why. Doesn't matter. She was wearing her hijab, so she was covered. They had no right to attack her. What about the men? Are you going to charge them as well?"

If he answered wrong, I might just choke him out. Tribal elder or not.

"I will question them. They may have a different version. Perhaps she came on to them."

"So that justifies them beating her to a pulp?"

"We don't know that the men in the video are the ones who assaulted her."

Was this guy an idiot or just a low-life bigoted scoundrel?

Bigoted was a given.

"Don't forget that I saw the men standing over her. When they saw me, they ran away. Why would they run if they weren't guilty? You saw the video. They sure looked guilty to me. I'm sure Amina can identify them as her attackers as well."

"The law requires that any charges against a man must be supported by the testimony of four men. Neither your testimony nor the young girl's will be admissible if it's not supported by the testimony or confessions of the other men."

"You have them on tape!"

"All I see on the tape is them walking to the car."

"Running to the car. Like they're guilty of something. Amina will confirm everything once she's able to talk."

"I'll say it again. A woman's testimony is not permissible in our court unless it's supported by the testimony of four honorable men. If she were to bring a charge against the men without the testimony of four witnesses, she'll be charged with an additional crime of slander."

I wanted to slap him across the head.

"This is the most ridiculous thing I've ever heard in my life. You're going to charge her with adultery, but the men get off scot-free."

"I didn't say that. The three men will be charged with having premarital sex, if they confess to the charges. The married man will be charged with adultery as well."

"What is the punishment for that?"

"That's up to the judge. Probably lashes. Maybe jail time."

Right at that moment, I wanted to scream at the top of my lungs.

"Amina will also be charged with the same crimes," he continued. "Three counts of premarital sex and adultery. She's already confessed to them. Her punishment is a hundred lashes and a year to two years in prison for each offense. The adultery charge is the more serious charge. The penalty can be lashes, imprisonment, even death, although I don't know if that will happen. Depends on the judge."

I let out an exasperated sigh, so he'd know how frustrated I was at him. The men get lashes and maybe prison time. Amina gets four hundred lashes and four to eight years in jail. Maybe death.

Maybe I'd just kill him and take Amina back to my plane and out of the country.

Truthfully, I wasn't totally surprised. This information wasn't completely new to me. I'd read the reports. Human rights violations against women and girls had been running rampant in the middle east for centuries. The UAE had made significant reforms over the years. Apparently, those reforms hadn't made it to this tribal area which was still operating in the dark ages.

I remembered reading about a woman, a hotel maid, who was raped by her employer. I don't remember where, although it wasn't the UAE. When she went to the hospital complaining of stomach pains, they discovered she was pregnant. She was arrested for having premarital sex but she wouldn't identify the name of the father which made things worse for her. The punishment was a hundred lashes even though she was pregnant. The sentence was carried out. They threatened to continue the beating until she divulged his name. When she finally revealed that he was married, the charge was changed to adultery, and she was sentenced to death. The media went ballistic.

Human rights groups condemned the actions, and the UN imposed sanctions. I seemed to think in the back of my mind that the woman went to jail, and the employer got off with a fine. While things may be getting better, I was witnessing firsthand how heavy handed the system still was against women in some areas.

"Amina should not be arrested. She did nothing wrong," I said to the man, after I had regained my composure and could speak in a calmer tone.

"That's none of your concern," he retorted. "That's for a judge to decide."

"I think it is my concern," I said. "I'm a witness to the attack. I can identify the men. I shot the video."

Something I regretted now. That was the primary evidence that could be used against Amina. I looked over at her. She let out a moan. Her face was almost unrecognizable because of the swelling. I wished the man would give me ten minutes alone in the room with the four men. I'd see that they get a beating they'd never forget. Put all four of them in the room with me at the same time. I didn't care. I'd beat them to a pulp, so they'd know how it felt.

Her eyes were still closed. I wondered if she could hear us. She was heavily sedated, but our conversation had been loud and heated.

"I need to confiscate your phone," the man said.

That wasn't going to happen.

"Sir, I'm here on business. I need my phone. I'm expecting a call from Sheikh Saad Shakir first thing in the morning. He won't be happy if he's unable to reach me."

Maybe throwing out the name of the powerful Sheikh might make a difference.

It did.

"Send the video to my email," he said. He took out his wallet and pulled out a business card and gave it to me.

Then he left.

I had no intention of sending the video to him. Especially if he were going to use it as evidence against Amina.

Shortly after the man left, Amina's mother arrived. She introduced herself as Samitah Noorani. By the look on her face, I could tell she was surprised to see me in Amina's room. After I explained to her all the details, her words and tone were even more ominous than the tribal authority and left me even more concerned.

"They want to arrest Amina for adultery," I explained to her. "The man wanted to take her to jail, even in this condition. I talked him out of it."

"Thank you," she said. "And thank you for helping my daughter."

"It's the least I could do. I wasn't about to leave her there on the side of the road. Clearly, I should've brought her home, though. I thought she needed medical attention."

I'd be kicking myself for that decision for who knew how long.

"They can't arrest her, can they?" I asked.

"They can and they will," Samitah said.

"That's so unfair. The man said they could sentence her to death."

"The courts are the least of our worries. More than likely, Amina will be sentenced to a hundred lashes and ten to twelve years in prison. That's what other girls have gotten in similar situations."

"The policeman said they could give her a hundred lashes for each charge. There were four men. That would be four hundred lashes."

"He's not a policeman. He's one of the tribal elders. He does have the power to arrest her, though. And the tribe can impose a sentence. They still have to follow UAE laws which limit lashes to two hundred at any one time. Amina wouldn't survive four hundred lashes. Her back would be decimated. More than likely, the punishment will be all together. Four charges, but one lashing. Maybe 140 lashes. But the court won't sentence her to death. That does happen, but not as much as it used to. Not for rape. For consensual adultery, maybe. Even though that's getting rarer."

"That's a relief. Still, ten to twelve years in prison is a long time."

"Unfortunately, I don't think Amina will ever go to prison."

"Oh good." Then I caught myself as the words sunk in.

"Why did you say, unfortunately?"

"Amina will likely be put to death because the man is married."

Samitah's tone was sober and with a hint of obvious resignation. I could tell she loved her daughter and was pained by this horrible turn of events. Samitah had shared with me how her daughter was a good student. Never got into trouble. Worked hard. And was a delightful daughter who had a bright future ahead of her. What did she mean by unfortunately? The words didn't make sense or match the tone.

"You just said the court wouldn't put her to death."

"I did say that. But her father is the one we have to worry about."

"Her father? What's he got to do with it?"

"My husband is a tribal elder as well. After the courts hand out their sentence, then the local tribes will impose their own."

"He's her father. Surely, he'll convince them to be lenient on his own daughter."

"My husband is an exacting man. He will not be lenient. He'll be leading the call for her stoning."

I slumped back in my chair and put my hand over my eyes and rubbed them roughly.

What a nightmare!

"I can't believe this is happening," I said. I was used to injustice. Saw it every day in my line of work. I'd just come from one emotional time with Bianca, now I was faced with another. This one even worse than Bianca's plight. I had to do something.

"Is there anything we can do to stop it?"

"She's already admitted to the tribal elder that she was raped. That's considered a confession of guilt to them. The man is married. The tribal law says it's adultery to have sex with a married man, even if it's not consensual."

"The only proof the man is married is the video. That's on my phone. What if I don't send it to him?"

"I'd be worried that you'll be charged with obstructing an investigation. You've already done enough for my daughter. I don't want you to get in trouble with the law."

"I'm not worried about me. I'm thinking of Amina."

We talked for another hour until it was time for me to leave.

I walked over to Amina's bedside. Leaned over and whispered in her ear. "I don't know if you can hear me or not. If you can, I won't let them do this to you. I promise."

The second promise I'd made today. Bianca. Now Amina. Neither of which, I knew for sure I could keep.

All I knew was that I had to try.

7

MJ

Tribal area outside Abu Dhabi City
One month before MJ's eighteenth birthday

MJ was in love.

Three months after her conversion to Christianity, she met Christopher. An eighteen-year-old from America whose parents had been in the UAE for more than a year. Christopher was the nicest boy she'd ever met, and they had an instant attraction. His dad worked for a banking conglomerate in Abu Dhabi.

They met strictly by chance. Christopher happened to be driving by at the exact moment a group of boys were harassing her while she was walking home from school. He ran them off and offered her a ride.

Even though riding in the car alone with him was against the law of her tribe, MJ had started testing the limits of her newfound freedom. She accepted the ride, and they hit it off immediately. He picked her up from school every day for two weeks and took her home so she wouldn't have any more problems with those boys. So no one would see her get out of his car, he stopped a block or two away from her home to let her walk the rest of the way.

MJ knew she was taking a serious risk, but she was taking them every day in other ways as well. She had taken her aunt's advice and only read the Bible at her aunt's house. Which was easy to do since she was over there almost every day. Most nights she even slept there, except those nights when her father was away on a business trip and someone needed to be there to watch the home.

Her father didn't seem to notice her extended absences and knew nothing of her so-called "apostasy." While apostasy was a crime in the United Arab Emirates, no one had been prosecuted for it in years. The plan was to keep it a secret from her father until her eighteenth birthday at which time she could do whatever she wanted.

When Christopher kissed her one day in his car, she'd broken more laws than just treason. Now, she'd broken sexual laws according to her tribe. Even though they hadn't actually had sex, they'd taken steps toward zina or sexual sin. They'd given in to their lusts. According to her father, it was better for a man to have a nail driven through his head, than to touch a woman who he didn't have a right to touch. Christopher didn't have that right until they were married which required her father's permission, which he would never give.

Dating, kissing, even holding hands with a woman who was not your wife was considered sin. Sin was subject to criminal punishment.

That's why MJ needed to introduce Christopher to Aunt Shule. They needed her advice. MJ was betrothed. Her father had promised her to another man on her eighteenth birthday. She intended to refuse, although her father didn't know it yet. In her own mind, she had no choice. Marrying the man was not an option. She was in love with Christopher. And he loved her. They had even talked about marriage.

She'd kept the relationship a secret from Aunt Shule until she was sure Christopher was the man for her. Not that she didn't trust her; she was just embarrassed. She didn't know if Auntie would approve of her kissing another boy or if she'd even like him.

But... she had nowhere else to turn. If anyone would understand and keep her secret, it'd be Aunt Shule. Her Aunt was the one who had led her to Christ and had practically raised her after her mother died in childbirth.

The day before, she asked Auntie if she could invite a friend for dinner. Even hinted that it was a male friend, although Auntie didn't ask. She said yes, and she spent all afternoon helping Auntie prepare.

When Christopher arrived, MJ was as nervous as a mouse around a cat. Auntie didn't seem surprised that the guest was a boy. She greeted him with a warmness even MJ didn't expect. Although, she ushered him into the house quickly, nervously checking the outside clearly to make sure no one saw him enter.

The meal was ready to be served, so they went directly to the kitchen table.

"Tell me about yourself, Christopher," Auntie Shule asked him warmly as they all filled their plates.

"My dad's a banker. I'm from America. I've been in the UAE for a little over a year."

"Do you go to school?"

"Yes ma'am. I go to a private Christian school in Abu Dhabi City."

Christopher was brown headed, with high cheekbones and baby-faced features. His eyes were soft and innocent. His manners were immaculate and his tone always respectful. Even though he'd kissed MJ, he was a perfect gentleman doing it.

"So you're a Christian?" Auntie asked.

"Yes ma'am."

"That's nice."

Aunt Shule looked at MJ and smiled.

For two hours they talked. The subject of the romance still hadn't come up, and the hour was getting late. Finally, Aunt Shule came right out and asked, since MJ was afraid to broach the subject.

"What are your intentions with MJ?" Auntie asked.

"I hope to marry her someday. After her eighteenth birthday."

In the UAE, a woman couldn't get married without her father's permission until she turned eighteen.

"Hmmm," Auntie said. Not giving anything away. MJ didn't know if she approved or not.

"How do you feel about that, MJ?" Auntie asked.

"I think it's great. I love him. I want to marry him."

"That's nice."

To MJ's surprise, Auntie Shule didn't say another word. The rest of the evening was pleasant and when Christopher said he had to go, Auntie excused herself so MJ and Christopher could be alone.

As he left, Christopher leaned in and gave MJ the second kiss of her life, sending chills down her spine. They turned off the porch light, and Christopher snuck away under the cover of darkness. It all felt so mysterious. Dangerous even, although MJ wondered if she really knew how dangerous.

She was reminded of that when she got back inside and found Auntie obviously ready to have a franker discussion. Auntie's mood was sober and her face tense with apprehension.

"What do you think of Christopher?" MJ asked before her aunt could speak.

"I like him. He seems like a nice boy."

"I want to marry him."

"I know, dear. I want you to marry a Christian as well."

"I can marry him when I turn eighteen."

"No, you can't!"

MJ's heart sunk to the bottom of her chest. "What do you mean?"

"The laws of our tribe don't allow you to marry a non-Muslim."

"Sharif married a Christian." Sharif was a boy in their village. Slightly older than her. Already eighteen.

"Muslim men in our tribe are allowed to marry a non-Muslim woman. Women are forbidden to marry outside of our faith."

"That's not fair!" Anger rose up inside of MJ like a sandstorm whipping through the desert.

"No one said life is fair, honey."

"What if I marry him anyway?"

"You could get in serious trouble with the tribal elders. You'd also be guilty of having sex outside of marriage. You could go to jail."

"We'd be guilty of sex outside of marriage, even though we're married?"

"Like I said, our tribe wouldn't recognize the marriage. In the view of the tribal elders, you're still single. You'd be having sex with another single man."

MJ started to cry.

"I'm going to ask you a question, and I want you to tell me the truth," Auntie said.

MJ stifled back a sob. "Okay."

"Have you and Christopher had sex yet?"

"No! We've only kissed twice. We're waiting until we get married."

"That's a relief."

"I know what the Bible says about marriage and waiting until you're married."

Auntie had actually taught MJ about sex even before the conversion. Her Aunt was the closest thing she had to a mother. Auntie, as she called her, taught her most of what she knew about the things of the world.

Auntie said, "You'll get in a lot of trouble if the two of you get caught. Promise me that you won't see Christopher anymore—"

Anger exploded inside of MJ and she raised her voice and said, "I have to see Christopher! I won't promise not to see him. I'll just die if I can't. I'm sorry, Auntie."

"You didn't let me finish. What I was going to say was promise me that you won't see Christopher except at my house. Not until we can figure things out."

"What can we figure out? It seems so hopeless. If the law won't let me marry him."

"You've got bigger problems than the law," Auntie Shule said.

"What do you mean?"

"On your eighteenth birthday, if you don't marry the man your father picked out for you, I'm afraid he'll disown you."

"Did he tell you who he picked for me?" MJ said in disgust.

"No."

"Abdul!"

"Abdul Sham?" Auntie asked.

"Yes! He's forty years old! He already has two wives and five kids."

"He can afford a plum dowry. That must be why. I'd hoped he'd pick a boy your own age."

"He didn't. I can't marry him. I want to marry Christopher."

"If you don't marry Abdul, your father will put you out of the tribe. He'll disown you. You'll be destitute."

"I don't care."

"Not only that... I'm afraid that he'll kill you."

MJ hadn't thought about that possibility. She'd heard of fathers killing their daughters for not obeying their wishes. She'd even seen the stonings in the square, although they were few and far between, and she hadn't seen one recently. Mostly, what she heard about were girls disappearing. Never to be heard from again.

Her father wouldn't dare! Or would he?

The reality suddenly hit her like she'd been hit by a truck.

Her father would kill her rather than let her marry Christopher. Especially since he'd lose the dowry.

She'd rather die than marry the man he had for her.

What was going to happen?

Her birthday was only a month away.

8

MJ

Abu Dhabi City
Three days before MJ's eighteenth birthday

Christopher introduced MJ to his parents shortly after they began discussing marriage. While Wayne and Ivory Tate expressed that they would've preferred their son wait until he was older to get married, they were sympathetic to MJ's plight. MJ's father had prearranged a marriage for her with a forty-year-old Muslim man who already had two wives and several kids.

As the Tate's got to know MJ better, they grew to love her and were thrilled by their son's choice of a wife.

The affection was mutual. MJ had never met a family so kind and generous. The total opposite of her own dysfunctional upbringing. Christopher's parents seemed like the perfect couple. Wayne treated his wife with respect. She seemed to be his equal in every way. While he worked and provided the income for the family, she managed the home and was active in the community and in church. They even took MJ to their Christian church on a couple occasions. Her father would go ballistic if he knew what she'd been doing behind his back.

She loved it. Her life had not been the same since her conversion. The best thing she'd ever done.

Because of the complexity of MJ's situation, the decision was made to bring in an attorney. A meeting was set at the Tate's home, so they'd have privacy, and Auntie Shule could attend.

MJ waited until her father was out of town on business to hold the meeting. Aunt Shule and MJ arrived at the Tates' apartment in center city together. If MJ had ever been more nervous than she was at that moment, she didn't remember when.

She felt better the moment she saw Christopher's parents. They greeted her and Aunt Shule warmly.

"We just love MJ so much," Ivory Tate said to Aunt Shule after handing each of them a glass of sweet tea.

"The feeling is mutual," Aunt Shule said. "MJ can't stop talking about how much she loves you. I certainly appreciate how kind you've been to her."

To be the center of attention felt weird to MJ. Everyone was talking about her while she was right there. She imagined she'd feel even more uncomfortable when the attorney arrived. The whole week since the meeting was arranged, she had dreaded it. Fearful the attorney would tell her she had to marry the Muslim man.

Wayne Tate stood across the room. "This is quite a mess the kids have found themselves in," he said. "Not of their own making, of course. I'm not blaming them. This isn't their fault. There must be a solution, though. Hopefully, the attorney will help us find one."

"What do you do for a living?" Aunt Shule asked Mr. Tate.

"I'm the CEO of digital banking for a local bank in Abu Dhabi City. We also have offices in Dubai, so I go back and forth. I'm under contract for eighteen months. I have six months left. Then we'll go back to the states."

"We want MJ to come back with us," Ivory said. "She can attend college. We'll pay for it, of course. Then we can take our time planning a wedding. I hope you can attend."

Ivory smiled at MJ who returned it. Christopher was sitting next to her on the couch and squeezed MJ's hand.

"That's very kind," Auntie said, "but I don't know if I'm up for it. That's a long trip. I'd love to see MJ start a new life in America. She's had a difficult life here, growing up without her mother," Aunt Shule said.

MJ could see her Aunt's eyes watering.

"I'd be happy to see MJ get a few good breaks in her life," Aunt Shule continued once she'd composed herself. "I don't know if it's possible, though. Her father can be a cruel man. When he finds out she's not going to marry Abdul, he's going to be extremely angry. MJ is a beautiful girl. A prized catch in our tribe. Her father has demanded a hefty dowry for her hand in marriage. He'll be upset that she has defied him, but also that he'll lose out on the money."

"It's hard to believe they still have arranged marriages in parts of the world," Ivory said. "How barbaric!"

Before anyone else could say anything, the doorbell rang, and Ivory sprang up out of her seat. Less than a minute later, they led a meek-looking man into the room. Short. Thin. Wire rimmed glasses sitting precariously on the front of his nose. They looked like they could fall off at the slightest tilt of the head. The man was dark skinned. Wearing a suit and tie and carrying a briefcase. MJ had never seen a lawyer before, but this was what she pictured one would look like.

"I'd like to introduce Anup Palan to everyone." Mr. Tate said. "You already know my wife, Ivory. This is our son Christopher and his girlfriend MJ."

When she was introduced as Christopher's girlfriend, MJ's heart leapt inside of her, sending a wave of euphoria through her entire body. She tried to imagine how it'd feel to be called his wife.

"This is MJ's Aunt Shule," Mr. Tate added as Auntie nodded to him.

Anup bowed his head slightly. "It's very pleasing to meet each of you," he said. "I hope I can be of service today."

"Anup is an expert on the laws of UAE," Mr. Tate said. "Particularly marriage and family law. He's from India but he studied Sharia law and has been practicing in the UAE for more than twelve years. He's also a strong advocate for women's rights."

He bowed his head again and smiled. "The law in the UAE is quite complicated," Anup said. "There are civil courts and Sharia courts.

Then there are the tribal courts. The law is not always applied equally. We must use it to our advantage when we can. While women have gained some rights, we still have a long way to go as a country to treat women fairly in every corner of our country. What is your situation?"

No one spoke right away. Everyone looked at MJ. She squirmed in her seat and her breathing became shallow.

Aunt Shule must've sensed it because she spoke up first. "My niece, MJ, and Christopher wish to be married, but her father has promised her to a Muslim man."

"The law does not require her to follow through with a prearranged marriage," Anup said. "For many years, girls had no choice. Now they do."

MJ didn't know that. She'd always thought she was obligated. Optimism was overcoming the fear that had gripped her since the meeting started as she suddenly let out a breath and flashed Christopher a smile which he returned.

"They're concerned that her father will kill her if she refuses," Mr. Tate said, causing fear to come racing back inside of her.

Anup nodded and let out a sigh. "That is a concern. I've seen it happen more times than I'd like. One time is too many."

"What should they do then?" Mr. Tate asked.

"Are you eighteen yet?" Anup asked MJ.

"I'll be eighteen in three days."

"My suggestion is that when you turn eighteen, you leave the country and marry in a country that allows an interfaith marriage."

"Her father would never approve of her leaving the country," Aunt Shule said.

"Once she's eighteen, she's free to do what she wishes. He can't stop her. There is the threat of violence to consider. I'd suggest she go into hiding."

"You can stay here," Ivory said.

"Thank you," MJ replied.

"Not yet," Anup said. "Not until she turns eighteen. You can get in serious trouble if you harbor her before she turns eighteen. She's under her father's dominion until her eighteenth birthday."

"Will she be safe until then?" Mr. Tate asked.

"We just have to make sure her father doesn't find out," Aunt Shule said. "She stays with me most of the time now anyway. Once her birthday comes around, he'll be out looking for her though. You can count on that."

"How long will it take for her to get a visa to the United States?" Mr. Tate asked.

"Two to three years. Maybe longer," Anup answered.

MJ felt her shoulders slump. Where could she hide for two years? She didn't want to be away from Christopher that long.

"Our work visa expires before then," Mr. Tate said.

"I'm not leaving without her," Christopher said.

"You might not have a choice," Mr. Tate said. "I don't know that we could even get your visa extended."

"If they're married, MJ can get into the United States right away," Anup said.

"I'll get married today," MJ blurted.

"Me too," Christopher said.

"I think the pastor of our church will marry you," Mr. Tate said, his voice raised a notch letting his excitement show.

"You must wait until she turns eighteen," Anup warned. "If you present the marriage certificate to the court and she's underage, it must have a guardian's approval. Her father is her legal guardian."

Christopher said. "We'll get married the first thing in the morning on your birthday. That'll be your birthday present."

"I suggest you make arrangements to leave the country right after," Aunt Shule said. "MJ's father will come looking for her. Don't forget, he's expecting her to marry Abdul on her birthday."

"That's a good idea," Anup said.

"I'll miss you," MJ said. She got up and walked over and sat next to her aunt.

"You can go back to America," Ivory said. "The two of you can stay at our home until we get back."

"Thank you, so much, Anup," Mr. Tate said. "You've been very helpful."

"I just hope this works," Aunt Shule said.

"Me too," Ivory added.

"It will," MJ said.

"I suggest that the two of you not see each other until your birthday," Mr. Tate said. "You don't want to take a chance that her father finds out before then."

"What can he do?" MJ said. "If he finds out."

"We are members of the Al Parsa tribe," Aunt Shule said. "They are very strict in following the tribal laws. Her father is a tribal elder. They could put MJ in jail."

"Let's make sure they don't find out," Anup said. "My suggestion is to get married, file the certificate, and get out of the country before your father has a chance to contest it. Once you're in America, he has no control over you. Neither do the tribal elders. Until then, the tribe can do anything they want. They can even put you in jail for zina charges. Charges of sexual sin. Your tribe may not recognize the marriage. If they don't then they could sentence you to lashes or prison. Possibly even death. You can always hope for the best, but my experience is to stay out of the tribal courts if at all possible."

"That's a good suggestion," Mr. Tate said. "That's why I think you two kids should stay away from each other until the wedding. We'll get you married in the morning, and on the first flight out of here."

"What do you think, Auntie?" MJ said.

"It sounds complicated," she answered. "The main thing is that we have to make sure your father doesn't find out. That's what I'm worried about."

MJ was suddenly worried about it as well, and the fear returned with a vengeance.

9

Bianca

Last night had not gone as Saad had hoped. The American woman, Jamie Steele, had rebuffed all of his advances. Much to his disappointment. The woman was feisty. Resourceful. A strong business woman. Rich. Gorgeous. Blonde which was always his preference. In spite of his strict upbringing, he liked a little fire in his paramour. Which was probably why he sought beautiful girls from other countries to satisfy his carnal affections. The Arab women were too passive and too submissive.

Which was why he was feeling unsatisfied this morning. The French girl, Bianca, had been a huge disappointment last night as well. Despite his many attempts to seduce her with his charms, she was unenthusiastic in their lovemaking. Barely attentive to his needs at all. At one point, he was so frustrated with her, he wanted to strike her. He held back and just roughly kicked her out of the bed after he finished.

Not only was it frustrating, but it made him angry. He paid these girls a lot of money. His fashion company put their faces on international magazines. The opportunities he gave them in modeling were once-in-a lifetime, career changing, chances for fame and fortune. He bought them expensive gifts. At the end of one year, he paid the girls three hundred thousand euros. Ten-years' wages for most of them. What they gave him in return paled in comparison to what he did for them. Some were appreciative, but not all. Perhaps he was too easy on them.

Maybe the American woman was to blame for distracting Bianca the night before. They had spent the entire evening deep in conversation. Unfortunately, he'd gotten distracted by a phone call that went on for almost an hour. Some problem in an oil field that didn't get resolved anyway. He'd cursed his employee for interrupting his evening.

Another call this morning had been even more unsettling. Perhaps, the main reason for his angst. A Turkish man called, upset because he had heard Saad was selling the painting to the American. The man identified himself as a member of the White Wolves, an offshoot of the Turkish mafia. They felt like the painting belonged in the Arab world.

"Why would you sell it to the infidels?" the man had asked.

"Money. They are the highest bidder. Make me an offer I can't refuse, and I'll sell it to you."

While he had signed an agreement to sell the painting to AJAX corporation, he could easily get out of it. The American woman wouldn't be happy, but what was her recourse? She couldn't sue him. No court in Abu Dhabi would rule against him.

What he really wondered was how the Turks knew about the woman and the sale of the painting. He quickly dismissed the thought without much introspection. Nothing surprised him anymore in this day of information technology available through so many mediums.

"We're prepared to pay you twenty-five million for the painting," the man had said.

"I'll sell it for thirty-five million." If he could make an extra two and a half million dollars, he'd do it.

Saad was, after all, a businessman first and foremost. The White Wolves could certainly afford his asking price. If they wanted it, they could come up with the money.

The man on the phone turned him down. The call ended badly, with both sides making all kinds of threats. Saad dished out as many as they gave to him.

"I'll sell the painting to whomever I damn well please," he had shouted and then hung up on the man.

Which was exactly what he planned to do. This morning. To the American. Which reminded him that he'd better get moving if he were going to make their meeting on time. Before Mrs. Steele had left the night before, they agreed to meet at eleven. If he left now, he'd barely make it.

Before being interrupted by the call, he'd been listening to the audio from his security system which had picked up the entire conversation between Bianca and Mrs. Steele the night before. Both the inside and outside conversations were recorded, but the two ladies were speaking in French the entire time. Which made him suspicious. Or maybe he was just being paranoid. The banter seemed friendly, casual, and harmless enough, but not knowing what they were talking about.

He picked his cell phone up from off his desk and dialed a number he knew by heart. The man answered on the first ring.

"Salam," Jeric Hashmi said. Jeric was a professor at the University and a friend who went all the way back to childhood.

"Good day," Saad replied. The two were men of the world and didn't bother with the longer traditional Muslim greetings.

"My good friend, Sheikh Saad, how are you today?" Jeric said enthusiastically.

"Very well," Saad said. "Shukran." *Thank you very much for asking*, he added.

"Why am I deserving of such an honor this morning?" the professor asked.

Saad loved listening to the professor talk. A linguist, the man was fluent in many languages. Even as a child, Jeric's speech was refined and proper. Like an adult. Certainly, in a way well beyond his years. Saad wasn't surprised that Jeric had made such a successful career as a professor which he seemed destined to excel at.

"As I remember, you speak French. Is that correct?" Saad asked.

"Fluently."

"I have a conversation I'd like for you to translate for me."

"I'd be happy to. Do you want to play it for me?"

Saad looked at his watch. The conversation between the two ladies had lasted almost an hour. He was to meet the American at eleven. There wasn't time.

"I'll send it to you. Listen to it at your convenience and get back with me. Mostly, I just want to know what was said. Of course, I'll pay you for your time."

"Not necessary. I'll let you buy the next time we have dinner."

"I always buy!"

"Then we should dine together more often."

The two men laughed heartily.

"We should have dinner soon. After you've finished with the translation, let's get together."

"I'd be happy to translate that for you as soon as I get it. Send it to my email address."

Saad wrote it down even though it was probably in his contacts. Then he hung up from the conversation and pulled up the file of the conversation and saved it to his computer which was linked to his security system. It took a while for the large audio file to download. When it did, he sent it to the professor's email address and closed his computer.

Then he went to see if the girls were ready to leave.

They'd better be.

He hated it when they kept him waiting.

* * *

Art Gallery
Abu Dhabi City

Saad and his entourage of four girls and two security guards, along with his driver, arrived at the art gallery fifteen minutes late. Mrs.

Steele was already there. Her rental Lamborghini was parked in front. The guards exited his vehicle first. Then Saad and his four girls filed out of his stretch limousine and entered the gallery. Per Saad's instructions, the painting was already packaged and ready for Mrs. Steele to take with her, although he wondered how she would fit it in her sports car. Not his problem. Once the transaction was finalized, she could make whatever arrangements she wanted.

Mrs. Steele's face lit up as soon as she saw him. He couldn't tell if she was genuinely interested or just trying to close the sale.

Seeing her caused the desire in him to reignite. She was wearing a black form-fitting dress and high stiletto heels. A scarf she'd use to cover her head if necessary, which wasn't around him, lay around her neck. Another thing he preferred about foreign girls. Mrs. Steele was much too lovely to hide her face and flowing blonde hair under a hijab, burqa, or scarf.

Seeing her reminded him of why he wanted her so much. He didn't remember the last time he met a woman as mesmerizing as Mrs. Steele. Such a shame she was married. He'd marry her himself if she weren't and if his religion allowed it.

He went right up to her and kissed her on both cheeks, leaving the other four girls behind. Jamie's fragrant hair and soft cheeks sent waves of desire through him. Perhaps he'd ask one more time if she wanted to stay the night in Abu Dhabi. He'd take her to a fine restaurant. Someplace where they could be alone. He'd leave his girls at home. Mrs. Steele didn't seem like the type that would consider a threesome.

A long shot, but it never hurt to ask. Before he could ask, a commotion at the front of the art gallery startled him.

Behind him.

He had just walked in, so he was still facing away from the entrance.

He heard shouting.

Mrs. Steele shrieked and then cowered down like something had frightened her.

Saad turned and looked to see what the commotion was all about.

What he saw turned his lustful desires into feelings of utter panic. A man in a ski mask was brandishing a gun. He'd already disarmed his two security guards.

The worthless fools.

They obviously hadn't been paying attention. When they followed him in, they should've watched his back. They were too complacent.

The gunmen ordered the security guards to the floor. To Saad's dismay, they obeyed him. He wanted them to attack the man. *The cowards.*

Was this an assassination attempt? Was he the target?

Then the man mentioned the painting. Speaking Turkish.

Ah! The White Wolves.

They had obviously sent this man. Saad could hardly believe it.

Did the White Wolves intend to kill him? Or just steal the painting?

Had he underestimated them? Perhaps he should've taken their offer of twenty-five million. His life was worth more than a measly seven and a half million dollars that he gained by selling it to Mrs. Steele. If they stole the painting, he'd get nothing.

Without warning, the gunman had his arm around Bianca.

She screamed.

The masked man pulled her close and had his gun to her head. All the blood had left Bianca's face, and she was white as a sheet.

"Anybody moves and I'll shoot her," the man yelled out. Violently. Like he meant what he said.

Saad recognized the man's voice. It was the same one on the phone that morning.

"Don't shoot," Saad shouted. "Take the painting, but don't harm the girl."

He needed to diffuse this situation. Surely the Turks didn't intend to harm anyone. They only wanted the painting. But why was he threatening the girl? While the girl had been frustrating last night, she was still his property. He considered this a personal attack. One that the White

Wolves would pay dearly for. It took a lot of nerve for them to come into his city in broad daylight, threaten his girls and him, and steal his property. If the White Wolves wanted a war, he'd give it to them.

Right now, though, he needed to get out of this alive.

Mrs. Steele was shaking. Her arms were on his back, and she peeked around him. Saad kept himself between her and the gunman. With his right hand, he placed his arm on her for reassurance.

"Don't do anything stupid," Saad said to everyone. "Just take what you want and leave," he said to the gunman.

"Where's the painting?" the gunman shouted. "Give me what I want, and no one gets hurt."

"It's by the door," Mrs. Steele said, pointing at a package by the entrance, inside a sturdy, wooden box frame. Safely wrapped for Mrs. Steele to take with her after they finalized the transaction.

The gunman inched back toward the door dragging Bianca with him. He swung her around, so she was behind him. Then backed her out the door. With his free hand, the gunman grabbed the painting. The man was big and strong. Bigger than most Turkish men. He picked it up with one hand like it was a toy.

The gunman backed out of the gallery with the weapon still pointed in their direction.

"Count to two minutes," he said. "Don't follow me. If anyone sticks their head out the door, I'll shoot it off."

Saad believed him. The man was clearly Turkish, but Saad couldn't place what region the gunman's accent was from.

Less than a minute later, Saad saw a white van flash by the front of the building. He rushed to the entrance.

His worst fear was realized.

The gunman had taken Bianca hostage.

10

A-Rad opened the back door of the van and carefully set the painting inside. He'd just exited the art gallery with his gun drawn, dragging Bianca along with him while clutching the painting. He ordered Bianca to get into the back of the van.

She hesitated.

"Now!" he shouted.

From the look of utter terror on her face, she clearly still had no idea what was going on.

"All the way to the back," he said.

She navigated around the painting and sat down on the floor of the van, which was clearly not easy to do in her high heels and tight dress.

Now was a critical time in the plan. A thousand things could go wrong. A-Rad had to hurry. He'd left the van running for a quick getaway.

They sped off.

Once he was out of sight of the art gallery, he ripped off the ski mask and threw it in the back. Bianca was still crouched on the floor, but now facing him, staring right at him. Panic gripped her face as every muscle from her chin to her forehead were tensed. So hard, lines were showing, which he doubted she actually had.

"Please don't hurt me," she said.

A-Rad smiled. He meant to comment, but the beauty of the woman and her vulnerability left him momentarily speechless. That, and he had to get his eyes back on the road or he'd crash the van which would put a significant glitch in the plan.

"I'm with Mrs. Steele," A-rad said to her. "You're safe now."

He heard her let out a huge sigh and say, "Thank you, God."

That wasn't entirely true. Bianca was in more danger now than she'd been in ten minutes ago. It still felt good to say it, though. A-Rad felt like her knight in shining armor saving the damsel in distress. While he'd risk life and limb for this woman he'd just met simply because Jamie asked him to, he hoped to keep further risk to a minimum.

"I thought... maybe," she said, stuttering somewhat. "You know. I thought you might be with her. But I didn't know. I was scared. You made it seem like you really were a bad guy."

"I am. For them. I'm their worst nightmare. My job was to get you out of there and take the painting. I'm glad it worked out."

Jamie had put together a good plan. Something A-Rad wasn't good at. He was better at executing other people's plans. In his mind, rushing in brandishing a gun wasn't the hard part. He had the element of surprise on his side, and the two guards were easy enough to disarm. The real challenge was getting Bianca and the painting to the plane without getting caught. He figured the police were already looking for a white van.

He wouldn't allow himself to relax until he had both safely on board. A task he figured would take about thirty minutes. He actually wouldn't rest until Jamie was on the plane too, and they were all safely in the air. Jamie had her own issues to deal with.

The important thing for him to do was get the van off the road as soon as possible. His route had been planned out in detail. Jamie forced him to memorize it. Something he wasn't good at doing. Fortunately, the preparation paid off, and he found the parking garage right where Jamie said it would be. It looked familiar because they had been there earlier in the morning to park a second getaway vehicle in one of the stalls.

A four-door white sedan was parked in level D, space 23. A-Rad backed the white van into the space next to it. The van had been stolen before dawn from a dry-cleaning pick-up and delivery service. The parking lot of the business had more than thirty such identical vans, and the hopes were that they wouldn't miss this one. They took one of five that had no lettering on the side.

"Put that burqa over you," A-Rad said to Bianca.

The black, traditional Muslim garment was laying on the floor next to Bianca. If somehow they were discovered, Bianca was to simply walk off wearing the burqa and blend in with the rest of the women walking around Abu Dhabi City in the same attire. A-Rad would deal with the threat while she got away. Hopefully, it wouldn't come to that, and Bianca could stay hidden in the van, and they could stay together. A-Rad would feel a lot better if Bianca never left his sight.

He explained the plan to her and where to meet Jamie if they got separated for any reason. He could see her tense up, probably feeding off his own concern. The thought of being separated from him was probably terrifying to her as well. Fortunately, she did what he asked and had the garment on in a matter of seconds.

"Stay out of sight," he instructed her. The last thing they needed was for someone to see an American male with a Muslim in a burqa sitting in a van. A police officer would arrest them on the spot and ask questions later. A-Rad wouldn't let that happen. While he wouldn't kill an innocent policeman just to get away, he wouldn't let them take him willingly. A-Rad touched his hip to make sure the gun was still there and within reach.

"I'll have us out of here and on the road within five minutes," he said. That was being optimistic.

A-Rad went around to the back of the van and opened the double doors. He ripped off the packaging on the painting and flipped it over, so the back side was facing up and the front side was lying on a protective cloth spread out on the van floor. With a screwdriver, he pried the painting out of the frame. Then broke the frame into pieces and put them on the ground next to the van.

He took out two layers of smooth, archival glassine paper, chemical free so as not to damage the painting. The paper was already cut to dimensions two inches larger than the painting all the way around. That's what he loved about Jamie. She didn't leave any detail to chance. Even though she'd been up all night dealing with some girl in a hospital she was trying to help, she never went to bed. Instead, she stayed up getting everything ready so things would go easier for A-Rad.

"I can sleep when I'm dead," Jamie had said.

Something A-Rad heard Curly say in training on more than one occasion.

A-Rad continued to work with the painting. Now came the tricky part. Jamie had shown him how to do it, but it still made him nervous.

"Roll it up like a sushi roll," she'd said. "Don't fold it. Roll it." She'd demonstrated the technique a number of times until he got it. Or at least got it enough to where she was satisfied. He still wasn't sure he could do it properly.

"It's okay. I trust you," Jamie said. "Don't even think about the fact that it's a forty-million-dollar painting, and that you'll ruin it if you roll it wrong."

By the sly grin on Jamie's face, he could tell she was joking. By the narrowed eyes, he could tell she was nervous about it.

"I'm just kidding," Jamie said. "We can restore it if we have to. But we won't have to *if* you roll it properly. Don't roll it too tightly. Do it gently. Like you're changing a baby's diaper."

"I've never changed a diaper before!"

"Picture your hands on a pretty girl's face. You're about to kiss her for the first time. That's how gently I want you to treat the painting."

"That I know how to do."

He tried to do it exactly like she'd said. Sweat was about to drip off his brow, so he wiped it with the sleeve of his shirt. Though hot outside, he was mostly sweating because he dreaded having to touch the painting. He'd much rather be touching a girl's face. That didn't make him nervous. Well... girls made him nervous, too. Not like this, though. He might as well be getting ready to perform surgery on someone. That's how nervous he felt.

Bianca was still crouched in the back of the van looking on. The only part of her body he could see were her eyes and hands. Even her eyes were stunningly gorgeous peering through the slit in the burqa. Olive colored. If that was a color.

Focus dummy.

He finished rolling the painting and felt like he'd done it right. At least the best he could under the circumstances. He took two steps back from the van to make sure the coast was still clear and that no one was around. The garage was mostly abandoned at that time of day.

The next step was to wrap a thin sheet of pre-cut bubble wrap around the painting and tape it in place. Then slide the painting into a tube and seal it shut.

After one last glance around the garage to make sure no one was watching, A-Rad said to Bianca in a serious tone, "Let's move. Take off the burqa and get out of the van."

He opened the passenger side door of the sedan and told her to get in. In the seat was a blonde wig and a pair of designer sunglasses.

"Put those on," he said.

While he didn't like ordering her around, time was of the essence, and she needed to act without hesitating. He took out all of the contents of the van and put them in the trunk of the sedan. The gun he kept on him. He put the tube with the painting in the backseat.

They sped out of the garage and headed toward the airport. He felt better and actually allowed himself to take in a few deep breaths.

"I'm Willy," he said, holding out his hand for Bianca to shake. Willy Shoemaker was his nickname on missions.

Her hand was trembling as she shook his which caused him to smile.

"You're going to be okay, now," A-Rad said reassuringly. "I won't let anything happen to you. We're going to get on a plane and get you back home."

"Thank you," she said with her voice cracking. A-Rad could see a tear or two escape her eyes and flow down her cheek, leaving a streak in her makeup. Wearing the wig, she actually did look like Jamie. Hopefully, the security guard at the airport would be fooled. If not, A-Rad would have a mess on his hands.

"When we get to airport security, you're going to pretend you're Mrs. Steele. In the glove box is her passport. Get it out and hand it to me. Mine's in there too. Give 'em both to me."

A-Rad pulled up to the security gate, rolled down the window, and handed the man both passports.

The man had an assault rifle over his shoulder and a firearm at his side. Another armed guard was in the guardhouse.

A-Rad could see their plane out on the tarmac, fueled, and ready to go. They were so close to safety.

They arrived at the entrance to the section of the airport where the private planes were parked. Security wasn't as tight as it was at the main airport, for obvious reasons, and A-Rad and Jamie had been there for several days and had come in and out of the gate multiple times without incident. The only difference this time was that they weren't in her Lamborghini. The security guard studied them closely. He looked down at the passports then leaned in and looked over at Bianca who was staring straight ahead.

"We're going to be leaving soon," A-Rad said to the man. "That's our plane over there. This is the last time you'll see us." He pointed in the direction of their jet.

Generally, passengers leaving didn't get the same scrutiny as arriving passengers. At least that's what he was hoping for. It would help if the man remembered him. A-Rad didn't recognize this particular man, but all the guards looked similar to him with their dark hair, scraggly beards, and thin faces with pointy chins.

"Have a good trip," the man said as he handed the passports back to A-Rad. He wanted to express the sudden elation he was feeling but maintained his stoic but friendly demeanor.

They drove through the guard gate and past the guard. As the gate closed behind them, both let out a collective sigh of relief. A-Rad parked next to their plane. Bianca was almost giddy, and her demeanor totally changed. She clapped her hands together and rocked back and forth in her seat with delight. A-Rad could only imagine the joy she must be feeling. Almost like she was getting out of jail. In a weird kind of way, she was.

A-Rad didn't completely share her enthusiasm. Although he was pleased this part of the plan had gone well and Bianca was safe, he wouldn't rest until Jamie was on the plane and they were in the air.

A number of things could go wrong for her. Would the police be called? Would she get caught up in an investigation? Would the Sheikh suspect anything?

A-Rad had tried to be believable with his accent on the phone with the Sheikh and again at the art gallery. Was Saad fooled? For whatever reason, A-Rad had a gift for sounding middle eastern. They'd discovered it during training on the Farm as A-Rad was constantly making fun of terrorists. Trying to talk like they talked as a joke.

Curly said it could be used on a mission. So, he made A-Rad study Arabic and Turkish and practiced speaking them for months until he perfected it. This was the first time he'd used it in the field. He thought it went well, but he wasn't sure. He tried to assure himself that everything would be okay, and that the Sheikh was duped.

If for whatever reason he wasn't fooled, Jamie could handle herself. Even if she ran into trouble, she could fight her way out of it if she had to. A-Rad would make sure the plane was ready to go in case she came speeding into the airport, crashed the gate, and was being shot at. Admittedly, his imagination was running wild. Still, he couldn't help but be concerned. When Jamie was in harm's way, he always felt whatever she was feeling as if he were right there beside her.

The biggest issue she might face was the security guard at the airport gate. A blonde-haired woman named Jamie Steele had already gone through security once. A-Rad had her passport. Jamie said she had a plan to get through a second time. He could always bring it out to her if she ran into trouble. The guards generally took a lunch break at the same time every day. As long as Jamie timed it right and arrived while they were on break, the new guards wouldn't know about the first Jamie.

Once the painting was securely in the plane and Bianca was comfortable, A-Rad took a seat by one of the windows. An assault rifle was now over his shoulder.

He kept his eyes peeled on the front security gate.

Just in case.

11

"You stole the painting," Alex said to me. The tone was between a statement of disbelief and a question. I wasn't sure which he intended.

"Yep," I said.

"You took the painting without paying the Sheik for it?"

"Yep."

"Just so I'm clear, Jamie, you left Abu Dhabi with the painting *and* the money?"

"Right."

"The Sheikh is out the painting, and he's also out—"

"Alex! How many times are you going to ask me the same question, just worded differently?"

"I'm just trying to understand what happened."

"I'll explain it to you."

"This I've got to hear."

"First of all, the Sheikh's a bad guy. He's trafficking women or at least holding them as sex slaves, so to speak. Against their will anyway. It's complicated. I don't feel bad about taking the painting without paying for it."

"How did you manage to do that?"

"I'm getting to that!"

"Sorry. Continue."

"A-Rad called the Sheikh, pretending to be a member of the White Wolves."

"The Turkish Mafia?"

"Right."

I wished he wouldn't interrupt me. It broke my train of thought. Alex knew who the White Wolves were.

"Anyway, A-Rad offered to buy the painting from the Sheikh at a lower price. Of course, he refused. So... we stole it from him. The Sheikh thinks the White Wolves stole it. So, we're in the clear."

"Won't the Sheikh call the cops?" Alex remained as serious as a preacher delivering a Sunday morning sermon.

"I don't think so. What are they going to do about it? I think the Sheikh will try to seek retribution from the White Wolves. Maybe start a little mini war over it."

I couldn't help almost laughing out loud about that.

"I suppose he'll be reimbursed by insurance," Alex said.

"He wasn't insured. At least that's what he said to me as I was leaving. You shoulda seen the look on his face when I walked out of the art gallery with the money. He didn't have the painting or the money, and one of his girl's was kidnapped. He was spitting mad."

"I made it back to the plane with no problems," she continued, "and we took off shortly after. We're somewhere over the Mediterranean Sea on our way to Switzerland. I took a nap for a couple hours and then called you as soon as I woke up."

"What are you going to do with the painting?"

"Sell it to our buyer. I'm meeting Mr. Takumi in Geneva Switzerland."

"Jamie! You're going to sell him a hot painting? Does he know that?"

"It's not hot."

"Please explain."

"I have a bill of sale. Sheikh signed it yesterday when we agreed on the price. He forgot to ask for it back."

"But he doesn't have the money."

"That's his word against mine. I've got a signed bill of sale. I also have a transaction receipt from the bank saying I got a cashier's check for the same amount."

"You've got to be kidding me!"

"Don't worry about it. I have a paper trail. Besides, it's never going to come up. Mr. Takumi is buying the painting for personal reasons. He wants to leave it to his kids. It's not like it's going up for auction anytime soon. Doesn't matter anyway. Saad isn't going to report the painting as stolen, and he certainly doesn't run in those circles where he'd see it up for sale."

I was depositing the cashier's check in Switzerland on purpose. If it ever did become an issue, the Swiss banks prided themselves on secrecy. Saad would never be able to prove that the money didn't go to him.

"Sounds like you've covered all the bases."

"I have. When I get to Geneva, I'll deposit the thirty-two million in our account, plus the forty million from Mr. Takumi. That'll give us a nice profit for the month."

"You can definitely make a good profit when you have no cost of acquisition."

"No doubt. Maybe we'll make a living stealing artwork from dirty oligarchs."

"Hey! I thought it was thirty-two and a half million. Are you skimming some on the side?"

"No. I'm giving Bianca a half million dollars. For her trouble. Although, skimming is a good idea. Thanks for that. I'm the one getting shot at. I should take a commission."

"I didn't know you were shot at."

"I wasn't. I just said that for dramatic effect. I should negotiate combat pay into my contract."

"Who's Bianca?" he asked, ignoring my jokes. I owned half the company, so I didn't have an employment contract. I could take whatever

I wanted. AJAX had been so profitable our first year, we hadn't yet dipped into the hundred million dollars allocated for our budget.

"Bianca is a girl I rescued from the Sheikh."

"I don't need to know the details. I'm glad everything went well. Good job. Does this mean you're coming home to me soon?"

"No. Sorry. As soon as I'm done in Geneva, I'm going back to Abu Dhabi."

"You're joking!"

"Not at all."

"Do you think that's a good idea? Showing your face around there again. What if the Sheikh figures out that you were the one who took the painting?"

"I have to go back."

"Why?"

"There are more girls to save."

* * *

The blueprints for the Sheik's house were on a laptop sitting on a table in the living area of our jet. Bianca and I were at the table going over them. After I pried her away from A-Rad. The two had really hit it off and neither had barely noticed me since we left Abu Dhabi. She was clearly smitten by him, and he was like a starry-eyed schoolboy over her.

Curly called it a "bullet romance." He said that when bullets were flying, emotions ran high. When the fighting stopped, the emotions didn't always go away immediately. It wasn't unusual for romantic feelings to emerge between two people in the throes of battle. I'd seen it a number of times with my husband, Alex. The passion between us often intensified after getting shot at.

I didn't try to put a damper on it. I let A-Rad enjoy it. Bianca was a beautiful and sweet girl. She'd been through a lot though. She'd have a lot of emotional scars to get over once she got home. Letting them both have a break from reality and some fun together for a few hours seemed like a good thing.

In the year I'd known A-Rad, I never once heard him mention a girl or even going on a date. Despite his manly exterior, he was a shy and introverted teddy bear on the inside. He'd never have the courage to go up to someone like Bianca and introduce himself. This opportunity fell in his lap. She was smitten by her hero, so to speak.

Right now, though, I needed intel. The romance would have to wait for a few minutes.

"Show me where the girls are staying?" I asked.

"Right here. We each had our own room."

"You said Anya wanted to leave. Are you sure?"

"Positive. I'm worried about her. I'm not there to protect her. We sort of protected each other. Or at least helped each other get through it. Are you going to try and help her as well?"

"Yes. Which one is Anya's room?"

Bianca pointed it out.

I asked Bianca a series of questions. How many guards were there? Where did they stay? How often did they change shifts? Was there a security system? Where were the cameras? Was there a motion detector system? How often were the girls there alone? Did the Sheikh have a routine?

Bianca had little information, but asking the questions helped jog my memory of what I'd observed. When I had all the information I needed from her, I excused myself and told Bianca to wait there. That I'd be right back. I went and got a briefcase out of the vault.

The vault was a secret compartment in the plane. Before we left Abu Dhabi, the authorities searched our plane. Standard procedure, and I had expected it. Bianca, the painting, and the cashier's check were stashed in the vault, which was built specifically for that reason. A hiding place, but also a safe room. It couldn't be detected without tearing out walls. We also had our stash of weapons and tradecraft spying gadgets in the vault. It had served us well on many occasions, flying in and out of hostile environments.

Alex and I had even used it to smuggle Bibles into Senegal, Nigeria, Kenya, and Mali where owning one was illegal. It had certainly come in handy in Abu Dhabi getting Bianca out of the country undetected.

I returned from the vault with a satchel in my hand. When I sat it in front of Bianca, she asked, "What's this?"

"Open it," I said.

When she opened it, her mouth flew open as she took some of the money and held it in her hands. When I went by the bank in Abu Dhabi, I also took out a half million in cash.

"What's this?" she asked again.

"Let's just say it's your payment from the Sheikh for services rendered."

"How much is it?"

"A half a million dollars. That's more than the three hundred thousand euros you would've made had you stayed the full year. That's assuming the Sheikh was even going to pay you."

"I don't know what to say."

"Say that you've learned your lesson, and you won't fall into one of these traps again."

"I can say that for sure."

"When we get to Geneva, Switzerland, we'll go to the bank and set up an account for you. Once you get back to Paris, you can do whatever you want with it. Wire it to your own bank. Keep it in there. Take it out when you need it or all at once. It's your money to do with as you wish."

She threw her arms around my neck and hugged me tightly.

"I don't know how to ever repay you. Thank you for the money and thank you for saving me."

"You don't have to. You helped me get the painting. That's payment enough."

"What about Saad? Is he going to come after me?"

"When you get home, wait a couple of weeks. Then send him an email. Tell him that your kidnappers let you go, and you went home. That you're not coming back. You're too afraid. If the authorities question you, tell them he was holding you against your will, and you escaped from your kidnappers and flew back home."

"What about my contract? He'll have me arrested."

"Do you ever intend to travel to Abu Dhabi again?"

"Never! I don't ever want to step foot in that place. Ever again."

"Then it'll never be a problem. He can't enforce the contract in France. I'd like to see him try. All you have to do is tell Interpol what the Sheikh has been up to and what he put you through, and he would be the one with a warrant out for his arrest. I assume he'll let the whole thing go. By emailing him, he'll quit looking for you. He might even send you the six months' pay he owes you. Although, I wouldn't count on it."

The cockpit door flew open and A-Rad appeared. The plane was obviously on autopilot.

"Are you guys done yet?" he asked. "I promised Bianca I'd let her fly the plane."

She looked at me and I nodded my approval. I almost felt like a mother telling her daughter she could go to the school dance.

Bianca bolted out of her seat, and the two disappeared almost before I could blink.

I felt suddenly tired again and went back into my room.

"Sleep and eat when you can," Curly always said. "You never know when you'll get another chance."

I had no idea what was facing us back in Abu Dhabi.

Amina.

Anya.

My phone rang interrupting my thoughts.

"Hi honey," I said with a yawn.

"I did some checking on that girl from Canada. Odille Coste."

Odille was the girl Bianca said went missing one day after she refused to service the Sheikh anymore. The Sheikh took her out to his yacht, and Bianca hadn't seen or heard from her since. I'd asked Alex to see what he could find.

"What did you find out?" I asked.

"She's missing. Her family hasn't heard from her in over a month. They're starting to get concerned."

Add Odille to the list which kept getting longer.

Another girl who needed saving.

If she was still alive.

Were there others?

12

MJ

The International Evangelical Community Church of Abu Dhabi
MJ's 18th birthday and wedding day

MJ had counted down the days to her eighteenth birthday with excitement and trepidation. Now the day was here, and she felt unspeakable joy that she was marrying the boy of her dreams. Christopher and MJ took the attorney's advice and didn't see each other until the wedding. The first time she'd see him was when she walked down the aisle in a few short minutes.

On the other hand, she saw his mother, Ivory, every day. She took it upon herself to plan every aspect of the wedding and tried her best to make it special for MJ. They went dress shopping, shoe shopping, and by the time they were done, MJ had an entirely new wardrobe including a white wedding dress that was the most extravagant piece of clothing MJ had ever seen, much less worn. Together they went to a spa, and MJ had her hair, nails, and makeup done by a professional for the first time ever.

"You're like the daughter I never had," Ivory had said.

"You're like the mother I never had," MJ replied.

MJ almost couldn't believe her good fortune. Every morning, she'd wake up in a panic thinking it all was a dream. Then she'd run to the bedroom closet at her Aunt's house and see her wedding dress hanging regally next to her new clothes, above her torn and tattered old clothes lying on the floor in a heap, and realize it really was happening to her.

Fortunately, she only saw her father twice in that time. Once in passing when she went by the house to pick up some things, and again when he came by the Aunt's house to go over the wedding plans with Abdul Sham. On that occasion, he behaved nicely to her. She guessed so as not to abuse his possession from which he was about to make a mini fortune.

He gave her permission to miss school that day. He'd pick her up at noon. Take her to the mosque. They'd say their vows, and she'd be out of his hair for good. Those were his very words. She couldn't expect him to be completely nice.

MJ almost couldn't keep from smiling. She wasn't going to school that day anyway. In fact, she'd never go back there again. After the wedding, Christopher and MJ would go to the passport office and pick up her papers. From there, they'd catch the first flight to America. Then she'd *be out of her father's hair for good*.

Those were her words.

MJ imagined her father's face when he came to her Aunt's house and MJ was nowhere to be found. When he finally figured out she wasn't coming back, he'd have to return the dowry. Some of which was probably already spent. He'd be beyond furious.

Her main concern was Aunt Shule. Her father would want to take out his rage on someone. Auntie would feign ignorance, of course, and it'd take her father days, if not months, to sort it all out and learn the truth. If he ever did figure it out. As far as he knew, she'd just disappeared like a vapor in the wind. He'd never think to look for other marriage documents or a passport application. Hopefully, he'd think she just ran away, maybe file a police report, and then eventually give up looking.

In a few hours, it'd all be a distant memory.

MJ was in a backroom at the church getting dressed with Auntie helping her. Ivory was out in the chapel making sure all the preparations were properly taken care of. She seemed almost as excited about the day as MJ did.

When the finishing touches were put on her hair and makeup and she was finally in the wedding dress, her Aunt gushed compliments, and MJ could feel herself radiating emotion like a bright sun lamp.

"I've never seen anyone as beautiful as you," Auntie said, "You're glowing."

"It's the makeup," MJ said. "It has glitter in it. Can you believe it? I feel like a princess."

"You look like one."

Auntie gave MJ an affectionate hug, trying not to displace any of the great care that had gone into the preparations of the bride.

"I want you to have this," Auntie said, handing something to MJ in a small box.

"What is it?"

"It was my mother's. She gave it to me. I'm giving it to you. I never had a daughter. You're the closest thing... " Auntie teared up and her voice cracked as she couldn't complete the sentence.

MJ opened the box and gasped. A beautiful necklace. A cross. Gold with a small diamond in the center. Elegant. Her grandmother's.

MJ threw her arms around Auntie's neck.

"It's so beautiful. I love it."

"You can only wear it at the wedding. Then take it off until you're out of the country."

"When I get to America, I'll wear it every day," MJ said, fighting back the tears. "It'll remind me of you."

"Don't cry, honey," Auntie said. "You're going to ruin your makeup."

"I'm going to miss you so much."

"I'm going to miss you, too."

A slight knock at the door and Ivory entered before they had a chance to say anything more. She must've seen them teary eyed, because her eyes suddenly teared up too, and she rushed next to them, putting her arms around Auntie and MJ.

"I know," she said. "I've been crying all morning. My baby boy's getting married. Can you believe it?"

She stepped back from MJ and looked her over from head to toe. With her hands clutching both of MJ's arms, she said, "You look stunning. You're the prettiest bride I've ever seen."

ML beamed like the bright desert sun. She could barely contain her excitement.

"Are you ready to do this?" Ivory said.

MJ's hands were shaking.

"I guess I am."

* * *

The wedding was a blur.

MJ barely remembered it. She knows she said, "I do." A ring was on her finger, so she must be married. She'd signed the marriage certificate, so it was official. Or at least would be once it was filed with the court. The preacher pronounced them man and wife. So, she was married in the eyes of God, which ultimately was the most important thing. She could hardly believe it. For days, she'd worried unnecessarily that it'd never happen. Now that it had, she was trying to let it sink in and feel the joy of it.

Truthfully, until they were on the plane, she wasn't going to let herself feel all the excitement. Something could still go wrong.

Christopher and MJ left the church in her Auntie's car to much fanfare. She drove them to the passport center. MJ made an application a couple of weeks before but couldn't officially get her passport until she turned eighteen. Without the passport, she couldn't board the plane and leave the country. Christopher had a copy of their wedding certificate in case they needed it. They'd definitely need it to enter the United States.

MJ wasn't sure what to think. Mixed emotions swirled around inside her like a blender. Things were going too well. She wanted to let the feelings of happiness loose inside of her, but she still had an ominous feeling lurking.

Auntie pulled into a parking space, and they all entered the building together. The line for a passport application was long, but they moved right through the one for picking up a passport quickly. MJ gave the lady who had what looked to be a permanent frown on her face, her name and information.

"I'm here to pick up my passport, please," MJ said.

"I need your birth certificate."

A bolt of panic hit her like a lightning bolt. *I knew this was too good to be true.*

"I gave a copy to the lady when I made the application," MJ insisted.

"It's not in the file."

MJ looked at Auntie who only shrugged her shoulders. Auntie was with her when they made the passport application. MJ specifically remembered giving it to the lady because she'd gone to great lengths to secure it. The birth certificate was in her father's files. She had to rummage through them to find it. She never took it back home. The original was at her aunt's house for safekeeping.

"I specifically remember giving it to her," MJ said. "Can you look through the file again?"

"It's not here," the lady said in an exasperated tone like they were bothering her. "Do you have a guardian's certificate giving you permission to leave the country?"

"They said I didn't need it if I had my birth certificate. Today's my birthday. I turned eighteen today. So legally, I'm old enough to get my passport without a guardian's certificate."

"That's true," the woman said tersely. "But you don't have a birth certificate. You'll need a copy before I can give you your passport."

MJ could see the passport laying there in the file. Opened. It had her picture on it. They were so close. For a moment, she thought about snatching it out of the file, but she thought better of it.

"Can I act as her legal guardian?" Auntie said.

"Are you her legal guardian?"

"I'm her aunt."

"That's not what I asked you. Do you have a court document showing that you are this girl's legal guardian?"

"No."

"Then I'm going to need your birth certificate."

"I don't have it with me."

"Then step out of line and let the next person in."

MJ started to object, but Auntie pulled MJ's arm and practically dragged her away from the counter. "We'll go back to my house and get the birth certificate and bring it back here," Auntie said.

MJ looked at the clock on the wall. It read 10:05.

"What about father? He's expecting me to be at your house at noon. That's when he's picking me up to take me to the mosque to marry Abdul."

MJ saw the hurt on Christopher's face as he grimaced, and his lips contorted.

"If we hurry, we can get there before he does," her Aunt said.

"I'm coming with you," Christopher said.

"No!" Auntie exclaimed. "You can't go anywhere near my house. If her father sees you, there's no telling what he'll do."

"What do you want me to do?" Christopher said.

"Wait here," Auntie said. "We'll be back in about two hours. Maybe I should just go. MJ, you stay here with Christopher."

"You'll never find where I hid the birth certificate," MJ said.

"Tell me where it is."

MJ tried to explain, but Aunt Shule didn't understand.

"I'll come with you," MJ said. "I know right where it is."

"If your father sees you, we'll act like everything's normal and then sneak away when he's not looking."

Christopher started to hug MJ, but Auntie pushed him away. "Don't Christopher! You kids have to be careful. No public displays of affection. You can hug and kiss all you want once you're safely on that plane. Until then, don't do anything to draw the attention of the authorities."

Several police officers were standing around. One looked their way.

"Let's get out of here," Auntie said.

"We'll be back soon, I promise," MJ said to Christopher. As they walked out the door, MJ looked back and waved. *I'll be back soon.*

13

Abu Dhabi International Airport

Brad, my CIA handler, wasn't supportive of me going back to Abu Dhabi. We'd just landed so he wouldn't be able to talk me out of it now.

"You're going to all this trouble and risk for one girl!" He'd said it with a rare show of emotion.

"It's two girls," I argued.

"You don't even know if the second girl's still alive."

"I meant Amina. Three girls if you include Odille."

Odille was the girl from Canada who disappeared off the face of the earth after refusing to have sex with the Sheikh. I didn't know if I could find her, but I was going to try.

"What can you do for Amina?" Brad said. "She might be in jail by now for all we know."

"I don't know. That's why I'm here. I'm going to assess the situation and come up with an MSO, and a plan." MSO was Mission Success Odds. I had no idea what the plan would be.

But I wasn't going to argue with him. I did want to assure him that I wasn't going to run off and do something stupid. He was right. Strategically, it didn't make any sense. Objectively, the rewards didn't merit the risk involved.

It costs thousands of dollars just to fly the plane back across the Mediterranean to get there. Something Brad never would've never let me do if the CIA were footing the bill. Since AJAX was covering it, he didn't have any say in it. And with the forty-million-dollar profit on the painting I stole from the Sheikh, Alex, my husband and business partner in AJAX, could hardly make a financial argument. Not that he tried. He was supportive of whatever I wanted to do.

Besides, the skeleton plan I had swirling around in my mind might bring a windfall to AJAX that would make the heist of the forty-million-dollar painting look like change for a parking meter. I wasn't ready to share that plan with anyone just yet. Not even A-Rad. Not even Alex.

"There may be more girls," I said to Brad as A-Rad walked into the center section of the plane after bringing it to a stop at the hangar.

"Don't expand the operation, Jamie," Brad said. "We have no way to extract dozens of girls."

I wanted to respond, but I knew he was right.

"If you need a fix, go down to the southern border wall. Now that we have an open-border policy, you can rescue four or five girls an hour down there."

What he said almost sent me into a rage. If I cussed, now would be the time I'd let one fly. I didn't rescue girls for kicks. Or for a fix. This was my life. While Brad cared about the girls in a weird and different way, for him, rescuing girls was wrapped up in missions. Operations. Strategic interests.

Rescuing girls from a horrible life of slavery was my passion in my life. My obsession. I cared about every single girl the same.

No man left behind.

Curly's words were drilled into me during training. It didn't apply to this situation in the way Curly meant it, but I had adopted it as my motto.

No girl left behind.

I didn't expect Brad to understand. It took Alex a long time to get it, but he finally did.

He gets me. It's who I am.

I was under no illusion that I could save the world. But I could do my small part. Bianca. Anya. Odille. Amina. They needed me. I didn't seek them out. They came across my path. Maybe by divine providence. I didn't know. All I knew was that I could help them. If it meant risking my life, then I would.

"I have to go," I said abruptly. "My plane's arriving."

Then I hung up the phone. Roughly. Brad would never know I'd done it in anger, but it made me feel like I was hanging up on him, and I felt better afterward.

Brad was right, though. I had to limit the operations. While I was able to extract Bianca easily enough, there was no way I could've gotten dozens of girls out of Abu Dhabi without getting caught. Not feasible. While Brad made me angry, I gave him grace. It'd been a long time since he'd been in the field. Looked in a victim's eyes. Watched someone die in front of him.

To his credit, he wasn't like a lot of the suits at Langley who treated girls like they were statistics. Numbers to be played with and manipulated. Brad genuinely cared. He'd been departmentalized. Meaning, his job was to analyze resources and allocate them where they made the most sense. Sometimes he said the wrong thing and sounded callous and uncaring. I knew his heart. He'd do the same thing if he were me and in the field.

What made the most sense to me was being exactly where I was. We had flown over the city of Dubai, and I could see the majestic skyline of Abu Dhabi as we were landing. Two majestic cities. By almost every measure, the richest cities in the world. Grand. Opulent. The towering skylines were monuments to extravagance.

I almost wept.

I'd read the threat assessment Brad had sent me. The report said Dubai now led the world in prostitution per capita. The information was staggering. I almost didn't believe it. Here was a country that would arrest you for holding hands or kissing in public but looked the other way when it came to illegal prostitution.

Sickening.

Something Brad couldn't understand without being here. He never saw Amina's face after being severely beaten and brutally raped by men who would probably face no consequences for their actions. I saw it firsthand. Amina's image was seared in my brain. How could I leave her here to be further abused by the legal system?

"What's the plan?" A-Rad asked, interrupting my thoughts.

"I'm going to the hospital," I said.

I had to see how Amina was doing.

I prayed to God she was still there.

* * *

Amina and MJ

Samitah dozed off in the chair in her daughter, Amina's, hospital room. She didn't know how long she'd been asleep when she was suddenly awakened by a commotion at the door.

A bolt of panic shot through her veins. At first, she thought it might be the police coming to arrest her daughter. It'd been two days since Amina was gang raped repeatedly by four men, brutally beaten, and then left alongside the road to die. While Amina was better, she was still in no condition to be hauled off and put in a prison cell with abhorrent conditions, no medical care, and scant food and water.

Samitah breathed a sigh of relief when she saw that the first person through the door was a nurse maneuvering a hospital bed through the doorway. An orderly on the other end steered the bed into the room, and a woman with a distressed look on her face entered behind them. Her eyebrows were furrowed, her lips pursed, and her shoulders as tense as a crane straining to lift a heavy load. Her eyes were red from where she'd obviously been crying.

From Samitah's vantage point, the person in the hospital bed was a girl. About Amina's age. Seventeen or eighteen. She couldn't be sure because the girl had bandages all over her. On her legs, hands, arms, and neck. Mostly on her right side. Each time the bed hit a bump the girl let out a moan. Even though she appeared to be heavily sedated, it evidently hadn't completely muted the pain.

They got the bed in position, and after the nurse left, Samitah offered the woman her chair.

"I don't want to take your place," the woman said with a sorrowful tone.

"I need to stretch my legs anyway," Samitah replied. She surmised the woman to be about her age.

The lady slumped in the chair like the weight of the world was on her shoulders. She rubbed her eyes roughly as tears began to trickle down her face. Samitah wanted to offer her some comfort but didn't even know her name. Instead, she just walked over to the sink and got the woman a glass of water from the tap.

"Thank you," the lady said, managing a smile. As quickly as the smile flashed across her face, the pained look returned.

"What's your name?" Samitah asked softly.

"Shule," she said.

"Is that your daughter?"

"My niece."

"This is my daughter," Samitah said, pointing at Amina, who had somehow managed to sleep through the commotion. She was still sedated as well. The swelling on Amina's face had diminished slightly but now had turned into an array of black and blue, almost purple colors. Samitah winced each time she looked at her daughter. Amina's right eye was still closed shut, and they wouldn't know if her eyesight was impacted until the swelling was completely gone.

"What happened to her?" Shule asked with obvious concern.

"Four men savagely beat her," Samitah responded bitterly. She wouldn't tell the lady about the rape. The rape by the married man was what could get Amina thrown in jail. Possibly even stoned to death. The woman in front of her seemed to be a kind and gentle person, sympathetic to Amina's plight, but the tribal authorities had a way of extracting testimony out of the most well-intentioned bystanders. Samitah could see this woman being dragged into court to discuss their conversations if she said the wrong thing. Saying Amina was raped aloud was almost like a confession.

"I'm so sorry," the woman said. "What's her name?"

"Amina."

To Samitah's surprise, the woman stood from her chair. walked over to Amina's bedside. put her hand on her daughter's head and stroked her hair. Mumbled a few words under her breath. Then sat back down.

"What's your niece's name?" Samitah asked.

"Majahammaddan, but we call her MJ."

"What happened to her?"

Shule's hands began shaking and her upper lip quivered. She clutched her hands to get them to stop.

Her voice cracked as she said, "Her father poured kerosene on her and then... set her on fire."

14

Gaziantep, Turkey

A steady rain beat down on Roha Zamani's head. Standing in the rain was unnecessary. The bomb would go off. He had no doubt about that. But Zamani liked to view his handiwork. Particularly when he'd been paid $100,000 in American dollars for it. Normally, he demanded less for his services. But the target was a mob boss in the Turkish mafia. Zafa Rafiq—second in command and a high-profile target.

The bombing would bring a lot of attention. Rafiq was a general in the White Wolves and a man of considerable power and influence. Whatever he'd done to deserve elimination from this earth was of no concern to Zamani. Sheikh Saad Shakir of Abu Dhabi wanted him dead and was willing to pay good money for him to make it happen. His line of work was an unemotional exercise. People hired him because he was the best. Methodical and ruthless. He didn't leave a trail. Things couldn't be traced back to him. As far as the White Wolves were concerned, Rafiq would be killed by a phantom ghost.

But for whatever reason, Shakir wanted his signature on the killing. He wanted the White Wolves to know it was him. Normally, the Turkish Mafia were not ones to be messed with or to be taken lightly.

Great care had gone into the planning. For two days, he followed his target. Learned his routine and watched for vulnerabilities. What he found was that the man had a penchant for the ladies as most men do. Bars and strip clubs were his main vices.

The Turkish man was careless. That happened to men of power as they begin to think they're invincible. Almost anyone in the world could be killed at any time if someone had the motivation and ability to do it. Even Rafiq, with four bodyguards and a driver, had vulnerabilities of which he was unaware.

He followed the same routine every night. That made Zamani's job that much easier. Eleven o'clock, the man said goodnight to his wife and kids and got into his car and his driver took him to a local club. Since Zamani knew when and where the man would be at that time of night, all he had to do was place the bomb in a trash can next to the car. Why the bodyguards were dumb enough to leave it there, was beyond Zamani's understanding. Not that it mattered. He could kill Rafiq in any number of ways. He just liked it when the target made it easy for him.

As soon as Rafiq walked past the dispenser to get in his car, Zamani would push the button, and the man would be history. The four, armed bodyguards were helpless to do anything about it. They couldn't protect him from a bomb. They couldn't even protect themselves. The bomb was so powerful, they'd all be killed.

The light in the upstairs children's bedroom flickered off. Zamani's heart raced faster. He took several deep breaths to slow it down. His only concern was the timing. If he pushed the button too soon, the target might not take the full force of the blast and would survive. Too late, and the man might be in the car. While it didn't appear that the vehicle was armored or built to withstand the blast, he didn't want to take any chances that the reinforced steel doors and windows of the high-end luxury limousine might blunt the force of the attack. The bomb needed to go off before the man entered the vehicle.

The front door opened, and the bodyguards appeared first. They looked in every direction. Instinctively, Zamani slinked back into the shadows, even though he was certain he couldn't be seen.

The first bodyguard walked down the steps and opened the car door. Two more men stood at the bottom of the stairs ahead of the target. As Rafiq neared the car, he looked around and tightened his jacket. Pulled the sleeves to the suit down on his wrists. Like he was a movie star. A big shot. His last act of arrogance on this earth.

Zamani pushed the button with perfect timing and precision. Not that there was ever any doubt. A second before to allow for the signal to travel the distance necessary to communicate with the bomb.

A fireball erupted.

The blast blew out the windows of the surrounding houses. Overkill perhaps. But Zamani didn't want to take any chances. When the smoke cleared, he observed five bodies on the ground. Rafiq and his four guards. The car had been lifted off the ground and moved several feet from the curb. No movement from the driver. He was probably dead as well. Obviously, not an armored vehicle.

Zamani pulled a mask down over his head and calmly walked across the street to the site of the bomb blast. He found the body of Rafiq, though barely recognizable. The remnants from the suit jacket and the expensive jewelry on his hands and around his neck gave him away. The man was obliterated. For good measure, Zamani took out his gun and fired three shots into the body. Unnecessary, but satisfying. If anything, the man was thorough. If he was paid to kill the man, he'd make certain the man was dead.

He then dropped a note From Sheikh Saad on the body and calmly walked away. He got in his car and drove away slowly in the opposite direction of the sirens that began to blare in the distance. He took off the mask and threw it in the back seat once he was several blocks away.

Then he dialed a number.

Sheikh Saad Shakir answered on the first ring.

"It's done," Zamani said.

"Excellent. The remainder of the money will be in your account in a matter of seconds."

"A pleasure doing business with you as always."

* * *

Sheikh Saad Shakir's house

The Sheikh stared at his computer screen, wondering how he felt about the message.

Saad. My kidnappers set me free once we got to Turkey. I've never been so scared in my life. I flew home. I hope you understand that I can't come back. Bianca.

Was he supposed to care? The kidnapping had been avenged. A member of the White Wolves was dead. From a bomb. The White Wolves now knew that he was a man not to be messed with. An eye for an eye. A life for a kidnapping and a painting. Actually, upon more introspection, he'd paid Zamani to avenge the stealing of the painting, not kidnapping the girl. Girls could be replaced. The painting couldn't. The fact that she wasn't coming back made him angry, but really, he had to force himself to feel any emotion. He hadn't missed her since the kidnapping and wouldn't miss her now.

Truthfully, he was glad she was gone. The last time they had sex had been boring at best. This way, he didn't have to pay her anything. The contract Bianca signed clearly stated that she had to stay the full year in order to get paid. That thought brought a smile to his face. He had saved three hundred thousand euros. Nearly four hundred thousand American dollars.

He picked up the phone and dialed a number he'd called hundreds of times.

"*As-Salam-u-Alaikum wa-rahmatullahi wa-barakatuh,*" the cleric said. *Peace be unto you and so may the mercy of Allah and his blessings.*

"*Wa Alaikum Assalam wa Rahmatullah,*" Saad responded.

"For what do I owe this honor, my friend?"

"I need a certificate of divorce. The girl, Bianca. I don't remember her last name. She is no longer of use to me."

Saad could hear the rustling of papers. Bianca didn't actually know they were married. When Saad initially approached the cleric about his scheme to bring girls from abroad to be his concubines, Sheikh Mo-hammad bin Lukman Ismael, a senior member of the Al Hafir order of Abu Dhabi, didn't approve.

"It is *zina*," he said in his usual loud and boisterous voice. "You will be damned to an eternity in hell!"

Saad was not a man to take no for an answer. He was used to find-ing ways around various laws in business and was determined to do so in his personal life as well.

"What do you suggest?" Saad asked.

"Have you considered a temporary marriage?" Sheikh Ismael said.

"Aren't those illegal?" Saad replied.

"Man's laws are not God's laws. God does not forbid it, so, neither do I. Besides, they will never know unless you or I tell them."

"How would it work?" Saad asked.

"You can only have four wives at a time. You can keep them for as long as you want. One hour or one year. That's up to you. When you're ready to divorce them, contact me. and I'll write a certificate of di-vorce. One final thing. The women must consent to the marriage."

That would be a problem. Saad tricked these women into coming to Abu Dhabi under the guise of being his models. With promises of mag-azine covers, fashion shoots, and stardom along with three hundred thousand euros. None of these women would've come had marriage been a requirement.

To get around that, Saad simply wrote a clause in the girl's contracts saying that they agreed to the union for one year. To his surprise, no one ever questioned it. As far as he was concerned, the union was an agreement to marriage. His word against theirs. No court in the UAE would take the word of a woman over a powerful Sheikh. What Ismael didn't know, didn't hurt him either. If he asked, Saad would show him the written contract. He never did ask. The cleric didn't require Saad to come into the mosque for the wedding ceremony. He simply asked him over the phone if he desired to be married and the legal name of the woman. According to Ismael, that made it all official, which was all Saad cared about.

"I have the marriage certificate in front of me," Ismael said. "When do you want the divorce to be effective?"

"Immediately," Saad said.

"Do you need another girl?" Ismael asked. "I have several to choose from. One just turned twelve. A virgin. Very beautiful. An orphan girl that I've taken in under my care. Only Seven thousand dirham." The equivalent of two thousand dollars. Young girls and virgins brought the most money. Saad paid a lot more than that for his professional girls, but they better suited his tastes.

"I'll get back with you on that," Saad said.

"*Assalaam-O-Alaikum Khuda Hafiz,*" he said. *Peace and blessings be unto you.*

Saad responded in kind and hung up.

He dialed Professor Jeric Hashami's number. He wanted to know what was on that security tape. The conversation between Bianca and Jamie Steele. When Mrs. Steele was at his house alone with her for nearly an hour. He'd emailed it to Jeric several days ago so he could translate it.

I have to find out what was said.

15

Amina and MJ

When I got to the hospital, I wasn't sure exactly what to expect. Was Amina still there? Had she been arrested? Was she still alive? While the quality of healthcare in the big cities of Dubai and Abu Dhabi were excellent, I didn't know if poorer girls like Amina got the same level of care. Her injuries didn't appear to be life threatening, but you never knew for sure when dealing with head injuries.

I was really confused when I opened the door and saw her mother, Samitah, sitting in a chair along the back wall with another woman sitting next to her. Their hands were clenched together and both of them were sobbing.

Was Amina dead?

I could see that she wasn't. The head of her hospital bed was elevated, and Amina was sitting up. Her eyes were closed, but she was clearly breathing, and the machine she was connected to, showed her vital signs were all normal. One eye was still swollen shut but looked better. She opened her other eye, looked at me and smiled faintly. I smiled back and touched her foot through the blankets.

My focus turned to the two ladies and why they were in so much pain.

Then I noticed another bed in the room in the far corner. A young girl. Maybe eighteen. Amina's age. She had heavy white bandages from the side of her neck all the way down the right side of her body. What struck me the most was the smell in the room. A lingering odor of kerosene and charred flesh overwhelmed the antiseptic smell of the hospital. I'd smell it before. After a suicide bombing and in a sex trafficking warehouse where bodies were being disposed of by burning them.

It didn't take long to figure out that this poor girl had suffered burns. If kerosene was involved, it was likely intentional. Somebody set her on fire.

When Samitah saw me, her tears stopped flowing momentarily, and she burst out of her chair. Her arms were around my neck before I could move toward her.

"I was hoping you'd come back," she said.

"I said I would."

The other woman stood. Still off to the side. Samitah grabbed her hand and pulled her toward us.

"This is Shule. That's her niece, MJ."

She pointed to the other bed.

"Shule, this is Jamie. The lady I told you about."

The woman put her arms around my neck and squeezed. I put my arms around her and returned the hug even though it felt awkward. Considering we didn't know each other, somehow, we already had a bond. Or at least the woman thought we did. She was clearly desperate for help. Something bad had obviously happened to her and to MJ. The woman's face was frozen in agony. Her brow was furrowed, her eyes, red from crying, and her jaw clenched.

"Let's sit down," I said, motioning for them to take their seats. "Tell me what's going on. How's Amina?"

"She's better," Samitah said.

"Has the tribal elder been back?" I asked.

"No. But I expect he will be soon."

I sat on the edge of Amina's bed. "Tell me what happened to MJ," I said as I reached out and touched Shule on the hand.

"It's horrible. Her father did this to her."

"What did her father do?" I asked, though I thought I already knew. I could guess why but wanted to hear their story.

Shule proceeded to tell me the entire story. MJ was her niece. Her mom was Shule's sister. MJ grew up without her mother. Her mother was married to a horrid man. MJ became a Christian. During that part of the story was the only time I saw Shule smile. She also lowered her voice to a whisper at that point. Even though the door was closed, she was clearly terrified that someone might hear her talking about MJ converting to Christianity.

MJ's conversion brought tears to my eyes. I feared that might be why her father had attacked her. I'd heard of "honor killings." A term used to describe it when Muslim family members killed their kin for converting to Christianity. I hated the name. There was no honor in killing someone for exercising their God-given right to accept or reject Christ. My anger for what happened to Amina was already high. This story was setting my resolve on fire.

Shule got to the part where MJ met Christopher. They fell in love. She relayed the whole story of the attorney and his advice to marry in a church then leave the country. It sounded like a wise thing to do. The kids were married earlier today. In a Christian church. By a pastor. A beautiful wedding.

Then the story turned to the passport fiasco. The bureau lost the birth certificate. MJ couldn't leave the country without the passport, and they wouldn't give it to her without the proof of age. They had to go back to Shule's house to retrieve the certificate. The whole time, Shule was worried that MJ's father might be there.

"We were only going to be a minute."

"What about Christopher?" I asked. "He must be worried sick. MJ never showed up. Do you know how to get in touch with him?"

Shule had little information. While Shule had a phone at her house, she didn't have a cell phone. Even if she did, she didn't know Christopher's number or his parent's phone numbers. The only thing she knew was their address in Abu Dhabi City. The Tate's knew Shule's address as well because Christopher had been there. My guess was that

Christopher and his parents had already been by her house. When they didn't find MJ or her aunt, they must've been beside themselves in worry.

Shule continued with her story. When she got to the actual attack, the tears returned like a flood.

"We were at my house. We went there to get MJ's birth certificate. Her father showed up... He was early... He wasn't supposed to get there until noon... MJ forgot to take off her wedding ring. And the cross necklace. I'd given it to her as a gift. I told her to take it off after the wedding. Foolish girl."

I could see how she could forget with everything she had on her mind.

"Her father saw the ring and the necklace and started yelling at her. MJ screamed back at him. 'I will not marry Abdul. I'm already married. And I'm wearing the cross because I'm a Christian!'"

Shule took a deep breath.

"Her father hit her. Slapped her hard across the face. MJ fell to the floor. He was so filled with hate. Like a madman. Totally out of control. I thought he was going to kill her right then and there."

Between each sentence were sobs. I got her some tissues and tried to comfort her.

"Take your time," I said.

"I ran into the other room and called the police. I didn't know what else to do. I couldn't fend him off. I knew she was in danger, but I didn't know he'd set her on fire. How could anyone be that cruel?"

Shule buried her head in her hands.

"I heard the door close. I thought he'd left. I hung up the phone and hurried to MJ. She was stunned, but still awake. We tried to get out of there before he came back. I saw him coming toward the front door, so I locked it. But he busted it down. He's a big man. He had something in his hands. I tried to get between them, but he pushed me aside and knocked me to the floor."

Samitah had her arm around Shule's shoulder and pulled her toward her. Shule let her as she slumped in her arms.

"I've never seen a man so angry."

She left out none of the gruesome details. He set MJ on fire just as Shule walked back in the room and went outside. Shule was able to get the fire out with a blanket. The police arrived at that time and called the ambulance and brought her here.

"It could've been a lot worse," the doctor had said. "A lot worse."

Apparently, he was only able to spray the kerosene on the right side of her body as she turned away from him. MJ had burns on forty percent of her body, but only the burns to her arm were severe. The main issue for the first forty-eight hours was the risk of infection.

"Did the police arrest her father?" I asked.

"Yes. They took him away, but he's probably out of jail by now."

"Any chance he'll come here?" I asked.

Shule shrugged her shoulders.

What I really wanted to do was take both girls out of the hospital, put them on my plane, and fly them to America. That's exactly what I would've done if they were in good enough condition to leave the hospital. But both of the girls would need several more days of healing.

I also had to deal with the Sheikh.

Rescue Anya.

Search for Odille.

After doing so, I'd come back for these girls.

"I'll find Christopher and tell him where to find MJ," I said. "Give me his address."

"Oh no," Shule said. "He can't come here. Please tell him to stay away. The tribal police will arrest him. And MJ. We can't tell anyone what happened."

"Why would they arrest MJ? What did she do wrong?"

"Nothing. But I don't want to take that chance."

The door burst open.

As if on cue.

In walked the man. The same one who'd been there the night I'd brought Amina in. He recognized me immediately.

"So... it's you again," he said to me.

"Good afternoon, Officer," I said, trying to be amiable.

I glanced over at MJ who opened her one eye but then closed it right away. Feigned sleeping. Probably the best thing.

The officer got right up in my face. I could smell the lunch on his breath mixed with the smell of nicotine.

"I never got the video from your phone," he said in an accusing and rough tone.

I lied. "I sent it."

"Give me your phone."

"I don't have it with me."

Another lie. If he searched me, he'd find it.

He also might lose a finger.

"I'll resend it when I get back home tonight," I said.

The man was still in my face. Less than twelve inches away. I refused to be the first one to move.

"The man on the video said you assaulted him."

If they thought that was assault, they hadn't seen anything yet. I now had several men in my crosshairs. The Sheikh. Amina's father. The four men who assaulted her. MJ's father. And this police officer, who'd back off if he knew what was good for him.

I let out a sigh of disgust. "How did I assault him? I was in the car the whole time."

"He said he reached into your car and tried to stop you from video-taping him."

"Sounds like he assaulted me. Is it permissible for a man in the United Arab Emirates to steal a woman's cell phone?"

"No. It is not permissible. It's also not permissible for you to assault him."

"Sounds like a case of self-defense to me."

"So, are you admitting that you did assault him?"

"No. But if his story is that he tried to steal my cell phone, then it sounds to me like he has already confessed to it and is the one with the legal jeopardy."

That caused him to pause.

"Have you arrested the four men who did this to Amina?" I asked, changing the subject off of me.

"That is none of your concern."

I wanted to continue the argument but thought better of it. In my mind, I was worried about a lot more than my welfare. The man was not there to talk about me. Was he there to arrest Amina? Did he intend to take her to prison? I considered a number of possibilities. None of them good.

Brad's words echoed through my mind. Was it worth the risk for one girl? Over the next few years, I could rescue tens of thousands of girls under the AJAX cover. If I resisted the officer and prevented him from taking Amina out of the hospital, my cover would be blown. If I did successfully get her out of the country, I'd never be allowed back in to help Anya or Odille or MJ for that matter. The better strategy was for me to stand down. As painful as it was to do so. Curly said that sometimes it was better to live to fight another day.

Turned out he wasn't there for Amina.

"Is this Majahammaddan Tabithe?" the officer said, walking over to MJ's bed.

I didn't say anything. I assumed he meant MJ.

"Yes sir," Shule finally said, as she stood from her chair and walked over to her niece's bedside.

"And who are you?" he asked.

"I'm her aunt. I'm the one who called the police on her father."

"It's a pity what happened to her," the officer said. My disdain for the man dropped a tenth of one degree out of hundreds.

"She's very fortunate to still be alive," Shule said soberly.

"Her father has filed a criminal complaint against her with the tribe," the man said, startling us.

I took a step toward them, so I was standing next to Shule whose mouth had gaped open.

"You're arresting the girl!" I said, more as a statement of disgust than a question.

I couldn't help myself.

"I'm investigating the complaint," the officer retorted. "Her father says she married a Christian man. Is that true?"

The three of us didn't answer.

He reached over and took MJ's hand and looked at the ring still on her finger. MJ let out a moan when he roughly dropped her arm back to the bed.

"I can see that it is," he said.

"Why would she be arrested for that?" I asked. I was proud of myself for toning down my anger and simply asking in my normal inquisitive voice.

"My understanding is that the man did *not* convert to Islam. It's against the law for a Muslim woman to marry a non-Muslim man."

"She's not Muslim," I argued. "She converted to Christianity several months ago."

The officer pulled out his notebook and wrote something down.

"We can add apostasy to the charges," he said almost gleefully. "It's also against the law for a woman to convert from Islam to another religion."

Shut up, Jamie.

I needed to keep my mouth shut. I'd made it worse for Amina bringing her to the hospital. Now I was making it worse on MJ. If I snapped the idiot's neck in two, I supposed I'd make it worse for all of them.

"I have everything I need," the officer said as he closed his little notebook.

He got back in my face. So close, I could've headbutted him into oblivion. It took all of my restraint not to.

"I'll deal with you later," he said. Then turned and walked out the door.

It didn't matter what he intended to charge them with. I was going to get the two girls out of the hospital and out of the country before they ever saw the inside of a prison cell.

The fact that he didn't arrest them on the spot, meant that I had time. Clearly, the hospital still had some say in the matter. How long would that last? Not long, I presumed.

I walked over to MJ, leaned over, and whispered the same thing in her ear that I had whispered in Amina's. "I don't know if you can hear me or not. If you can, I won't let them do this to you. I promise."

Another promise.

The first time I said it to Amina, I wasn't sure I could actually keep the promise. I was even less sure now.

16

When I left the hospital, I was in full-blown mission mode. Angry and resolved. Everything would be by the book from here on out. At least to the extent that I did things by the book.

A-Rad and I turned our focus to rescuing Anya. Not that we would forget about the two girls suffering in the hospital. But we had time to formulate a plan for them. From the conversation with the tribal elder, I gleaned that he wasn't going to arrest them anytime soon. Not until they recovered from their injuries.

I'd already given Alex and the AJAX team back home a list of things to do for our mission and decided to call him to find out how he was coming on that list.

We'd traded the Lamborghini for a black SUV with tinted windows. The SUV wasn't as flashy as the sports car. In fact, black SUVs dominated the roads in Abu Dhabi and Dubai. Like white cars and trucks back in the states. We'd blend right in which was vital for a spy mission.

Also, Saad had seen me in the Lamborghini. At some point, our mission was going to take us to his house. Sooner rather than later. Better he continued to think I'd left the country.

A-Rad was driving. I put the call on speaker so he could listen in.

"Hi honey," Alex said when he picked up.

"Hi sweetie," A-Rad said to him.

Alex let out more than a chuckle. "Sorry, A-Rad. But you're not my type," he quipped.

"You're not my type either. Your legs are too hairy, and so's your back."

"From what I hear, that Bianca girl is more your type," Alex said.

"Yeah!"

"I heard about a little lip massaging back in Geneva."

When Bianca had said goodbye to A-Rad, she kissed him. Out of the blue. On the lips. Hard. Taking us all by surprise. A-Rad more than anyone. Then she rushed off to her plane. I'd told Alex about it, but I didn't expect him to repeat it. I was a little ticked that he did. Clearly, this would only be the beginning. I could envision Alex and the other guys, razzing A-Rad about it for months.

He was already turning bright red.

I jumped in. A-Rad was embarrassed. Also, if I didn't cut them off, the two of them would banter on back and forth for five minutes.

"Did you get the picture of Anya I sent you, Alex?" I asked.

"I did," he said, getting right back into work mode.

I'd tell him later in private to drop the thing with Bianca. I could tell A-Rad was still sensitive about it.

"I'm working on it now," Alex said. "You should be able to pick up a passport at the US Embassy tomorrow morning."

Alex was creating a new identity for Anya. Using her picture, he was making her a passport under an assumed name. That way we didn't have to smuggle her out of the country. She could simply board a plane and leave. The fake passports we made would fool any customs security checkpoint in the world, including the U.S.

"Let me get Brad on the phone," Alex said. "He said there's been a development."

My heartbeat suddenly increased.

I had no idea what that could be. I'd already had my own major development. MJ. What happened to her was heartbreaking. Which reminded me that we needed to stop by Christopher's house on the way back to our plane. He and his family must be worried sick. That caused me to momentarily lose my focus on Brad's news.

When Alex had Brad on the phone, he explained the new development.

"A bomb exploded in Turkey. A high-ranking member of the White Wolves was killed. Zamani was behind the bomb attack. Or at least that's what we believe at this time. It fits his M.O."

I thought I knew where he was going with this conversation. "Someone made a call from a burner phone two minutes after the blast," Brad said. "A couple of blocks away. Guess who he called?"

"Sheikh Saad," I said, having already pieced it together.

"That's right," Brad said. "Your man hit the White Wolves. I don't have to tell you why."

"Retaliation for stealing the painting and kidnapping Bianca. That's too funny," I said.

Saad obviously bought the ruse that the White Wolves were behind the theft. I figured Saad couldn't care less about Bianca. The painting was now in the hands of the buyer from Japan. We were forty million dollars ahead, and Saad was out the money and the painting. While I expected him to be angry at the White Wolves, I didn't expect him to retaliate by killing one of them.

"You think it's funny that you're starting a mini-war in the middle east?" Brad said to me.

"I always think it's funny when bad guys are killing each other. Less people around for me to kill."

"Don't even think about killing the Sheikh," Brad warned. "Just rescue the girls and get out of there. Anyway, I'm telling you this new information, so you don't get caught up in the crossfire."

"Thanks. It warms my heart to know that you're concerned about me," I said sarcastically.

"Signing off," Brad said, and the phone went silent. That's the closest he got to an actual goodbye.

That made me think of something.

"Alex. How are you coming on finding the Sheikh's bank accounts?"

"Pretty good. We've found several hundred of them. He's got billions of dollars in accounts all over the world."

Alex was a master hacker. The best in the world. Especially now that he had a team of computer experts working behind him at AJAX. His team could hack into anything. Which was a scary amount of power for his team to possess. Fortunately, they were using it for good.

"Are they all legitimate?" I asked.

"They appear to be."

We were investigating the Sheikh to see if he had any ties to terrorism.

"Any accounts in Turkey?" I asked.

"Let me check."

I muted the phone and said to A-Rad. "Let's swing by the Tate's apartment in Abu Dhabi City. You know. MJ's husband, Christopher's house. See if anyone's there."

While A-Rad hadn't gone into the hospital with me, he waited in the car, and I filled him in when I came out. He was as fired up about helping MJ as I was.

I took their address out of my pocket and handed it to him, and he entered it into the GPS. A few seconds later, Alex was back on the phone.

"He has one account in Turkey," Alex said. "At the Bank of Ankora."

"What's the balance?"

"He's got a little over seven billion Lira in that one account."

"What's that come out to in dollars?"

"Let me add it up."

We could see the skyline of Abu Dhabi City on the horizon. Every time I saw it was like the first time. No downtown anywhere in the world was more magnificent. Too bad some of that wealth was in the hands of men like the Sheikh. Pure evil.

"Nine hundred million dollars. $985,463,277.45, to be exact."

I could feel my mouth gape open. A-Rad shook his head in disbelief as well.

"Can you take it out of the account and make it look like the White Wolves stole it?" I asked.

"Are you thinking what I think you're thinking?"

"Can you steal it, so it's never traced back to us?"

"That's brilliant. That'll really stir up a hornet's nest. Saad will go ballistic if that money goes missing. Naturally, he'll think the White Wolves are retaliating for the bombing. That'll take the war to a whole new level. I can put the money back later. Good idea, honey."

"Thank you."

"Brad's not going to like it, though," Alex said.

"That makes it an even better idea."

* * *

Abu Dhabi City

A-Rad found the Tate's apartment building with no trouble. We had to stop at the security desk, and the man had to call them before we could enter. I gave him our name. A woman's voice was on the other end.

"Tell her we have a message from MJ," I said to the man at the desk.

That got us through immediately. The door to their apartment was already open, and a woman and young man greeted us as soon as we got off the elevator. I presumed the young man was Christopher.

"You talked to MJ? Is she okay?" the woman asked me with a sense of urgency in her voice. She hadn't invited us into the apartment.

"We just left her," I said. "I'm Jamie and this is A-Rad."

"Where is she?" Christopher said. "I want to see her."

"She's in the hospital," I said. "Her father attacked her. Is there someplace we can talk privately?" I asked. The last thing I wanted to do was have this conversation in the hallway with security cameras watching us.

"Please come inside," the woman said, motioning for us to follow her.

The apartment was upscale which I already assumed given the address and the outside of the building. The Tate's clearly had means. The woman was in her forties. Styled blonde hair. Wearing red leggings and a white pullover shirt. Christopher was in jeans and a polo shirt. More of a preppie type. An unlikely pair, it seemed to me. MJ and Christopher. They came from two totally different worlds.

A contrast to my marriage. Alex and I were exactly alike. Which made us an even odder couple. Two Type A passionate personalities caused Alex and me to clash at the drop of a hat. We also moved on from things quickly which was why we were able to make it work. Thinking of Alex caused a twinge of missing him to shoot through my heart. Alex and I both knew the risk of someone knocking on our door someday and telling us that the other was in the hospital. Or worse.

I took a second to choose my words carefully. Christopher and his mom had no doubt been going through emotional hell for the last few days. Not knowing what happened to his new bride must've been excruciating. The details were even more horrific than probably they'd even imagined. While I couldn't totally lessen the blow, at least I could try and be reassuring first.

"MJ is hurt, but she's going to live and will recover. As you know, they went to Shule's house to get the birth certificate."

I wanted them to know that I had information that I couldn't possibly know without MJ or the Aunt giving it to me. I wasn't sure how much they trusted a stranger showing up on their doorstep. The fact they were starving for information was most likely why they let us in. I wanted to build their trust right from the beginning.

"Aunt Shule gave me your address and asked me to come see you and explain why they haven't been in touch."

"We went by her house," the mom said. "Several times. No one was there. Obviously. I'm Ivory Tate by the way. This is my son Christopher. My husband, Wayne, is at work."

"MJ's going to be okay," I repeated. "But she was burned. Her father poured kerosene on her and set her on fire."

Ivory let out a gasp.

"Oh, my word!" she said, as tears welled up in her eyes. "I was afraid something bad had happened to her."

Christopher began pacing around. His fists balled and his shoulders tensed. He was having the same reaction I'd have. While I didn't know exactly what he was thinking, he probably wanted five minutes alone with the father. Not that it would be a good idea. Christopher was a hundred and forty pounds sopping wet. I'd never seen the father, but I imagined that he could make mincemeat of Christopher in a matter of seconds. Better for Christopher to get his anger out here and never see the father.

"She's in the hospital recovering from her burns," I added. "The right side of her body was most affected. Her face wasn't burned at all."

"I want to see her," Christopher said, not even acknowledging my comment. I got the impression MJ's face could be disfigured and Christopher wouldn't care.

"That's not a good idea," I countered. "You may be putting her life in danger. The tribal police have already been by to see her. They intend to charge her with a crime. I suggest you get in touch with your lawyer. He should go by and see her."

"That's a good idea," Mrs. Tate said. "Anup will know what to do."

"Her Aunt is with her. I'm going to help as well."

"Thank you," Mrs. Tate said. "What can we do?"

"My understanding is that you want to go to America," I said.

"That's right," Christopher replied. "We were going to leave two days ago, but MJ had the problem with the passport. As soon as she's well, I want us to get out of here."

"The authorities put her on a no-fly list," I said. "They aren't going to let her leave the country."

"What are we going to do?" Mrs. Tate said.

"I have a plane. A-Rad is my pilot." I pointed over to him. "I just have to figure out how to get MJ on it without the authorities knowing about it."

"You'd do that for her?" Mrs. Tate said. "It sounds like you would be putting your own life in danger."

Of course, I couldn't tell them that I routinely put my life in danger. At some point, I might tell them that I work with the CIA but not yet.

"I'm going to help MJ," I said. "I just have to figure out how to do it." My first priority was to get Anya out of the clutches of the Sheikh, but of course, they couldn't know about that.

A loud rap at the door, startled everyone. Mrs. Tate stood and went to the door. I could hear a man's voice in the hallway but couldn't see his face.

A few seconds later I saw the person behind the voice.

The tribal elder.

Same guy. The one from the hospital.

When he saw me, his eyes widened.

"Why am I not surprised to see you here?" he asked me.

"I'm surprised to see you. What brings you to Abu Dhabi City?" I asked, even though I knew the answer.

Confirmed when he turned to Christopher and said, "I'm here for the boy. Are you Christopher Tate?" he asked.

"Who wants to know?" the kid said brazenly.

"You're under arrest!"

"On what charge?" I asked, trying to take the focus off Christopher before he said something to make matters worse.

The man said, "On the charge of proselytizing. Sexual indignities. And Taboos on Atrionization. Just to name a few."

I didn't know what atrionization was or maybe I'd gotten the word wrong in the translation. I didn't think it was a word. Whatever he said the charge was, I figured it couldn't be good.

17

Christopher was now in handcuffs.

"Is that necessary?" I asked Barney. My nickname for the idiot police officer, tribal elder, or whatever he was, who was trying to arrest these poor kids for no reason. For some reason he reminded me of Barney Fife from an old-time television show I watched as a kid on reruns.

Barney got in my face again like he had at the hospital. Lunch must've consisted of some type of fish. I had to back up or I would've gagged.

I could see A-Rad tense up.

Easy boy.

"I've got another set of handcuffs on me," Barney said. "I can easily put you in a set and haul your skinny little *al-hammar* down to the station. I think that word meant ass in Arabic.

Putting me in a set of handcuffs would not be easy for him to do. In fact, impossible. Easy for me to do to him. I could put him in a Curly Cuff. That's where we handcuffed a bad guy's wrist and ankle together. Behind his back. I've been in that position. After five minutes, you wished you were dead. It'd take me less than a minute to have his *al hammar* sticking up in the air in a most uncomfortable position.

Somehow, I had to get the pictures out of my mind so I could make my argument. "I'm just saying that the boy is not going to run. Where would he go? His parents live in Abu Dhabi. He goes to school here. I don't think cuffs are necessary. I'm sure he'll go peacefully. That's all I'm saying."

"Did you send me the video?" Barney asked me, trying to get in my face again.

I tried holding my breath. That didn't work, so I tried breathing through my mouth. What I really wanted to do was pinch my nose with my fingers. I'd offer him a piece of breath mint if I had one.

"I haven't had a chance yet," I said, turning my head away completely.

"Do it now. While I'm here."

"I don't have my phone with me."

My phone suddenly rang.

Shoot!

I pulled it out of the pocket where it was hidden.

Alex.

Of all times to call.

Barney tried to take it from my hand, but I pulled it away. A-Rad took a step in my direction. Fortunately, Barney didn't see him. While he was pushing the limits of my patience, I wasn't ready for a confrontation. A-Rad's signature move was a chokehold. I could see him preparing to execute one by the way he was holding his arms out.

"I'll send it now," I said, catching A-Rad's eyes giving him a look to stand down.

I pretended to be typing in the information. I pretended to hit send.

Barney pulled out his phone. "Let's make sure I got it."

Dang!

I went ahead and typed in the information and sent it to him. When I talked to Alex later, he'd take care of it.

Barney's phone dinged and he confirmed that he got it.

"Let's go kid," Barney said, grabbing Christopher by the arm. The boy pulled away.

Mom let out a squeal. More of a shriek.

"Why are you arresting my son?" she said, "He hasn't done anything wrong."

Mrs. Tate was almost pleading with the man. I could tell she was getting desperate. This was clearly an upstanding family. They probably freaked out when they got a parking ticket. I broke laws in other countries all the time when the mission required it. I was dangerously close to breaking one now. Assaulting a tribal officer.

"I told you why your son is under arrest," Barney said. "I read you the charges."

Barney didn't read Christopher his rights before he handcuffed him. I wondered if he was required to do so in Abu Dhabi. Regardless, I knew from experience that keeping quiet was the best thing to do with this detective.

I could sense a trap coming.

"One of the charges was proselytizing," Mrs. Tate said. "Christopher didn't do that. MJ was already a Christian when they met."

I winced.

Barney pulled out his little notebook and wrote something down. Mrs. Tate had just inadvertently provided evidence that MJ did in fact convert from Islam to Christianity. She'd made the same mistake I made. Twice.

"I think Christopher needs to talk to his attorney," I interjected trying to put an end to the conversation. Barney wasn't going to be talked out of arresting Christopher. The best thing to do was accept that and limit the damage.

Barney must've sensed an opening because he said, "Sexual indignities is another charge."

"What are sexual indignities?" Mrs. Tate asked.

"Having sex outside of marriage," Barney replied.

I knew exactly where he was going with that. Before I could stop her, Mrs. Tate said, "But they're married."

I don't know if my grimace showed on my face, but my heart dropped a couple of notches in my chest. She'd just provided testimony that implicated Christopher and MJ in a crime. Christopher was guilty because he married a Muslim woman without converting to Islam according to MJ's tribal law. MJ was guilty because it was against the law in her tribe for a Muslim woman to marry a non-Muslim man. Mrs. Tate was digging them a hole that they would not be able to get out of.

I stepped between them and took Mrs. Tate by the arm and whispered to her, "Don't say anything else. Christopher needs to talk to his attorney."

She pulled away. "I'm coming with you. Where are you taking my son?" she said angrily.

"You're not allowed in the building."

"I want to visit my son. I have that right."

"The only rights you have are what I give you! No visitors are allowed in the holding cell. Not until he's transferred to the main prison."

"Where do I post his bail?"

"He'll have to go before a judge to ask for it."

"How long will that take?"

"I don't know, but I doubt the judge will grant him bail until the trial."

"When can I see him?"

"Not until the trial."

"What about his attorney? When can he see him?"

"The boy is entitled to an attorney. He'll know how to get in touch with him."

"Are you saying I can't see my son until the trial?"

"That's correct."

Barney grabbed Christopher by the arm and led him away. Out of the room and toward the front door. Christopher kept straining to look back at his mom. His eyes were widened and his mouth agape in total panic.

"I'll call Anup," Mrs. Tate said to him. "We're going to get you out of there."

Mrs. Tate was almost hysterical. I grabbed her and put my arms around her to keep her from following them out the door.

"What are they going to do to him?" she asked, as she collapsed into my arms, practically sobbing.

"I don't know."

The truth. I had no idea what would happen next.

* * *

Mrs. Tate called her husband who called the attorney. I gave Mrs. Tate my cell phone number and told her to call me with any news and put her number in my phone. A-Rad and I left as soon as we could break away. What had transpired caused me to rethink my plans. I needed to get the girls out of the hospital sooner rather than later. As soon as I called Alex, we needed to head right over there and warn them.

"How ya doing?" Alex answered.

"Not good. Christopher's been arrested. The policeman just hauled him off to jail. I have no idea what they'll do to him in there."

"They won't torture him, if that's what you're thinking. He's an American. They don't want that kind of press."

"I'm concerned about the other prisoners. Who knows what kind of scum he might be in a cell with?"

"I wouldn't worry about that. Like I said, he's an American. They'll isolate him from the rest of the prison population. He should be fine."

"I hope you're right. Did you call me?"

"Anya's passport is ready early," Alex said. "It's at the US embassy for you to pick up."

"Great. We'll head that way now. Thanks."

"You're welcome. Sounds like you've got your hands full there. Do you need some help? I can send some reinforcements."

"Not yet. We're okay for the time being. I do need for you to do something for me."

"Anything."

"I'm going to send you an email address. I sent a video to it about five minutes ago. Hack into that email account and put a virus on the video."

"How bad a virus? Do you want to be a nuisance or go nuclear?"

I thought about it for several seconds.

"Go nuclear," I finally said. "Wipe out his whole email account. If you can, have the virus get on his phone when he opens it. I also want the video destroyed. So he never sees it."

"Somebody must've pissed you off."

"You have no idea."

* * *

We picked up Anya's passport from the embassy and then stopped for lunch. The diner was busy, so we kept our voices low as we discussed our next move.

"What's the plan at the hospital?" A-Rad asked me. "Where are we going to take the girls? Are they even in good enough condition to be moved?"

The questions came rapid fire, before I had the chance to answer the first one.

"I don't know," I said, answering the last one first. "But they're definitely not in good enough condition to go to jail."

A-Rad was smart to ask. I didn't want to compulsively go charging into the hospital and take the girls out without a plan. I had no way to take care of them if they needed medical attention.

"We could take them to another hospital," I said. "Check them in under assumed names."

"That's a good idea."

I pulled up my phone and began looking for hospitals.

"We need to find one outside the jurisdiction of the policeman," I said. "Someplace where he'd never look."

"If that doesn't work, we could take them to a hotel," A-Rad said. "You can connect with a doctor by the internet. He can write them a prescription, if they need medication which I'm sure they do. I can break into a pharmacy and steal some."

"A-Rad I'm impressed. You're actually doing field analysis."

"I'm more than just a pretty face."

"How are we going to get them out of the hospital, then? What would you do?" I asked.

A-Rad wrinkled his nose and put his hand on his chin like he was deep in thought. His eyes suddenly widened like a light bulb went off inside his head.

"I could dress up as an orderly," he said. "I'll just walk in and wheel them out in a wheelchair."

The idea was actually a good one. I was genuinely impressed. We always just thought he was the muscle. He was actually becoming useful in planning missions.

"That's a brilliant idea, A-Rad."

"Look on your phone and see if there's a place in town that sells scrubs," he said to me. "You know hospital uniforms."

He was on a roll.

A-Rad was freaking me out.

"And stethoscopes!" he said excitedly. "I could pose as a doctor instead of a nurse. A doctor could order people around."

I didn't want to stifle his enthusiasm, so I just let him continue to brainstorm and keep my mouth shut.

"I'm sure the hospital has medicine and supplies," he continued. "I'll take what we need from there. I won't even need to break into a pharmacy."

"You can go in first," I said. "You'll need an employee's badge. You can probably get one in the doctor's lounge."

"Won't they know that I'm not from that hospital?"

"Tell them you're from a different hospital. That you're there visiting two of your patients. Make up some story about what happened to them."

"My patient was in a car wreck. How's that?" A-Rad asked.

"That's good. She was burned. The passenger with her has a head injury."

A few seconds later, the light bulb look came on his face again. "Right!" he said. "That sounds like our two girls."

I couldn't wait to tell Alex about our conversation. He'd be shocked.

"Let's get to work," I said, as we both finished our lunch around the same time.

I couldn't help but smile. I hadn't seen A-Rad this excited since Bianca kissed him on the lips.

* * *

Sheikh Zimraan Jaber General Hospital

Abu Dhabi had several shops that sold scrubs. None that sold stethoscopes. A-Rad would have to steal one once he got in the hospital. We stopped somewhere for him to change. To my surprise, A-Rad actually looked the part. As long as he didn't have to open his mouth and have to sound like a doctor, he'd probably fool the people at the hospital.

I thought the idea of an orderly was a better one. That way he didn't need to have any expertise. But A-Rad was so excited about playing the doctor, I didn't want to suggest it.

We arrived at the hospital and walked right in. No one even gave us a second look. Hundreds of healthcare professionals were flitting around the hospital which was abuzz with activity. A-Rad went to find wheelchairs and I went directly to the girl's room.

As I walked down the hall, I could sense something was different.

Their door was open.

I didn't hear any activity.

I walked through the open door.

The room was empty.

Both beds were made.

Samitah and Aunt Shule were not there.

The girls were gone.

18

Christopher's trial started today. Any minute actually. A hearing more than a trial according to his attorney, Malak Abdallah, who was explaining the procedures to us. A railroading more than a hearing, after listening to him describe the process.

"Don't be under any illusions that this will be a fair trial," he said to those of us in the room. Aunt Shule was there. As were Mr. and Mrs. Tate. Samitah, Amina's mom, was noticeably missing. Her husband wouldn't let her attend.

MJ's trial was in three days, and Amina's was a week from now. According to Malak, the judge was from Dubai and traveled two days a week to preside over the cases in that particular village. Malak commented that the prosecutor was likely being strategic in scheduling Christopher's trial first to gather evidence to use against MJ.

The building was nothing more than an above average home that had been renovated to serve their purposes as a makeshift courthouse. It consisted of one large room where the trial took place, along with an office for the judge, and four small rooms for the parties to use. One room Malak described was basically a ten-foot by ten-foot prison cell. No bars, but locks and steel hooks on the walls where the defendants were chained while they waited for the proceedings to begin. A bench was attached to each wall around the entire room and seated up to a dozen or more people.

I was horrified to learn that all the defendants were kept in the ten-by-ten cell and tried on the same day. MJ would be in there with her father, who was being charged with domestic abuse. Amina would have to be in the holding cell with the four men who raped her. A guard would be in there to protect them, but the girls were victimized once again.

Not only was that unfair, but the charges were bordering on absurd. The father should've been charged with attempted murder. Domestic abuse didn't even begin to describe what he'd done to her by setting her on fire and permanently disfiguring her. The charges against Amina's assailants were even more outrageous. None were charged with rape. Three were charged with fornication. Meaning they had sex outside of marriage. Amina had the same three charges filed against her. A twisted and perverted way of thinking that somehow forcible rape was viewed the same as consensual sex.

The married man was charged with the more serious crime of adultery. As was Amina. None of the men were charged with assault. They all admitted to the sexual contact, but each denied hitting MJ and didn't know how she got her injuries. Lying and perjury must be permissible under their twisted rationalization of theology and sin.

I offered to testify, but Malak was against it. I could testify that I saw them hitting her. If they were going to lie to get off, I'd lie to get them convicted. Malak said that all I would do was make things worse because I'd also be testifying that the men raped her. That evidence would be used against MJ to prove the charges against her. Better for me to stay out of it, he argued, much to my consternation.

The only reason I was even in the room was because I was paying Malak to represent Amina. If I hadn't, she'd been given a court-appointed attorney, which would've been worse than having no attorney at all. The Tates were covering Christopher and MJ's legal fees. Malak was telling us what we were up against, only increasing the tension which was on everyone's faces.

"We got the worst possible judge," Malak said while adjusting his turban.

The attorney fit the part perfectly. Tall and thin. A whitish beard. His head was covered. He looked and acted like a typical Arab male and seemed genuinely concerned about Christopher and the two girls. Even though he came highly recommended by Anup, I had a hard time trusting anyone involved in the system, including Malak. He'd have to prove himself to me in the courtroom before I'd give him any respect.

"The individual emirates decide whether they want to enter the federal system of justice or maintain local control," Malak explained. "This village chose the latter. They have control over all their courts. The rules of procedure are set by the local tribes. Of course, they all follow Sharia law and the civil laws of the land and are subject to the appeals process, but they're basically given free rein to run their courts and dole out punishment as they see fit."

What he was saying didn't instill my confidence in him or the process.

"What can you tell us about the judge?" I asked.

"He's a fundamentalist. Sheikh Zariah Omair Mirza Hallal is his name. He's worse than most judges in the UAE. He'll interpret the tribal laws in the strictest possible way."

"Is he fair?" Mr. Tate asked.

Malak waved his hand in the air dismissively. "What is fair? Fair is a relative term. To this judge, fair is following the tribal laws. To some of us, if the law is unfair, then following it is as well."

"How's Christopher doing?" Mrs. Tate asked. They still hadn't been allowed to see him since his arrest.

"Christopher is being treated fairly well, under the circumstances. I met with him yesterday. He's lost a few pounds from the atrocious food which he complains about, but his situation is a lot better than what the girls face."

"How are the girls holding up?" I asked.

We'd desperately been trying to get information on Amina and MJ's health. Other than attorneys, the prisons didn't allow visitors. Now that Malak had seen the girls, I was anxious to find out their conditions.

"Not good," Malak said. "They're together in the same cell, which is a good thing. They can look out for each other. A lot of times they put girls in solitary confinement. That way no one knows what the guards are doing to them. That hasn't happened yet. Once they're convicted and moved to the regular prison population, their conditions will worsen."

My mouth almost flew open. *Once they're convicted!* Malak was their attorney, and he was already resigned to the fact that they'd be found guilty. Before they even had their day in court.

Malak continued before I could confront him with that statement. "Amina and MJ sleep on a mattress on the floor."

"That's not good," Aunt Shule said, speaking up for the first time. Shule seemed nervous at being at the courthouse. Not just for MJ, but she had expressed concern about her own safety. She was dressed in a burqa so as to not draw any attention to herself. While Christopher was charged with proselytizing, Aunt Shule was actually the one who introduced Amina to Christianity. A crime punishable by death according to the tribal law. I could see why she was genuinely concerned. Although, she didn't know that I'd never let them arrest her. I'd fight to the death to protect her. Aunt Shule and I had grown extremely close through the ordeal and shared the same Christian values.

"At least they have something to sleep on," Malak said. "A lot of girls don't. They also have a cell to themselves. Many girls are crowded into one cell, sometimes, ten or twelve at a time. The biggest problem for Amina and MJ is that they aren't getting any medical treatment."

Something I had worried was the case. "They should've never been taken out of the hospital until their wounds had healed," I said roughly.

"I don't disagree," Malak said. "They're lucky their wounds haven't become infected. The conditions are deplorable. The water's not fit to drink. They're each given a bar of soap and a rag to wash themselves. Amina got sick to her stomach from eating the food, so she's lost a lot of weight."

"She didn't have much to lose," I said.

Malak nodded. "All things considered, they're doing pretty well. Fortunately, I haven't seen any signs that either of them has been tortured or raped by the guards. It's only a matter of time, though."

"You act like it's a foregone conclusion that all three of them are going to be found guilty," I said to Malak strongly. I was beginning to question his competence and resolve to help the three of them.

"The fact is that they *are* guilty. Not of all the charges. But they have all confessed to their crimes in one way or another. Christopher and MJ did get married. MJ also converted to Christianity. It's against the tribal laws for her to do so, and it's against the law for them to marry unless he converts to Islam."

I started to argue with him, but Malak put up his hand to stop me from saying what he probably guessed I was going to say.

"I agree that these charges should not have been filed. In other jurisdictions, they wouldn't have been. But we are in the tribal areas. The local laws prevail. Regardless of what you think of the laws, they still exist. As does the punishment. My job is to minimize the severity of the sentences. The judge could make life extremely difficult for them if he so chooses. Our options on appeal are non-existent. This is our only chance to help them. It will not be easy."

A sober silence filled the room.

"I'm most concerned about how they answer the charges," he added.

"I don't understand," I said.

"Me either," Mrs. Tate said.

"This isn't like America," Malak explained. "There's no innocent until proven guilty standard in this court. There is, but it doesn't mean anything. There's no right to confront witnesses. All the prosecutor has to do is call the detective, and he's allowed to present what he learned from the investigation. Hearsay is allowed. Everything that's said can and will be used against them."

"Do you intend to call any witnesses on their behalf?" I asked.

Malak shook his head no. "Who would I call? Everyone I could call would only make the situation worse."

"I'll testify," Mrs. Tate said.

"What are you going to say?" Malak argued. "That they didn't get married? No. Our best strategy is to keep quiet. The problem is going to come when the judge asks Christopher a particular question."

"What question is that?" Mr. Tate asked.

"The answer to the charges," Malak replied. The second time he'd referred to answering the charges. I didn't understand why that had him so concerned.

"I'm sorry, but I don't know what you mean," Mr. Tate said.

Malak was speaking in English, and while his English wasn't bad, things were still being lost in translation.

"The way this judge runs a trial is that the prosecutor will read the charges. The detective will be called to provide the evidence. Then the judge will ask Christopher how he pleads. Guilty or not guilty."

In America, the defendants were asked up front. Before any evidence was presented.

Malak continued. "Herein lies the problem. If he pleads not guilty, and the judge finds him guilty, then he's committed another crime in his eyes. It's against the law in this tribal jurisdiction to plead not guilty to a crime that you've committed. If you plead guilty, then the judge goes right to sentencing. This judge is more lenient in sentencing if you plead guilty."

"That's ridiculous! So, if you're innocent, you make things worse if you plead not guilty?" I asked.

"If you're found guilty by the judge," Malak said, "then you are guilty in the eyes of the court. That's what makes things much worse. The judge will believe that you lied to him if you plead not guilty when he thinks you are."

"So, do the girls intend to plead guilty?" I asked.

"We haven't decided yet. I want to wait and hear what the detective says and how Christopher's trial goes."

"Don't you know what the detective's going to say. Doesn't the prosecutor have to provide you with pretrial discovery?" I asked.

Malak laughed. "No. He doesn't have to give me anything. I'll find out what he's going to say at the same time you do."

Things were much different here than in America. Not that I was surprised. But I hadn't realized how different and unfair.

"Also, be prepared. The girls will be treated much harsher than the men. My job is to keep the two girls alive. MJ's case will be easier. Even though apostasy is punishable by death, no one has been stoned for converting to Christianity for several years. Amina's is a different situation. Her tribe is calling for her death on the grounds of adultery. The judge won't sentence her to death, but the tribe might."

"Won't the judge have the final decision?" I asked.

"He'll listen to the evidence and then render his judgment. At that time, the tribal lawyers add their punishment. The judge has no say as to what they decide. All he can do is adjust his own punishment, which they sometimes do if the tribe's judgment is too harsh or cruel. Which I fear will be in Amina's case."

"It sounds so hopeless," Mrs. Tate said. She looked at me. I wasn't sure what I could do or say that would be reassuring.

"What about Christopher?" Mr. Tate asked. "What will the tribe do with him?"

"He's not subject to a tribal verdict," Malak replied. "He's not a member of a tribe. The judge will decide his fate according to civil laws. Christopher's problem is how he pleads."

"He'll plead not guilty, of course," Mr. Tate said.

"It's not that simple," Malak said. "If Christopher pleads guilty, then the judge will likely go easier on him and simply expel him from the country. No jail time and no lashes."

"That's what we want, anyway," Mr. Tate said. "We want him on the first plane out of here."

"The problem is that if he pleads guilty, he seals MJ's fate. His guilty plea is all the evidence the judge needs to convict her of marrying a non-Muslim. The judge will then assume that they consummated the marriage and find her guilty of sex outside of marriage. That won't get her the death penalty, but MJ will get lashes and jail time."

"How much jail time?" Mrs. Tate asked.

"That's up to the judge. Probably two to five years. But he could go up to twelve years. And sixty to a hundred lashes. Plus, whatever the tribe adds to the sentence. Her tribe may not add anything to the sentence, though."

"What happens if Christopher pleads not guilty?" Mrs. Tate asked nervously.

"If the judge finds him guilty, then he'll throw the book at him. He'll likely get prison time. Six months is my guess."

"Damned if you do, damned if you don't," I said sarcastically.

"Basically," Malak said while nodding.

I was warming to him. A little. He seemed to at least understand the system. I'd yet to see him in action in the courtroom. I wasn't sure what was going to happen in there. Sounded like he didn't know either.

My thoughts moved on to other things. Could A-Rad and I pull off a prison escape? How could we even get inside the prison? If we were going to do something, it should be there at the courthouse. The problem was that none of the three were there at the same time.

"How is Christopher going to plead?" Aunt Shule asked, which brought my attention back to the problem at hand. The most important question asked so far.

"I don't know," Malak said. "I explained everything to him yesterday. It's his decision. We'll know once we get inside the courtroom."

"It sounds like MJ is going to be found guilty no matter what Christopher does," I said. "It pains me to say it, but maybe Christopher needs to save himself and get out of the country."

"I agree," Mr. Tate said.

"Knowing him, he won't do that to MJ," Mrs. Tate said.

"I suspect that's what she'd want him to do," I countered. "Jail could be hard on him. No telling what he'd be subjected to."

I didn't want to elaborate, but I could envision how the guards and other inmates might treat a rich, white boy from America.

A knock sounded on the door. Several of us jumped.

The judge had arrived at the courthouse, and the court was convening. We'd soon know what Christopher was going to do.

19

I'd only been seated in the courtroom for less than two minutes when Barney walked in. He took one look at me and made a beeline in my direction. His eyes were on fire with rage. I knew why.

"That video you sent me had a virus on it!" he said to me roughly.

"I know, right! I had to get a new phone. I can't believe your email gave my phone a virus. You should really get that fixed."

"I want that video."

"I don't have it. Like I said, my phone was ruined. So was the video, I guess."

"I should arrest you on the spot," he said.

"On what charge? You're the one who gave me the email address with the virus."

Barney glared at me and then stomped off to take a seat by the prosecutor.

Aunt Shule was sitting next to me. Mr. and Mrs. Tate were two rows in front of us. Right behind where Christopher would sit with Malak who was in place with papers strewn in front of him. Otherwise, the audience area in the courtroom was empty.

The room was nothing like an American courtroom. A small table sat in the front of the room where the judge would sit. It had no front, so his legs were showing. Malak said they didn't have jury trials in the tribal region, so there wasn't a jury box. Two small tables had been placed in front of the judge's table. No witness stand. Apparently, statements were just read, and the judge or the attorneys asked questions from their table.

The side door opened, and Christopher was brought in.

Mrs. Tate let out a muffled squeal. Malak had warned her not to try and approach Christopher, so she kept her seat. Christopher let out a broad smile when he saw her. He seemed in good spirits, considering. His hands were bound, and his feet shackled. The chains echoed eerily through the small room which was dead silent. He had to move furtively to keep from stumbling. A guard had a firm grip on his elbow and pushed him roughly down onto the chair beside Malak. I imagined he had received worse treatment when out of our watchful eye.

If I remembered right, Christopher was wearing the same clothes he wore when he was arrested that day at his parent's apartment. His hair was mussed, and I could see slight stubble on his cheek. Such a sad sight, even though he seemed to be doing okay. I couldn't imagine what was going through his mind. Here he was, an eighteen-year-old boy, facing a judge who held his future in his hands. Made worse by his agonizing decision to plead guilty or not guilty. MJ could be facing years in prison or even death if he said or did the wrong thing.

If the decision was weighing on him, it didn't come through in his demeanor. I was torn and agonizing over it. If Alex were in that situation, I'd want him to save himself and let me figure out my own plight. But I was more resourceful than MJ. She could die in prison with her wounds untreated. The guards could make her life unbearable. The guards might eventually subdue me but not before I made their lives unbearable.

If Christopher did plead not guilty, what could he do about it anyway? He'd be rotting in jail as well for six to twelve months. If Alex were out of jail, at least he might be able to develop a plan to rescue me. Christopher had no such abilities. The best thing for both of them to do was to plead guilty and throw themselves on the mercy of the court. What other choice did they have? They could both plead not guilty, but it seemed like Malak wasn't prepared to put up much of a defense. If they were going to be found guilty anyway, better to take the lesser-of-two-evils approach.

So unfair that these two kids were being tried for unfair laws. I'd broken more laws in foreign countries than I could count. Even in the UAE. We'd stolen the Sheikh's painting and almost a billion dollars out of his account. Kidnapped a girl and smuggled her out of the country. The thought almost made me smile. What would Barney think if he knew what I'd done?

What I was going to do! That night even.

We were biding our time before we raided the Sheikh's house and rescued Anya. A-Rad and I had been doing reconnaissance every night. Alex had hacked into the security system, so we were watching and hearing everything happening inside the house in real time. Several more laws I was currently breaking.

After the bombing in Turkey, the Sheikh had stepped up security and hadn't gone out of the house. That's the only reason we hadn't acted to rescue Anya yet. We'd make our move tonight.

The back door opened, and a police officer appeared, followed by a man I presumed to be a judge. A younger man. Not at all like what I expected. Sharply dressed and immaculately groomed. He was wearing a black robe, with a blue vestment under it, along with a white collar and a white turban. More like a hat. Like a Russian would wear. White as the driven snow turban. His beard was of moderate length. Jet black color. The judge wore what appeared to be expensive glasses.

The judge began. "We're here on the matter of Christopher Tate. The prosecutor will read the charges."

The man sitting next to Barney stood and read them in Arabic. The prosecutor used fancier words and cited some penal code numbers, but from what I gathered, they were basically the same charges Barney had mentioned at the apartment. Proselytizing. Illegal marriage. Fornication. Meaning, since the marriage wasn't legal, then they were having sex outside of marriage.

B.S. charges in my mind.

A travesty.

I'd asked Brad to have the President of the United States make a plea on their behalf, but I didn't know if he had or not. Our relationship with the UAE was complicated. While we openly expressed concern about their human rights violations, the political scales of balance in the Middle East were more important to the powers that be than the lives of a few, poor, Arab girls. If Christopher was treated badly in the courts, then being an American citizen, the politicians might make more of an issue out of it. As of now, they probably wouldn't get involved.

The wheels of justice spun quickly here. The prosecutor asked Barney a few questions. He mostly referred to the little black book I'd seen him writing in at the apartment and the hospital.

Mrs. Tate's words were the most damning thing he read.

"Majahammaddan Tabithe was already a Christian when they met," Barney said, reading from his notes. Mrs. Tate's words almost verbatim.

I knew it at the time, and I knew it now. The biggest problem for MJ was converting from Islam to Christianity.

He read another of Mrs. Tate's statements. "Mrs. Tate said they were already married when I read the charge of sex before marriage," Barney said. Then he added, "Majahammaddan was wearing a wedding ring when I saw her at the hospital."

The judge took a lot of notes. Barney said a few more things, then sat back down. The prosecution's case took less than twenty minutes. By the demeanor of the judge, and the way he glared at Christopher, it seemed to me like he'd already made up his mind. The best thing for Christopher to do was plead guilty and hope for the best.

The judge asked Christopher to stand. "How do you plead to the charges?" he asked.

"Not guilty," Christopher said, raising his chin defiantly.

I was shocked.

My heart skipped a beat as I feared he might be making a big mistake.

I guess we now knew.

Foolish boy.

Love above all.

Christopher would go to jail before he'd do anything to harm MJ.

While I admired his commitment to her, I couldn't help but wonder if he was making a terrible mistake.

* * *

Since Christopher pleaded not guilty, Malak was going to have to defend him, like it or not. I hoped he had a rabbit to pull out of his hat.

Malak stood slowly and deliberately. Whether he was thinking or stalling for time, I wasn't sure. Either way, he had a monumental task ahead of him. We'd see if he was worth what we were paying him.

"Your honor, if I may, I'd like to discuss these charges one at a time, if it would please the court," he said.

"Go ahead," the judge said.

"Let's begin with the charge of proselytizing. A very serious offense under the tribal laws. The law provides up to five years in prison for blasphemy or for proselytizing of Muslims."

I didn't think he was off to a good start. Why remind the judge of the sentence?

Malak continued, "No evidence has been presented that the defendant has ever made any statements insulting God, the prophets, the holy books, or the houses of worship."

"The prosecutor has made no such charge of blasphemy," the judge said.

"But he has made a charge of proselytizing. As the court is aware, proselytizing is a form of blasphemy and is a crime against God."

"As is apostasy, which the girl is charged with," the judge added.

I didn't know where Malak was going with this.

"Based on the severity of the punishments for crimes against God," Malak said, "the law requires that the punishments should be averted by the slightest doubts of ambiguities. No evidence was presented against my client that he induced the girl to convert to his faith."

"Mr. Prosecutor, do you wish to respond?"

"No, Your Honor. We will let the statement of the detective stand for itself. The mother of the defendant clearly stated that the girl converted to Christianity."

"If I remember the statement correctly," the judge said, "she stated that the girl converted before she met her son."

"My point exactly, Your Honor," Malak said. "Clearly, that statement creates doubt and ambiguity. I'm curious as to why that charge was even brought, considering the evidence, or lack thereof. If the prosecutor wants you to accept the statement as true—that the girl converted to Christianity—shouldn't the court also accept the statement that she converted before she met her son as true?"

"Would you care to respond?" the judge asked the prosecutor, who declined.

It seemed as though the prosecution was willing to concede that point and focus more on the charges of fornication. My view of Malak went up a notch.

"Let's deal with the next charge," Malak said. "The prosecutor has claimed that the couple was married. Where is the proof of that?"

The prosecutor stood and said, "The proof is in the mother's statement. She confessed to their marriage. The girl was also wearing a wedding ring."

"Why hasn't the prosecution produced a marriage certificate?" Malak asked.

This might be an interesting and persuasive argument. Anup had told the pastor who performed the ceremony to wait until the kids were out of the country before filing the marriage certificate. Apparently, he waited. Probably, when Christopher was arrested, he didn't file it at all. That sounded like a good development.

"The mother's words are proof enough," the prosecutor said.

"Proof of what?" Malak argued.

"Proof of marriage."

"Your Honor, what constitutes a legal marriage under Islamic law? A marriage is not legal until it's registered in a Sharia court and MOFA attests to the marriage certificate."

"A technicality," the prosecutor said.

"An important one, don't you think?" the judge asked.

I could feel the excitement building in Malak as he seemed more energized. His words were coming faster and his manner more demonstrative.

But the prosecutor came fighting back, "The charge against Christopher is not that he's married. It's zina. Fornication. Even if the marriage certificate were filed, the marriage would be invalid. The girl cannot marry a Non-Muslim unless he converts to Christianity. Because the marriage is not valid, they have committed fornication."

"Where is that testimony, Your Honor?" Malak said. "What evidence has been presented to the court that the couple has had sexual relations?"

"They were married, Your Honor," the prosecution argued. "Of course, they did."

"I don't have to remind the court that zina is also a crime against God." Malak stood tall, confident. "In these most serious crimes, there are not to be any doubts or ambiguities in the charges. The prosecutor has provided zero evidence that the couple has engaged in any sexual indignities. In fact, my client is prepared to testify and give a statement that they haven't."

"The defense is asking us to believe the unbelievable," the prosecutor said. "No one is going to believe that the couple didn't consummate their marriage."

"They weren't married!" Malak said raising his voice for the first time. "Christopher is a Christian. In his faith, it's appropriate to not have sexual relations until you're married. The girl, Majahammaddan didn't turn eighteen until the day she was arrested. She could not have been married before her eighteenth birthday. Is the prosecution suggesting that the sexual indignities occurred before her birthday? If so, she cannot be charged with a criminal offense. As you know, Your Honor, minors cannot be subject to punishment in the criminal courts. They are only subject to reprimands and or rehabilitation."

"What say you, Mr. Prosecutor?" the judge asked.

"The sexual indignities could've occurred on that day. After they were married."

"Could've is not proof. An ambiguity. The court should also be reminded that the girl was at her Aunt's house when she was attacked by her father. Just a few short hours after this alleged marriage. The two were never alone together. From her Aunt's house, the girl went straight to the hospital. She wasn't even with the defendant."

"I've heard enough," the judge said. "I'm ready to rule."

I thought that was good for us but couldn't be sure.

"On the charge of proselytizing, I find the defendant not guilty."

Mrs. Tate let out a shriek. The judge looked up and stared at her.

"Sorry," I heard her say.

"In addition, the prosecutor hasn't proven that they were married. And has presented no evidence that the defendant and Majahammaddan were engaged in sexual indignities. So, on the second charge I find the defendant not guilty."

I couldn't believe it. Malak had pulled it off. My view of him had totally changed.

"Your Honor, may I speak," the prosecutor said.

"Do you have something to add?" the judge asked.

"The detective would like to read one more statement for the court to consider."

I wanted to ring Barney's neck.

"Go ahead," the judge instructed.

Barney said, "When I was putting the boy in my cruiser to take him to the station, he said, 'You can't stop me from seeing her.'"

The judge's tone turned more serious, "Counselor, does your client still intend to have a relationship with the girl?"

"Your Honor, the girl is in prison. They don't have a relationship at this time."

"Young man," the judge said, addressing Christopher. "Do you intend to still have a relationship with the young girl?"

"Yes," Christopher said.

I winced.

Lie! I wanted to shout to him.

"Do you intend to convert to Islam?" the judge asked.

"No sir," Christopher said.

"Then I find you guilty of verbal abuse!" Verbal abuse was disrespecting the laws of Islam by what you said.

"Your Honor, may I speak?" Malak asked, but the judge ignored him.

"The sentence is six months in prison!" the judge said emphatically.

"Your Honor, if I may?" Malak said.

"Go ahead."

"My client misspoke. His intention is to leave the country. He has no intention of returning. I would respectfully ask that you not sentence him to prison but let him leave peacefully and put this situation behind him."

"I will sentence him to time served. I'm ordering the detective to take the boy immediately to the airport. I assume he has the means to purchase a ticket, is that correct?" the judge asked.

"Yes, Your Honor."

"Then detective, see that the boy is on the next flight out of the country to a destination of his choosing. I'm ordering that he not return. If he does, he will be arrested immediately, and begin serving out his sentence."

"That is acceptable, Your Honor," Malak said. "My client appreciates the court's mercy."

The prosecutor left with Christopher.

All in all, the best possible outcome.

The Tate's wanted their boy gone anyway. It took a long detour to get there, but at least he didn't have to go to jail.

I had a feeling, based on this judge, that Amina and MJ were not going to have it so lucky.

20

Anya

Sheikh Saad Shakir's house

T he White Wolves hadn't retaliated. Yet.

Saad could feel it coming. He'd killed one of the generals in the Turkish mafia with a bomb. They deserved it. He didn't start this war, but he had taken it to a new level. They'd stolen his painting and kidnapped one of his girls. He killed one of their important men. Tit for tat. An eye for an eye was ingrained into the Turks and in him since childhood. Only a matter of time until they made another move.

Saad had beefed up security in and around his home for that exact reason. He'd suspended all travel and hadn't been out of the house in days. The safest place was probably on his yacht. He considered making himself a moving target and going out to sea. But boats were easily tracked on sonar. Sitting ducks, so to speak, if attacked by a helicopter or a submarine.

Not that the White Wolves were that resourceful. They were much more effective at ground attacks. The deciding factor to stay on land had been the thought of spending days on the water which wasn't appealing to Saad. He hated the water. The only reason he had a yacht was for the prestige of it. A man of his means was supposed to have one.

That, and he could keep on it the girls he wanted to make disappear. Odille. Seno. Rosita.

Another reason he didn't want to go on the yacht. Those three girls were there, and he'd long since quit trying to force them to service him. Too easy for them to kill him in his sleep. The girls at his house were much better at pleasing him. Although Rosita, a Spanish girl, had at one time been one of his best girls. One he particularly liked in bed, until she demanded more pay for her services. As if three hundred thousand euros wasn't enough. He could easily afford it, so that wasn't the problem. It was the principle of the thing. The girls signed a contract. They were in no position to demand anything from him.

When he refused to increase her pay, she refused to provide any services. Now she'd been held on the yacht for no pay. That served her right. At least she was on a luxurious yacht. He could've turned her into the authorities and had her thrown in jail but didn't want to draw attention to himself. Someone somewhere might believe her story. This way, he could just make her disappear anytime he wanted to.

The other thing the yacht was good for.

The girls had no way off. The four-hundred-and sixty-five-foot super luxury mega yacht was parked far enough away from the shore that the girls couldn't escape. If they tried to swim, they'd drown before they reached land or be bitten by a stonefish or sea snake. At some point, all three girls would no longer be of use to him, and he'd simply make a trip out into the Persian Gulf, attach a weight to their legs, and throw them overboard. Never to be heard from again. A dozen or so girls had met that fate over the years.

The three currently on the yacht would meet a similar fate, sooner rather than later. He was tired of them. Actually, he was tired of all his girls. This last batch hadn't been one of the best. Maybe it was time to rethink his plan.

A ding on his computer interrupted his thoughts. The sound meant he had an email. Nighttime had set in, and the Sheikh was in his office, wrapping up the last of the day's business. Anya was waiting for him in his suite. She was another problem girl. Had been ever since Bianca left. The two of them had been inseparable, and now that Bianca was gone, Anya was different. Less attentive to him. Not as uninhibited. Boring. He hated boring.

Perhaps those contracts should only be for six months, he mused. Most of the women tended to lose enthusiasm over time. Maybe it was he who lost enthusiasm. He might be the one who needed more variety. If he weren't limited to four wives, he'd have a hundred. He didn't understand why he couldn't.

His last conversation with the cleric had been interesting. He said Saad could marry as many girls as he wanted and divorce them at any time for any reason. The only caveat was that he could only have four at a time. That didn't seem to be a problem. With a temporary marriage, he could have a hundred girls in the span of a couple of months if he wanted. When he was done with them, he could just send them back. That sounded good to him. Stick with Arab girls. They knew their place.

Boring.

Arab girls were dutiful. He didn't want obedient. He wanted feisty and alluring. Girls who had experience in the real world. That's why he sought fashion models all across the world. Those girls were vulnerable as well. Flash the possibility of money, glitz, and glamour in front of them, and they became easily manipulated. For a while anyway.

Girls like Anya. Beautiful. Thin. Experienced in the ways of the world.

Perhaps the answer was to get a hundred like Anya and then divorce them when they lost their allure. He could certainly afford it.

He started to ignore the email and go to his suite to see her. The thought of the potential of hundreds of girls had him excited. Instead, he pulled up the email. The curiosity was too strong, and Anya would have to wait a couple more minutes.

Jeric.

The Professor of Linguistics at the University was emailing him. At first, Saad wondered why, then he remembered he'd asked him to translate the conversation between Mrs. Steele and Bianca. With everything else going on, he'd forgotten about it. Why did it matter now?

Bianca was gone and wasn't coming back. The painting was gone forever, and he'd likely never see Mrs. Steele again.

The email was marked urgent.

His heartbeat was already elevated from thinking about Anya. The urgent designation caused his heart to pick up a few beats per minute. What about the conversation could be considered urgent?

When he opened it, his curiosity turned to trepidation.

Here is the translation. You need to read it. Sounds like you may have a problem on your hands.

What kind of problem? That didn't make sense. How could Mrs. Steele or Bianca cause him a problem?

The email had an attachment. The transcript. He began to scroll through the pages. The words leapt off the screen like a news alert on television.

Why don't you go to the police?

Mrs. Steele said those words. A litany of emotions exploded inside him. Fear. Anger. Anxiety. Confusion. Bianca had confided in Mrs. Steele and told her what was going on. The girls had a confidentiality agreement. Bianca had violated it. Although, that might be the least of his worries. He'd gone to great lengths to keep his private activities private.

What he did with his girls was none of Mrs. Steele's business!

What's her name? Mrs. Steele asked.

Odille Coste. Bianca answered.

Saad couldn't believe the words he'd just read. Bianca told Mrs. Steele about the Canadian girl! She mentioned the yacht.

Then he became totally confused.

I'm going to get you out of here, Mrs. Steele said to Bianca.

Then she started giving her instructions.

Make sure you're at the art gallery tomorrow.

Whatever happens, go with it.

Before he had a chance to wrap his mind around the conversation, he read something that turned his anxiety into rage.

Anya wants to leave too.

He didn't bother reading the rest. Saad bolted out of his chair and walked rapidly toward his suite.

What does Anya know?

He was about to find out.

He'd kill her if she didn't tell him.

* * *

A-Rad and I were at the Sheikh's house ready to make our move and get Anya out of there. Saad made a strategic mistake in the placement of the guards around the house. They were too spread out. To the point that they couldn't see each other. I would've placed them at the four corners of the house. That way each of them could see two of the others at all times. The guards had radios and could communicate, but I placed a device near the house that blocked all radio frequencies except one. The one A-Rad and I were communicating on. The device also blocked all cell phone and internet communications. From this point on, the house was dark from a communications standpoint. No one could communicate in and no one could call out.

When A-Rad gave me the signal, the entire house would literally go dark. I was prepared to shut off the electricity, so all the lights went out. I'd disarmed the guard on the back side of the house. He lay on the ground, zip tied and gagged. Another guard, who'd been patrolling the beach area, was now shackled to the underside of the dock. A-Rad took care of the two guards at the two entrances to the house. I assumed he had no trouble because I hadn't heard from him. He was to radio me when he got inside the house.

Alex, my husband back at AJAX headquarters, had turned off the security system. He set the feed to run on a loop, so if Saad were to look at it for any reason, he'd see the guards in their positions.

I intended to stay outside the house and let A-Rad go in and get Anya. Better that Saad didn't see me. While I was wearing a mask, he might detect my gate or mannerism. As far as Saad was concerned, this was another White Wolves attack. To my knowledge, he hadn't made any connection between me and the stolen painting or the kidnapping of Bianca. I wanted to keep it that way.

Tonight's attack would be just like the first. All Saad would know was that the same guy who hit the art gallery was now in his house. That'd put the fear of God in him if he actually believed in God. I wanted him to believe that the White Wolves could get to him at any time. That'd cause Saad to panic. Make a mistake. Escalate the war with the White Wolves. My plan had several layers. Like peeling an onion. Anya was the first layer. After she was safely out of harm's way, I'd execute the second part of my plan.

A static in my ear told me A-Rad was about to speak into the radio.

"I'm at the door," he said.

"I'm ready."

"I'm in."

The plan was for him to go straight to Anya's room. If he could get her out without being detected, then all the better. A-Rad had a note in his pocket to leave for Saad.

To avenge Rafiq. Check your Turkish bank account. WW.

Saad would know who the note was from. The White Wolves. Their signature trademark. Also, the fact that they mentioned Rafiq meant they knew he was behind the killing.

"Going up the stairs," A-Rad said. "To get the package." Anya was the package. I hated calling her that, but better to keep her name off the radio. I wanted Saad to believe that taking Anya was random. Like Bianca.

"Roger," I answered. "All clear here."

If he ran into any trouble, I'd kill the lights. A-Rad had night-vision goggles on his head, so he'd be able to see in the dark by simply flipping them down.

I could hear yelling coming through A-Rad's headset.

Then a blood curdling scream.

A woman.

I could hear A-Rad breathing heavily. Like he was running.

As much as I wanted to say something, I was trained to keep quiet. A-Rad would tell me what I needed to know. If I needed to infiltrate the house, I could within seconds. As excruciating as it was, I had to hold my position.

Another scream.

Coming through the headset. Only this time louder.

A-Rad must be getting close to the commotion.

What's going on?

"I'm at the Sheikh's suite," A-Rad said. "The door's shut. The screams came from inside."

Before I could ask if he needed me, he said, "I'm going in."

21

Anya

Sheikh Saad's suite was the most luxurious room Anya had ever been in, but it still felt more like a prison than anything else. Tonight was her night to be with the Sheikh, and she was dreading it. She'd lost count on the number of times she'd had to endure his rough and unwanted advances. Eleven or twelve was her guess. Since she'd only been in the UAE for three months, she had dozens more to go to before her twelve months of hell was up.

She'd done the math in her head. Three hundred thousand euros was twenty-five thousand a month. She had to be with Saad three or four times a month. About 6250 euros each time. That thought made her feel worse, not better. No matter how much she was getting paid, she was nothing more than a prostitute. In reality, a sex slave. She'd never voluntarily do it for any amount of money. She'd rather be back working at the diner for a pittance than enduring one more night with the monster.

How did I get into this mess?

One day she was working as a waitress in Denmark, struggling to pay her tuition at the University of Copenhagen. The next day she was being whisked away to Abu Dhabi to start a new job as a model. How could she have been so stupid? Her dad always told her if it seemed too good to be true, then it was.

As luck would have it, she happened to be working on the day the Arab man, Zain Cahn, entered the diner and sat down at one of her tables.

"Why is a pretty girl like you slaving away in a restaurant?" he had asked when she brought him the check.

The man was smartly dressed. Expensive suit and tie and wearing a Rolex watch. He was smooth and debonair. Charismatic and persuasive. Believable.

"I don't mind. It's a job that pays the bills," Anya said.

"Have you ever thought about being a model?"

"No!"

The truth. She'd never even thought of the possibility that she was pretty enough to be a model.

"How would you like to make some real money?" he asked.

Alarm bells went off in her head right from the start. The man was feeding her a line, and she could tell it. Girls were recruited all the time to go to Amsterdam to work in the red-light district. Promised more money than they could imagine, many fell for it. Anya wanted to study literature. Maybe go to America someday.

"I'm not interested, but thank you," she said politely.

"How do you know? I haven't even told you what the job entails."

"I think I can guess."

"It's not what you think. I work for a fashion magazine. We're always looking for girls to be on the cover and work photo shoots."

He handed her his card. It looked legitimate. Raised gold lettering. An Abu Dhabi address. She'd never heard of the fashion magazine, which should've been her first red flag. Actually, one of about a dozen. Mostly, she should've listened to the voice inside her head and just walked away.

"I'm not pretty enough to be a model," she answered instead.

"You're exactly what we're looking for. An everyday girl. Today's models look just like you. Pretty. Wholesome. Nice figure. An honest face. That's what we want in our girls."

Anya could feel her cheeks blush. "I don't know anything about modeling."

"We'll train you. Don't you want to travel the world? Get out of Copenhagen? The pay is three hundred thousand euros for a one-year contract."

Anya could almost feel her eyes widen and her mouth fly open. Now she knew the deal was too good to be true. Why would anyone pay her that much money to be a model? Out of the blue.

The money would be amazing if it were true. She'd have to work ten years to make that much as a waitress. That much money would pay for her college. Maybe she was pretty enough. Her dad always said she was beautiful. What about school?

She could take classes online for a year.

Stupid.

Anya wanted to cry.

Now that Bianca was gone, she was all alone. Two other girls were in the house, but they didn't understand the torture she was going through. They liked working for the Sheikh. Anya was taught to value herself more than that. Her dad would roll over in his grave if he knew what she was doing.

What choice did she have?

Bianca had told her about girls disappearing. If she didn't do what the Sheikh wanted, he would have her thrown in jail where she'd be tortured and raped by the guards. Or worse. Make her disappear like Odille did. The best thing for her to do was to tough it out. Make the best of it. Hope she got paid.

To this point, she hadn't seen any money. Except ten thousand euros for signing the contract. Nor had she been on the cover of any magazines. She wondered if she ever would see the rest of the euros. All she could do was keep forcing herself to pretend like she was enjoying herself. Make the Sheikh happy and hope for the best.

She knew what was expected. He'd left a skimpy lingerie on the bed for her. She put it on and sat on the chaise lounge waiting for him. Feeling insecure. Nervous. It didn't matter how many times she went through this, she'd never get used to it.

Her heart started racing when she heard footsteps. Not the normal sound she heard when the Sheikh was coming. More stomping. Like he was angry.

The door flew open.

The Sheikh's eyes were ablaze like burning embers of coal.

She instinctively put her hands over her chest and cowered back.

He was on her in a second. The Sheikh grabbed her by the hair. Anya let out a scream. By the look in his eyes, he was going to kill her. She wanted to scream again, but no one was around who could help her even if she did. The other two girls were in the house, but what could they do?

The Sheikh was spewing out words like venom. Expletives. Something about Bianca and Mrs. Steele.

"You're hurting me," Anya said as she tried to tilt her head, so it didn't hurt so badly.

The Sheikh let go of her hair but then stood over her. Crowding her. Pushing her roughly with his hands.

"What did you say to Bianca?" he shouted in her face.

"I don't know what you mean."

The Sheikh backhanded her across her cheek.

It stung like a thousand wasps had landed on her face.

For a moment, things went black.

"What did you say to Mrs. Steele?" he demanded.

"I didn't say anything. I've never spoken to her." Anya scooted back on the chaise lounge, but she had nowhere to go to get away from him. He held her down with one hand and had the other raised like he was going to strike her again. Anya let out an even louder scream.

"Did you say to Mrs. Steele that you wanted to leave here?" he asked.

"I've never talked to Mrs. Steele."

He grabbed her hair again and jerked back hard. She could feel chunks being ripped out. The pain shot through her like a knife. Between her throbbing cheek and burning scalp, Anya was racked with searing pain.

"You're lying! Was Bianca really kidnapped? Did Mrs. Steele help her escape?"

"I don't know. I swear. Please don't hurt me." Anya was desperately begging the Sheikh to calm down.

He looked like he was going to hit her again.

Anya saw movement out of the corner of her eye. The Sheikh must've heard it too because he turned around.

Suddenly the Sheikh was on the ground.

A masked man stood over him with his foot on his chest and a gun pointed at his head. The Sheikh's hands were in front of his face, as if that would stop a bullet.

"Who are you? What do you want?" the Sheikh said.

The man answered him in Arabic.

Something about a bomb. He mentioned a name. Rafiq.

The masked man waved his gun at Anya. "Go to your room and get dressed," he ordered. "When you're done, come back down here. You have three minutes."

Anya was too terrified to even move. Her mind couldn't process what was happening.

"Go! Now!" the man said. "Don't make me shoot you."

Anya covered herself with her hands and ran out of the room. She went upstairs. The other two girls were at the top.

"What's going on?" one of them whispered.

"There's a gunman in the house," Anya said. "He's got the Sheikh."

The girls hurried back to their rooms.

Anya only had three minutes. She had to hurry. She went into her room and rapidly changed clothes and put on a pair of sneakers. Her heart was still pounding in her chest, but she was beginning to think more clearly.

I have to get out of here.

Once she was dressed, Anya grabbed her phone off the table by the side of her bed and stuck it in the back pocket of her jeans. She then tiptoed back to the top of the stairs and listened for any signs of the gunman. The Sheikh's master suite was at the back of the house. She could sneak out without the gunman knowing. Were there more masked men outside?

A risk she had to take.

Anya went down the steps and opened the back door carefully and slipped out, shutting the door gingerly so as to not make a noise.

She paused to get her bearings. From her vantage point, she was looking out on the Persian Gulf. A moment of indecision froze her. Should she run north to the road and try to catch a ride or run along the beach and try to find a house where someone might help her?

She chose the beach. Anya went down the steps, past the swimming pool and onto the beach. Her heart was still racing and her breathing labored, but the adrenaline propelled her forward. Running on the beach was hard. She might've made the wrong choice. On the road, she could get away faster.

Anya was suddenly tackled from behind.

When she landed, the person fell on top of her knocking the wind out of her.

She tried to scream, but nothing came out.

A gloved hand was on her mouth.

The man was holding her down even though she tried to fight him off.

Maybe a woman?

For some reason, it seemed like the man might be a woman.

"Anya," she said. "Don't scream."

Definitely a woman. *How did she know my name?*

"I'm here to help you. I'm going to take my hand off your mouth, but don't scream."

Anya was on her stomach and the woman was on her back, holding her down with her hand over Anya's mouth.

"Promise me you won't scream," the woman said.

Anya nodded her head.

"I'm here to help you. I helped Bianca, and I'm going to get you out of here."

The voice sounded familiar. The night was dark, and the moon was blocked by the clouds.

Mrs. Steele!

Anya rolled over. The woman was still on top of her. Anya's eyes began to water, and tears started to escape her eyes and run down her cheeks.

"Can you really get me out of here?"

"Yes. But we have to be quiet until we're safely away. Let me help you up."

The woman took Anya's hand and lifted her up from the ground.

They both shook off the sand.

The woman listened to something in her ear. A radio or something.

"Let's move," she said.

The last thing Anya wanted to do was walk back toward the house.

It seemed like she had no other choice.

* * *

The Sheikh was trying to process what was happening.

A man was in his house. Wearing a mask. Pointing a gun at him. Where were his guards? How did the man get past the security system? He could only assume his guards were dead.

The gunman had mentioned Rafiq. Obviously, he was with the White Wolves. From his manner, it appeared the man was there to kill him. Maybe Mrs. Steele didn't have anything to do with Bianca's disappearance or the stealing of the painting after all.

"I'll double whatever they're paying you," Saad said.

"You killed Rafiq. He was my brother."

"You stole my painting and kidnapped one of my girls."

"You should've sold me the painting when you had the chance."

"I'll buy it back from you."

The man laughed. "You're lucky I don't kill you."

That caused Saad to let out a sigh. The man wasn't there to kill him.

"What do you want?" Saad asked.

"I want you to know that I can get to you anytime I want. Even in your own house."

"I can get to you, too!" the Sheikh said, even though he immediately regretted the words. That only made the gunman angrier. He waved the gun in Saad's face again like he was going to pull the trigger. The Sheikh was a proud man. He'd rather die than let someone disrespect him in his own house.

The man took a piece of paper out of his pocket and threw it on the bed. "Check your bank account," he said.

What did he mean? What bank account?

Before he could ask, the man was gone.

The Sheikh jumped to his feet and ran to a room off his master suite. There he found a gun. He looked at the security cameras. What he saw had him perplexed. The guards were still at their posts. How did the man get inside without them knowing it?

Saad heard a car speeding away. He looked on the camera feed and didn't see one. Then he noticed that the feed wasn't changing. It kept showing the same movements from the guards. Clearly, he'd been hacked. The White Wolves were playing a loop over and over again. He'd underestimated them. The White Wolves were much more sophisticated than he'd imagined them to be.

He went back into his room and looked at the note.

To avenge Rafiq. Check your Turkish bank account. WW.

A wave of panic went through him like he'd been hit by a lightning bolt. He had almost a billion dollars in his Turkish bank account.

Saad practically ran to his office. He furiously typed in the secured link to his bank. He typed in the username and password.

His heart sank when he saw the numbers.

00.06

All zeros in the account except for a few cents. His money was gone!

The White Wolves had retaliated. They hit him where they knew it would hurt him the most. His money. They may have also taken Anya. He couldn't care less about her.

All he could think about was the money.

And revenge.

He picked up his phone and dialed Zamani.

When he answered on the first ring, the Sheikh said, "I want to strike the White Wolves again. This time it must be big. We must bring them to their knees."

22

MJ

Siraj Jabara Correctional Facility for Women
Two days later

For the last three weeks, MJ had lived in constant pain. Ever since that fateful day when her father doused her with kerosene and set her on fire. Sometimes, she woke up in the middle of the night sweating in terror as she relived the moment over and over again in her dreams. What started out as the happiest day of her life—her eighteenth birthday and marriage to Christopher—had turned into the biggest nightmare with no end in sight.

All because she couldn't keep her big mouth shut.

They'd gone back to Aunt Shule's house to get her birth certificate because some fool at the passport center lost the copy she provided to them. They knew they were taking a risk going back to the house, but she couldn't get her passport without the certificate. With the passport she could leave the country with Christopher and start a new life in America.

The plan was to get in and out of Aunt Shule's house as quickly as possible. Three minutes. That's all she needed to find the certificate, and she'd be away from her father forever.

Then he showed up.

In a good mood.

After all, he was going to collect a huge dowry that day from Abdul. She'd relived the conversation again and again in her mind. Now, she knew exactly what to say. Then, she was a stubborn and obstinate teenager who thought there was nothing her father could do to stop her from leaving the country.

"Are you excited?" her father had said to her. "You're getting married."

All she had to do was play along.

Instead, she said defiantly, "I'm not marrying Abdul," immediately escalating the situation.

Her father went into a rage. He hit her in the face which only made her angrier. That's when the pain started and had continued to this day. His thick and rough hand stung her cheek.

Then he saw the ring on her finger and the cross around her neck.

"What's that?" he said pointing to her hand and neck.

Now she knew what she should've said. "Aunt Shule's. She let me try them on."

Instead, she said, "I'm already married! That's right. I'm a Christian now. I married a Christian man. There's nothing you can do about it!"

She thought he was going to hit her again, but he suddenly left the house.

Aunt Shule came rushing in and said to her in a panicked voice, "We've got to get out of here. He'll be back."

Before they could leave, he was back. He tried to grab her hair, but she pulled away and ran to her room. He followed her and busted through the door before she could shut it. He then hit her so hard, she fell back onto the bed. Then he did the unthinkable. Poured kerosene on her.

When she let her mind go there, she could still smell the stinging chemical that burned her eyes and skin. Then she heard the sound of the lighter. A clicking sound. She could still hear it sometimes at night when everything was quiet.

All her senses were heightened that day. While she wanted to forget every detail, they were etched in her mind.

Especially the agony.

When her father set her clothes on fire with the lighter, the pain was unlike anything she'd ever experienced before. She was so paralyzed in fear, she didn't know what to do other than just thrash around in the bed. The more she tried to put out the flames, the more they spread.

Why did she keep reliving it?

Today would be bad enough without living the horrors of the past.

Her trial was today.

MJ lay in her bed. Not a bed. An old moldy mattress laying on the concrete floor. The darkness of the night engulfed her. So did the now-familiar putrid smell of the prison. A mix of urine, sweat, vomit, and stale air from the lack of ventilation. The only other thing in the room was a broken toilet and a sink with unclean water. That, and the cock-roaches, ants, and the occasional rat who frequently invaded the cell and were not afraid of them.

Amina lay next to her. MJ hadn't been able to sleep. She was careful not to wake her friend. Amina tried to make herself stay up but suc-cumbed to sleep several hours before. MJ could only lay on her left side. The slightest movement or touch sent pain shooting through her body from the still-unhealed burns on the right side of her body.

Tonight, she was left to her thoughts. Regrets from the past. Fear of the present and the hopelessness of the future. Her attorney wasn't op-timistic about today. The only thing that was bringing her peace were the Bible verses she'd memorized and kept saying in her head over and over again.

I will never leave you nor forsake you.

Love your enemies and pray for those who persecute you.

How could she pray for her father? Her attorney said she'd have to face him today. She tried to say a prayer for the prosecutor and the judge, but the words seemed insincere.

One verse did bring her comfort. She knew it by heart. Aunt Shule had made her memorize verses and then recite them to her. This was one of her favorites which now had new meaning.

Blessed are those who are persecuted for righteousness, for the kingdom of heaven belongs to them. Blessed are you when people insult you and persecute you and say all kinds of evil things about you falsely on account of me. Rejoice and be glad because your reward is great in heaven, for they persecuted the prophets before you in the same way.

Malak, her attorney, had warned her that they were going to say all kinds of evil things about her today. They'd try to get her to recant her faith. Promise her leniency in exchange for renouncing Christianity. That was her biggest fear. Would she be strong enough to stand firm in the faith? She'd rather die than deny Christ. That's how strong she felt now, but what about in the courtroom? In front of all those people? Under the threat of more pain? The judge could make her life even more miserable.

A verse she remembered sent chills down her spine.

Everyone who confesses me before men, I will also confess him before my father in heaven. But whoever denies me before men, I will also deny him before my father in heaven.

MJ began to cry.

What if I refuse to deny him?

What will they do to me?

Even worse, *What if I do deny him?*

She prayed fervently and asked God for strength. She didn't think she could do it on her own. She couldn't deny Christ, but she didn't know how to endure the lashes or possibly even the stoning.

MJ felt so alone.

The prison cell was dark except for a dim light in the hallway. The conditions were harsh. She felt such pain in her soul. Agony. Fear. That she'd make a mistake and say the wrong thing, like she did with her father.

Then she remembered a verse. Or maybe the Holy Spirit brought it to her mind. She suddenly knew what to do.

When you are brought before judges, rulers, and authorities, do not worry about how you will defend yourself or what you will say. For the Holy Spirit will teach you at that time what you should say.

Don't say a word, she heard a still small voice say.

Then she thought about what Jesus did when he faced his accusers. When Jesus was before Pilate, they hurled all sorts of accusations at him. Reviled him. Accused him of crimes he didn't commit. The verse suddenly popped into her mind.

When Jesus was accused by the chief priests and elders, he answered nothing. Then Pilate said to him, "Do you not hear your accusers? Will you not answer them?"

She wasn't sure she remembered the verses word for word. But this was the essence.

"He answered not a word," MJ said aloud.

That's what she'd do. She wouldn't answer them. She'd keep her mouth shut. Her attorney could mount her defense, but she would remain silent. Like Jesus did. If the Holy Spirit told her to say something, then she would. Otherwise, she'd keep quiet.

MJ suddenly felt peace. For the first time. She even fell asleep and didn't wake up until morning when she felt Amina stir.

"I'm so worried about you," Amina said as they lay on the mattress together.

"Things will be okay," MJ said, still feeling the peace that had come upon her during the night.

"How can you be so calm?" Amina said. "I'd be a nervous wreck. I am a nervous wreck. My trial is in four days."

"I'll be fine. God will be with me."

"They have to find you not guilty. Like they did Christopher. If they do, you can go to America and be with him. I'll miss you, though."

"Everything's going to be fine. I know it. I trust God."

MJ didn't know what was going to happen today. One thing she was almost certain of was that they weren't going to let her go. She didn't know if God was preparing her for it, or if it was her imagination running wild, but she was expecting the worst.

She'd be punished. MJ could sense it. Almost picture it. Like a sandstorm. An ominous cloud in the distance slowly moving toward her. Soon, it would envelope her with the fury of an unrelenting storm.

One thing was for sure.

She wasn't through with the pain.

*   *   *

The guards took MJ out of the prison and drove her thirty minutes to a town outside her village. There she was led into a building that looked like a house. In the back of the building was a small room with benches. The guard chained her to the wall. She was wearing a black burqa and only her eyes were showing. Just as well. She didn't want anyone to see her face. It'd be easier to keep quiet if her mouth were covered. It might not hide the tears, though.

The plan was to stay silent. No matter what happened. She felt the strength to do so. Her hateful father had demanded silence around him most of her life, so she was used to it. While she felt more peace, her emotions swirled around like a jetty in an oasis. They were like two men fighting. Each trying to get the better of the other. Sometimes peace got the upper hand. Other times anger, fear, bitterness, or unforgiveness was winning the day. The burqa would hide the confusion.

The door opened, and the rage rose to the surface and overwhelmed every other emotion she'd been experiencing as her father was led into the room and chained to the wall right across from her. His eyes were filled with crazed fury when he looked at her. His jaw clenched and his fists balled up. She got the feeling he would've killed her if he wasn't chained to the wall.

Don't say a word.

"You are no longer a daughter of mine," he said with vitriol dripping from every word.

She wanted to ask him why he set her on fire. Why did he hate her so much? What did she ever do to deserve it? She'd always been an obedient daughter. Until now.

But MJ remained silent.

"It's like I don't even have a daughter."

Fortunately, they weren't together long. The guard showed up and led her father out of the room. Then another guard came for her. She was led into a larger room and made to stand alongside the wall just inside the door. Her father was sitting at a table with another man. Presumably, his attorney. Two other men were sitting at another table. One of them she recognized as the man who arrested her.

MJ could see her attorney sitting in the back. Next to Aunt Shule on one side and Mrs. Steele on the other.

In the row behind them were Christopher's parents. At that moment, she wished the burqa weren't covering her face so they could see her smiling. It warmed her heart that they were there. Her attorney said the Tate's were paying her legal fees. She had wondered if they hated her because she had brought this on their son.

Her eyes met Mrs. Tate's. She smiled. That brought her comfort. Reassurance that they didn't hate her.

A guard entered the room through another door followed by a man in a robe. Presumably the judge. He sat down at the table in the front.

When the judge began speaking, MJ's heart started pounding even faster and stronger. All her confidence and resolve left her like a balloon released in the sky. How could she get it back?

"This is the matter against defendant, Emir Tabithe, who is present in the courtroom. Mr. Prosecutor, what are the charges?"

Clearly, her father would be tried first.

"Domestic abuse, Your Honor," the man at the second table said. "Emir's daughter, Majahammaddan Tabithe married a Christian man against his wishes. According to the tribal customs of his village, the father chooses a husband for his daughter. His daughter refused to marry the man, costing Emir his dowry and his reputation among the other tribal elders. Then he learned that his daughter had committed crimes against God. Apostasy and blasphemy. According to the laws of the tribe, the punishment for denouncing Islam is death. Emir was simply doing his duty to the elders of his tribe and protecting his honor."

Who's on trial here?

It sounded like the prosecution was reading charges against MJ and not against her father.

"I understand all that," the judge said. "According to the complaint, the defendant set his daughter on fire. Is that the allegation and the reason for the charge?"

"Yes, Your Honor," the prosecutor said.

"How does the defendant plead?" the judge asked.

The man sitting next to her father stood and said, "Emir pleads guilty."

"I sentence you to two years in prison and fifty lashes," the judge said. "However, I reduce the sentence to six months and no lashes, since Emir pled guilty."

"We thank Your Honor for the consideration," his attorney said.

"Is Emir's tribal elder in the courtroom today?" the judge asked.

A man in the audience stood.

"Do you wish to add any punishment to the sentence I've imposed?"

"No, Your Honor." The man said. "I'd actually like to speak on Emir's behalf if I may."

"Of course."

"Emir is a well-respected man in his tribe. He's also a tradesman providing essential services to his Emirate. A number of businesses and employees are counting on him for their livelihood. Considering the guilty plea, might the court consider a suspended sentence so that there is no disruption in his work."

The judge rubbed his beard like he was thinking. "If Emir agrees to fifty lashes, then I will suspend the sentence to time served."

Her father's attorney stood and said, "Emir will agree to that with appreciation to the court."

MJ could hardly believe it. Her father had practically killed her, and he basically got a couple weeks in jail for it.

Don't say a word.

The judge abruptly turned and looked at MJ. "Is it true that you re-fused to marry the man God had chosen for you?"

Don't say a word.

Actually, Christopher was the man God had chosen for her. It took all of her self-control to keep from saying so.

"I'll ask again," the judge said. "Did you marry a Christian so that you wouldn't have to marry the man your father chose for you?"

Yes!

That's what she wanted to say, but instead, MJ stood against the wall in silence.

"Did you convert to Christianity?" the judge demanded, his voice getting louder.

I love the Lord.

MJ bit her lip. Hard.

"Have you blasphemed God?"

"Do you refuse to answer my questions?" The judge was practically shouting now.

"If I may, Your Honor," Malak, her attorney, said. "May I have a moment to confer with my client?"

"No! Sit back down. Do you refuse to answer my questions?" he said to MJ.

She stood there like a statue and didn't answer. Her gaze was fixed on the judge, so he'd know she'd heard him.

The judge picked up his gavel and hit the table.

"I find the defendant, Emir Tabithe, not guilty on the charge of domestic abuse. You are free to go without punishment. As to the fifty lashes, his daughter will take those upon her back for disrespecting this court."

A murmur went through the crowd. Then a gasp. Coming from Aunt Shule.

The judge hit the table with the gavel two more times. Hard. Like he was furious.

"After the punishment is carried out, we will begin her trial. Hopefully, she will learn to respect this court."

He looked over and glared at MJ.

MJ let out a breath she'd been holding.

Not a word.

The guard took her arm and led her out of the courtroom, through the cell, and outside around back of the courthouse. He threw MJ roughly to the ground.

Another guard emerged with a cane. Her burqa was raised over her head exposing her back. She got on her knees and put her hands in front of her to pray.

She heard the swoosh of the cane. The exhale from the man as he brought it down upon her back.

Then she felt the pain.

The worst pain she'd ever felt in her life as the cane hit on her right side. Against the unhealed burns.

Don't say a word.

Don't even let them hear you cry out.

After five lashes, the resolve left her and she could no longer keep from crying out in pain.

23

Inside the Courthouse

If I could, I'd burn the whole place down.

Then kill every single person involved in a system that would let the father go free and subject an eighteen-year-old girl to fifty lashes for falling in love.

When they brought MJ back inside from her beating, her burqa was stained in blood. She walked gingerly and hunched over. If the guard wasn't holding her up, I was concerned that she would've fallen over. When she sat in the chair, she leaned forward so her back wouldn't be up against the seat.

The tragic part was that her ordeal wasn't over. The trial hadn't even started, and the worst might very well be ahead of her. If she made the judge angry again, he could send her right back to the yard for another beating. One thing I'd learned from Malak was that the law allowed up to two hundred lashes at a time. While rare, he'd seen the maximum punishment meted out several times. Even against women and girls. Theoretically, MJ could be facing up to a hundred and fifty more lashes with the cane.

The other thing I'd learned was that a courtroom in the tribal region was like the wild, wild, west. The judge ruled. He set the procedures and doled out the punishment. The appeals court rarely overturned the judges. I understood why MJ refused to answer his questions. Had she answered yes to any of them, she'd been found guilty of the charges. The result would have been lashes anyway. Probably jail time. Maybe even death. MJ did the right thing by not even dignifying the judge's questions with an answer.

Aunt Shule was sobbing, so I reached over and squeezed her hand. I could hear muffled cries coming from the row behind me. Probably Mrs. Tate.

As much I wanted to, I couldn't act now. I had other things to consider. Anya was safe and out of the country so one thing was off my list of worries. But I still had Odille to think about and search for. Anya said there might be even more girls missing. Both Anya and Bianca said the girls were taken to the yacht and they never saw them again. I had to find a way to get on the yacht and see if there were any clues as to their whereabouts.

Then there was Amina. In four days, her trial would begin. If I helped MJ, I risked the possibility that my cover would be blown, and I couldn't help Amina or the Sheikh's girls. The problem was that I couldn't rescue both MJ and Amina. They were never in the same place at the same time. I'd looked at a possible mission at the prison, but that wasn't feasible. Alex and I went over the plans and satellite images of the facility for more than an hour and came to the same conclusion. Any rescue attempt was a suicide mission.

If I was going to rescue MJ, it had to be now. Once she was sentenced, she'd be behind bars for an extended period of time. Or perhaps even executed. I went through a plan in my mind. All I had on me was the knife hidden in my skirt. Two guards had guns. Barney probably did as well. I'd need a diversion. Maybe wait until after the trial and act while they were taking her away. Then I'd only have one or two guards to contend with.

Really, the best time would've been while she was in the yard getting a beating. I could sneak out of the courthouse, disable the guards, and get MJ out of there before anyone inside knew what had happened. But they'd know it was me who took her.

Then what about Amina?

I could come back to get her on her trial date, but the place would be crawling with guards if they even tried her in the same location. I'd need my whole AJAX team to fly to Abu Dhabi to help me. Alex already said he would, but I dismissed the idea. Right now, no one knew I was a threat. That gave me the advantage. A whole team could make a big play and bring a lot of firepower to a rescue attempt, but that many people weren't as good at integrating undercover into the situation.

I was already as close as we were ever going to get without using force. No question in my mind that I could save one of the girls with just me. Even get her on my plane and out of the country and still be able to look for Odille and potentially other girls.

But I couldn't save both of them by myself.

So... I had to pick one of the girls to rescue.

Gut wrenching.

Not the first time I couldn't help someone and wouldn't be the last.

Which one?

Amina was my first choice. I had slightly more of an affinity with her because I came upon her the night of the attacks. I'd seen her attackers and even injured one of them. In some ways, I was to blame for taking her to the hospital instead of to her home. That's why, if push came to shove, I'd rescue her over MJ.

The timing was better with Amina as well. I needed a few more days to see if any more of the Sheikh's girls needed rescuing. I could rescue those girls, then come back in three days and snatch Amina at her trial and get her out of Abu Dhabi for good. Having saved everyone except MJ.

That seemed like the best plan. Not that it made it any easier.

Watching MJ suffer was breaking my heart. I didn't always do the smartest thing. In some ways, MJ would be the easier girl to rescue. Getting her to America would be simpler. She already wanted to go there, and Christopher was waiting for her. I'd promised I'd help them. The opportunity to rescue MJ was right in front of me.

Poor Amina.

How could I leave her behind?

I couldn't.

No girl left behind.

I had to figure out how to save them both.

That caused me to rethink my plan. First, I needed to let things play out with MJ's trial. Perhaps Malak could pull another rabbit out of his hat and, by some miracle, she'd be found not guilty. That wasn't likely to happen, given the judge's animosity toward her, but better to wait and see.

The courtroom was completely quiet. If a mouse were making a noise, we would've heard it. The solemnity of the moment was not lost on even the prosecutor and the guards as no one was talking or moving around.

The judge broke the silence when he returned and sat down at his place behind the table.

"Before this court is the trial of Majahammaddan Tabithe. Will the prosecutor read the charges?"

"There are two charges, Your Honor. The first is apostasy. The girl has admitted that she converted to Christianity and abandoned her faith. The second is zina. The girl admits that she married a Christian man against the teachings of our faith. Because the marriage is invalid, the sexual relationship between the woman and the man is fornication. The charge is sexual indignities."

"Present your evidence," the judge said.

"I think the evidence is already before the court. You have the testimony of the detective at Christopher's trial. His mother said to the detective that Christopher and the defendant were already married. The girl was wearing a wedding ring at the hospital when the detective came to question her. Additionally, you have the testimony of the father. In his own words today, the girl's father said that she told him she was already married. She also admitted to her father that she was a

Christian. As you know, Your Honor, a woman or girl can be convicted on the testimony of a reputable man. The father's word is enough for this court to render a verdict. I can provide more evidence, but what's the point of wasting the court's time?"

"Thank you, counselor. Malak, how does your client plead?"

"Your Honor, if it please the court. I'd like to remind you that you have already ruled in this matter. In Christopher's trial, you found that the boy and girl are not legally married. In addition, the prosecutor did not present any evidence in that trial of a sexual relationship between the two and has not presented any evidence today. Christopher was charged with the same two things. On both counts, Your Honor found him not guilty. Therefore, the court should defer to its previous judgment and find Majahammaddan not guilty as well. Thank you, Your Honor."

"I didn't ask for arguments. I asked how your client pleads."

"With all due respect, a pleading is unnecessary if you've already ruled."

"I haven't ruled on this girl's guilt or innocence. Therefore, I need a plea."

Malak paused and looked down at his notes. I knew his dilemma. If he pled not guilty and the judge found MJ guilty over some technicality, she would've committed a third crime and the judge was harsher on defendants who pleaded not guilty. If she pleaded guilty, the court's finding of Christopher not guilty would be nullified. The judge also hadn't ruled on the apostasy charge. To me, it seemed almost certain that he'd find her guilty of converting to Christianity.

Malak had no choice in my mind. He must've been thinking the same thing because he said, "My client pleads not guilty." Malak sat back down.

"Thank you. The court finds the defendant guilty of marrying a non-Muslim and for having an improper sexual relationship with him."

Malak burst to his feet. "Your Honor, the defense hasn't even had a chance to offer evidence!"

"The court doesn't need to hear any further evidence. I have the testimony of the father. He is a man of fine reputation and the girl's very words condemn her."

"Your Honor, I have an affidavit from a doctor who examined Majahammaddan and found that, in his opinion, she is still a virgin."

"Let me see the affidavit."

Malak approached the judge and handed him the paper. He looked it over.

"Does the prosecutor have a response?" the judge asked.

"No, Your Honor, other than that the court has already ruled. It defies common sense that the couple did not consummate their marriage."

Malak continued to press his argument. "Your Honor, to find a man guilty of sexual indignities requires four witnesses. As you know—"

"Only one witness is required to convict a woman of zina," the judge said, cutting him off.

Malak was still standing. "My point, Your Honor. You don't even have one person who's come forward to present any evidence of a sexual relationship. You do have one male witness, Christopher, who testified that no sexual contact has occurred between the two. My client is willing to testify to that fact as well."

"The law requires that the witness be a follower of Islam and be a man of reputable standing," the prosecutor said. "May I remind the court that Christopher has been convicted of a crime."

"So has the father," Malak said. "Can he really be considered a man of high reputation when the court found him guilty of domestic abuse?"

"The court found him not guilty," the judge said.

"After a guilty verdict," Malak retorted. "Even after you sentenced him to punishment."

"Let me make this easy for everyone," the judge said. "I'll find the defendant not guilty on the charge of zina. On the charge of marrying a non-Muslim, I find her guilty, and sentence her to time served. Is that satisfactory, counselor?"

"Yes, Your Honor," Malak said.

My heart leapt with joy. It looked like Malak had pulled another rabbit out of his hat. Time served meant she was free to go with no further punishment. A smile came on Aunt Shule's face for the first time as she looked up to heaven to thank God.

"As to the charge of apostasy," the judge said. "How does your client plead?"

My heart sank to the bottom of my chest.

"Let me confer with my client, Your Honor," Malak said.

He leaned over and began whispering in MJ's ear. They talked for nearly a minute.

"My client is not prepared to enter a plea at this time," Malak said.

The judge's whole demeanor changed again. He leaned forward in his chair. His eyes were furrowed, and his jaw tensed. His shoulders raised in obvious anger.

"Young lady, have you renounced your Islamic faith and converted to Christianity?" the judge asked harshly.

MJ was silent.

"I'll ask you again. Are you a Christian?"

MJ refused to answer.

"If you don't answer, I'll sentence you to fifty more lashes!"

MJ stared straight ahead. It appeared from my angle, that she wasn't even looking at the judge.

"Your Honor, my client has the right to remain silent," Malak said. "She has an attorney who can speak on her behalf."

"Then speak. What is her plea?"

"I don't know."

"Guard, seize the girl and administer fifty more lashes!"

"No!" Aunt Shule cried out.

I put my arm around her and pulled her close and whispered for her to remain silent. I didn't want Aunt Shule to get lashes as well.

The guard jerked MJ from her seat. Violently. She cried out when he grabbed her right arm. The one with the burns and now the torn flesh from the caning.

She stumbled from the shackles that got caught up in the table and chair.

The guard pulled her up. Another guard came and took her other arm and they lifted her off the ground and carried her out of the room.

The judge stood and left.

What do I do?

I could go out and stop them. That wasn't wise. Curly always said not to act out of emotion. Act because the facts dictate a certain response. Saving MJ meant risking being able to save the other girls. The risk was too great that I'd blow my chance to help Amina and Odille.

As agonizing as it was, the prudent thing was to wait.

There might not be another opportunity.

When I heard the first scream, tears filled my eyes, and I clutched Aunt Shule harder. I'm sure she didn't realize that she was the only thing holding me back. Her hands clutched to mine, or I would've taken my knife, killed the two guards and driven MJ away from this heinous travesty.

We could almost count the lashes by the number of times MJ cried out in agony. The father sat on the other side of the courtroom with an evil smile of satisfaction on his face. I wanted to walk over and hit him so hard that he'd never smile again.

When the beating mercifully came to an end, I dreaded what I'd see when they brought MJ back in the room. As expected, her burqa was a bloody mess. The guards literally had to carry her in.

They practically threw her down in the chair. Malak spoke to her. MJ turned her head toward him. Her look was vacant. The once vibrant and outgoing teenager looked like the life had been beaten out of her. She needed medical attention for her wounds. I doubt she'd get it.

The judge returned. I wanted to take the knife out of my skirt and fling it at him. I was very efficient with knife throwing up to about thirty feet. He was at the far end of my range, but with adrenaline pumping through my veins, I had no doubt that I could kill him from where I was sitting. I could only picture myself doing it. I had to control my anger. Now was not the time.

Don't act out of emotion. Curly's words were the only thing restraining me. That, and I'd missed my opportunity. I should've acted before she was beaten a second time. I'd probably relive those last few minutes over and over again. Second guess myself. Alex would help me get over it. We'd both seen worse. As if that was any consolation.

The judge said, "Majahammaddan, how do you plead on the count of apostasy?"

MJ didn't speak.

"I can sentence you to fifty more lashes if you don't answer me! I'll ask one more time. Will you renounce Christianity?"

MJ put her hands on the table and pushed herself to a standing position. Her knees almost gave way, but she was able to hold herself up. Malak put his hand on her back to steady her.

"I will never deny that Jesus Christ is my Lord and savior."

A gasp went up on our side of the room. The other side erupted in shouts of derision.

"Apostate!"

"Treason!"

"Blasphemer!"

"Stone her!"

The judge hit his gavel against the table three times. MJ gingerly sat back down in her chair.

"Based on your confession of guilt, I sentence you, Majahammaddan Tabithe, to ten years in prison and one thousand lashes. The lashes are to be carried out at the rate of one hundred a year. If at any time in the ten years, the girl renounces Christianity, I will reduce her sentence to time served."

Malak remained seated. He didn't even try to present an argument on her behalf. He probably thought he'd only make things worse.

"Does the tribal attorney wish to add to the sentence?"

Her father stood.

"Yes, Your Honor. I am the tribal elder. We desire that the girl be sentenced to death by stoning."

Malak stood to his feet, "The law allows for stoning for apostasy, but may I remind the court that it has been discouraged by the Supreme Court. No person has been stoned for apostasy for several years."

"The tribe has the right to offer a sentencing suggestion," the judge said.

"And you have a right to reject it."

"I will not sentence the girl to death. But I will also not stand in the way of the tribe's judgment. I wash my hands of the matter and will turn the girl over to the tribe after she has exhausted her appeals."

He hit his gavel and said, "This court is adjourned."

I was trying to process it all.

After the courtroom cleared, Malak explained it to us. "We will appeal to the Supreme Court. That'll take about ten days for them to render a decision."

"What are our odds?" I asked.

"Fifty-fifty," Malak said. "They don't often intervene in these low-level cases. At the same time, they sometimes get involved in death penalty cases. Especially a woman of this young age."

I walked out of the courtroom and got out my phone. I saw the van driving MJ away. Our eyes met. I wanted to run after her.

I dialed Alex. Tears were running down my cheeks. I had to take a deep breath just to get the words out.

"Hi honey," he said. "How'd it go?" I knew he was probably sitting by the phone, anxiously awaiting my call.

"Not good. I need you here. Bring the whole team. Bond and Josh. Get here as soon as you can."

"What are we going to do?"

"Make these people wish they'd never been born!"

24

Diyarbakir, Turkey

Baha Dalman had not risen to the highest rank in the White Wolves without understanding what was happening around him. That's why the events of the last two weeks had him totally baffled. One of his generals, Rafiq, and four of his bodyguards, were killed in a car bombing outside his home. A Sheikh from the UAE, Saad Shakir, claimed responsibility.

While Baha had heard of the Sheikh, he'd never had any dealings with him. As far as he knew, the White Wolves hadn't had any run-ins with him either. Why would the Sheikh be targeting one of his men? The Sheikh wasn't a player in the drug trade or in arms dealing. All he knew about the Sheikh was that he was a playboy and had earned most of his money legitimately.

He hadn't retaliated against the Sheikh for a number of reasons. One, he wasn't certain the Sheikh was even behind the attacks. Sometimes rivals spread disinformation and blamed an act on a third party who had nothing to do with it. Baha didn't want to kill associates of the Sheikh who might be innocent until he had more definitive proof of the Sheikh's involvement.

Secondly, he wasn't sure he wanted to start a war with such a powerful man. The Sheikh was a cousin to the Crown Prince of the UAE. He had a net worth of fifty-to sixty-billion dollars. While the White Wolves had resources at their disposal, the sanctions against Iran and Russia by the US had cut their income in half. He wasn't sure he could win an all-out war with the Sheikh without killing him.

The most prudent thing to do was to wait it out and see what happened next. Perhaps the attack on Rafiq was personal and didn't involve the White Wolves at all. The Sheikh was a womanizer and maybe Rafiq had gotten involved with one of the Sheikh's women.

Baha sat at his desk in the headquarters of the White Wolves, contemplating his options when his phone rang.

Zamani.

The bomb expert. A freelancer who Baha suspected of killing Rafiq.

Why would he be calling me?

He started to let it go to voicemail, but curiosity got the better of his judgment.

"Salam," he answered.

"A bomb is going off in your building in less than two minutes. I saw you were there in your office. I wanted to warn you. I didn't want you to die."

"Thank you," he said to the familiar voice. Definitely Zamani. He realized how stupid it sounded to say thank you after he'd said it. Why was he thanking him for blowing up his headquarters?

"Who's behind this?" Baha asked angrily.

"Saad Shakir."

If Zamani said Saad was behind it, then he was. Zamani was a man of his word. Strange, considering he was a killer. With ethics. At least when it came to telling the truth.

A chill went down Baha's spine. If Zamani said a bomb was about to go off, that meant it was. He had to get to safety. Two minutes wasn't much time. Something he had to know first.

"Why is Saad targeting the White Wolves?" Baha asked.

The line went dead.

Baha had to hurry. He crawled under his desk. That wasn't a safe enough place.

The closet.

He got out from under his desk and practically ran to the closet off of his office. No sooner had he slammed the door shut, than the bomb exploded.

Below him. The entire building shook. He could hear a loud crashing sound coming from his office. Probably ceiling tiles falling as the entire structure of the building was likely compromised.

He waited for the shaking to stop and opened the door to his office to assess the damage. To his horror, his entire desk was gone. All that was left was a hole in the floor. Had he stayed under the desk, he would've gone crashing down a floor or two as well.

The room filled with smoke. He put a handkerchief over his mouth and went out into the hallway. Only one of Baha's lieutenants was still there, walking around in a daze. Baha took him by the arm and led him to the stairway where they made their way down to the first floor.

There, they found unspeakable carnage. The entire floor was destroyed. Several people lay dead or dying on the floor. Fearing that the building was unstable, he made his way to the outside. His lieutenant stayed behind to help the wounded. The fire inside the building was growing and now engulfed one side of it. His phone was still in his hand, so he called for fire trucks.

He tried to remember who would be inside at that time of the night. A cleaning crew. Four people probably. Three of his lieutenants were meeting in the downstairs conference room. Their bodyguards were probably inside. Two each. That totaled thirteen.

Maybe more.

Seeing the entire building about to go up in flames infuriated him. Powerful man or not, the Sheikh had crossed the line. Baha could've been killed in the attack, and he now had confirmation the Sheikh was behind it.

He was already planning his revenge.

The White Wolves didn't start this war, but he intended to finish it.

The Sheikh would die for this.

* * *

Sheikh Saad Shakir's house

The Sheikh made a decision. The models were too much trouble. After Bianca and Anya were kidnapped, only two were left in the house. Those two were taken to the yacht earlier that day to join the three already there. In a few days, he'd get rid of all five girls. He'd make them disappear in the Persian Gulf.

In the meantime, he needed to replace them.

He picked up the phone and called the cleric of his mosque.

The man answered with the traditional long Muslim greeting. The Sheikh responded with the short version.

"I want to divorce all three of my wives," the Sheikh said. He'd not yet had a chance to call the cleric to get a divorce from Anya. With the other two soon to be at the bottom of the gulf, the Sheikh, by law, had four slots available to fill with other wives.

"I can handle the paperwork immediately," the cleric answered. "Remember, that you cannot have sexual relations with your former wives from this point on."

"Understood. Take care of the paperwork so they are no longer legally my wives," the Sheikh said. "I don't want to do anything that would displease God."

The cleric began a long salutation, but Saad hung up before he finished.

He had an incoming call.

"Salam," the Sheikh said.

Zamani.

"It's done," Zamani said. "The entire building is destroyed."

"How many dead?"

"I don't know, but I saw thirteen people go in earlier in the night. Baha made it out safely."

"That's probably better for now. I'd rather he be alive to see the aftermath. He now knows that I'm not one to be messed with."

"I believe that's true. I told him you were responsible."

"Good. Next, we will demand that he return my money and painting, or I will destroy his entire organization."

"I presume *my* money will be in my account shortly," Zamani said.

"I'm sending it now. Thank you."

The line went dead.

Saad was glad Zamani was on his side.

* * *

Amina

Women's correctional facility.

MJ never came back from her trial.

Amina hadn't heard from her lawyer either. She had no clue what happened.

Did the judge find MJ not guilty and let her leave the country to be with Christopher?

Was she found guilty and sent to another jail?

Was she executed?

Amina tried not to let her imagination run wild but couldn't help it. She lay on the mattress in her cell and sobbed. While she had no idea what had happened to MJ, she feared the worst. And her trial was in three days.

To make matters worse, a guard had started to show an interest in her. Amina was allowed outside of her cell one hour a day. A guard was eyeing her and taunting her out in the courtyard. He said he was going to come into her cell in the middle of the night while she was asleep and do all kinds of disgusting things.

She'd tried to make herself go to sleep but couldn't. The fear was overwhelming. The internal injuries from the gang rape hadn't fully healed. It still hurt to walk. Her eye was better, although her vision was still blurry. It had felt good to get out of the cell and into the sunshine. She missed MJ, though.

She felt safer when MJ was there. Not that the two of them could've done anything if a guard came in. But at least having her there had made her feel like she wasn't alone.

A noise startled her.

Amina sat up from the mattress. She heard footsteps coming down the hall and stopping right in front of her cell door.

She pushed the tears out of her eyes.

MJ?

The cell door creaked open.

Not MJ.

The guard.

He walked into her cell and closed the door behind him.

25

Abu Dhabi International Airport

Alex and the AJAX team arrived at the airport the following morning. Unexpectedly, they were rested and ready to hit the ground running, showing no effects of jet lag at all. As I expected, they were already at each other's throats.

Especially Bond Digby and my husband Alex, who had the proverbial love/hate relationship. Bond was complaining because he had to fly in coach. Alex explained that they only had two first class seats. Bond lost the game of sharks. Some silly game they play when one of them had to do something or be the odd man out.

Alex and Bond were too much alike which was the problem. That, and the fact that Bond was constantly flirting with me. At first, he was halfway serious. Now I think he did it just to get under Alex's skin. The only reason Alex put up with it was because Bond was good at his job and had saved his life once. Something Bond reminded Alex of often.

A-Rad and I met them at the airport. As soon as Bond saw me, he came right up and kissed me on both cheeks.

"Hey!" Alex said. "I'm her husband. I should get to go first."

"I'm just getting her warmed up for you."

"I can do that myself, thank you very much," Alex said, as he leaned in to kiss me on the lips.

I pushed him away.

"Hey!" he said for the second time.

"It's against the law to have any public displays of affection," I reminded them. Not that they needed it. All three of them had run many operations in Arab countries. They knew the laws as well as anybody.

"You guys haven't been here for five minutes, and you're already breaking the laws," I quipped.

The reality was that they'd probably break a lot more before we were finished.

"I never did like that law," Alex said.

"You can kiss me when we get back to the plane," I joked.

"What about me?" Bond asked. "Do I get a kiss back at the plane as well?"

Alex glared at Bond. Josh pushed Bond toward the back seat of the SUV. I couldn't help but smile. It was good to have the team back together again. Before getting in the SUV, Josh gave me a wave.

We'd lucked out when we formed this team. Bond Digby was a former MI6 British intelligence officer. Everyone called him 007 for obvious reasons. If anyone could look or play the part of a James Bond, Digby could pull it off. His expertise was intelligence. He was one of the best in the business at operating in the field. He could take information, analyze it, and draw conclusions which were right more often than not.

Colonel Josh Hawley was a battle-tested veteran who did four stints in Iraq and Afghanistan during the height of the wars. His nickname was Private. The guys' way of razzing him. If it bothered him, he never let on. No one was better at battlefield strategy than Josh. Having him on our team had saved all of our lives on more than one occasion.

Our first mission together was almost a disaster. Brad, our CIA handler, sent us to Uganda to rescue a group of seventy-five school-aged girls, kidnapped from their classroom by local rebels. We found their hideout, and Josh developed a plan to attack them. Even though we were outmanned four to one, the plan worked, and we killed most of the rebels and took the others prisoner.

The problem was that the rebel's reinforcements arrived before our extraction team. A major gun battle ensued. Josh took charge and, somehow, we held them off until we ran out of ammunition. Even then, through a series of crafty maneuvers orchestrated by Josh, we were able to secure some of the enemy's weapons and stay in the fight.

Eventually, the cavalry arrived, and the girls were rescued without one of them losing their lives. That experience drew the team together in a way that three months of training with Curly never could. For all the bantering and harsh words between the four men, A-Rad, Josh, Bond, and Alex were a band of brothers. Any one of them would risk life and limb to save the other. If you asked who they'd want in a fox hole with them, they'd choose each other. If you caught them at a time when they weren't joking around.

When we got back to the plane, I gave them the mission objectives. I explained everything that had happened with MJ and Amina, Bianca and Anya, and what we might be facing in the next couple days.

Josh was tasked with developing the operational plan and was listening intently.

Bond was in charge of securing intelligence, and was staring off into the ceiling like he was deep in thought.

Alex was an expert in cyberwarfare. He suggested looking for MJ, although I didn't hold out much hope of rescuing her even if we did know where she was.

"Two days from now, Amina goes to trial," I said.

The group was huddled around the kitchen table in the center section of our luxury jet.

"This will be a simple extraction," I continued. "They'll drive Amina to the courthouse in a van. One guard. Two at the most. Rent-a-cops. After the trial, they'll bring her back out to the van. Grab her then."

"Do you want us to kill the guards?" Bond asked.

"I don't think that'll be necessary," I said.

"We'll know what to do when the time comes," Josh added.

Josh was the calmest person under fire I'd ever seen. Bullets could be flying, but the fog of war never overwhelmed him. He could still see the battlefield clearly and almost always knew exactly what to do. I'd never seen him hesitate under fire.

I'd first met him on a mission to Cuba. He was leading a team for the Air Force that flew planes into hurricanes to get weather readings. A-Rad was his pilot. Josh and I parachuted into the eye of a hurricane together in Cuba. Something we lived to tell about. But not before Josh killed four bad guys when we ran into trouble trying to rescue four teenage girls.

The mission was successful, and Josh was the first person I thought of when Brad presented us with the opportunity to build our own covert team.

"I agree with Josh," I said. "However, if the guards pose a threat to you or Amina, then take them out. Whatever it takes."

"Why don't we grab Amina when she's going *into* the courthouse?" Alex asked. "That makes the most sense."

I shook my head no.

"We need to let the trial play out. Amina's attorney thinks he can get her off on the charges. Amina was a minor when the rape occurred. The UAE civil laws don't allow punishment for minors. If she can walk from the charges, then we don't even have to do anything. Better to wait and see what the judge does."

"That makes sense," Josh said.

"But if you see Amina come out of that courthouse with a guard, you move immediately," I said.

I told them about how MJ was taken out in the yard twice and beaten.

"Don't let that happen to Amina," I added soberly. "If they bring her out to cane her, then kill the guards, and get her out of there."

"We won't let them lay a hand on her, I promise," Alex said.

The other guys voiced the same resolve.

"Let's talk about the Sheikh's house," Josh said. "Satellite imaging shows that he's got twenty to thirty guards around the house now. That'll make it more difficult to penetrate."

"I guess he did that because we snatched Anya from the house," I said.

"You didn't hear, I guess," Alex said. "A bomb went off at the White Wolves headquarters in Turkey. A dozen or more people were killed. Their leader was in the building but walked away unscathed. As you can imagine, he's on the warpath. The chatter is that he's planning an attack at some point on the Sheikh for retaliation. I'm sure the Sheikh is worried."

"Looks like you've stirred up a hornet's nest," Bond said, talking about me.

I looked over at A-Rad and he smiled, so I returned it. I explained how A-Rad used his Turkish accent to kidnap Bianca and Anya, but make it look like the White Wolves did it.

"That was the plan," I said. "I wanted the Sheikh to think the White Wolves were behind the kidnappings and that they stole the painting. I preferred them fighting each other to fighting us."

"Your plan worked to perfection," Alex said.

"We actually don't need to attack the house," I said. "The yacht is my concern."

"Aren't there still two girls in the house?" Alex asked.

"Yes. But as far as I know, they want to be there. I want to find the Canadian girl who went missing. According to Bianca, she was last seen on a boat headed for the yacht. The yacht hasn't moved in three months, so there's a chance she's still on it."

"If she's there, we'll get her off," Alex said.

"Josh, we need a plan to get to the yacht without being seen. There will likely be a couple of guards there as well."

"Step ahead of you," Josh said.

"I got the layout of the yacht," Alex explained. "And satellite images. Brad sent them to me. The bird showed there are three guards on board. With assault rifles. We didn't see the girls."

"That tells me the girls must be on the boat," I said, as my heart started beating faster. "There wouldn't be guards unless they had something to protect. There also wouldn't be three guards for just one girl. There must be more than one girl on board."

"My thoughts exactly," Josh said. "Bond and I will go to the house and check it out. We'll see what we see and get back to you with a plan."

"I'll go with you," A-Rad said. "I know where the house is. I'll drive you."

The guys went in the vault, picked out weapons and supplies, and soon were on their way. I could tell they were all excited to be back in the field and on a mission. This was what we lived for. The men had really embraced the challenge of rescuing girls which made it easier for me. These guys wouldn't risk their lives if they didn't believe in the cause.

Once they were gone, Alex looked at me with his little boyish smile that I'd grown to love.

"Now that all the kids are out of the house, maybe I can get that kiss!" he said.

I'd forgotten about giving him one when we got back to the plane.

"You can have more than that," I said, as I kissed him passionately. Hard and firm and let it linger.

After the emotions of the last two weeks, having him there was good for my soul.

I needed it.

I had a feeling the next few days were going to be just as trying if not more.

26

Amina

Courthouse

Being back at the courthouse where MJ had been so badly mistreated brought back a flood of anger and sadness as the images played in my mind like a movie. Curly always said to get rid of them as soon as possible. I liked to let them linger near the surface, so the righteous indignation stayed at a boiling point, ready to erupt at the right moment.

I didn't think I'd get my satisfaction today. The plan was to rescue Amina and get out of there as soon as possible, without anyone knowing I had anything to do with it.

The courtroom had more people in it than when MJ went through her trial. Malak and I were the only ones there representing Amina's side. The Tates and Aunt Shule thought it best not to attend, though they sent their prayers and support.

We were clearly outnumbered. Sitting behind the prosecutor were the four defendants who attacked Amina along with their attorney. Amina's mother, Samitah, sat next to her husband. Fidgeting. Because of her burqa, I couldn't see her facial expressions, but her body language said it all. She kept wringing her hands and looking around nervously. If I could see her face, I was certain it was pained. Samitah loved her daughter and hated what her father was doing to her.

Amina's father looked angry, resolved, and determined to see that his daughter got what he thought she deserved. He was looking around nervously as well, sitting on the edge of his seat like a tiger about to pounce on its prey. I was surprised he sat on the same side of the courtroom as the four men who had raped his daughter. Probably because he blamed her more than them.

Malak told me that Amina's tribe would be pushing for the death penalty for her. He was still confident that he'd get Amina off on a technicality. She was a minor at the time the rape occurred. Minors, by law couldn't be punished for crimes. Not even with lashes. Certainly not stoning. His main concern was what would happen to Amina as soon as she was set free. He worried that Amina's father would do the same thing MJ's father did and try to kill her.

I wasn't worried about that at all. He would never get the chance.

Malak sat next to me waiting for Amina to arrive.

"Have you heard from MJ?" I asked him.

"I met with her yesterday."

"How's she doing?"

"As well as could be expected, considering. She seemed more worried about Amina than anything else. She's resigned to her fate."

"There's still the appeal."

"I don't think there's much chance the Supreme Court will even hear it, much less act on it. As crazy as it is, the judge did follow the tribal law. He has a lot of latitude in handing out sentencing. He only sentenced her to lashes and jail time. The tribe sentenced her to death. The civil courts are extremely reluctant to overturn a tribal verdict. They maintain their power by keeping the tribal leaders appeased. Unfortunately, MJ is a poor girl. There's no one out there advocating on her behalf or clamoring for her release."

"Where is she?" I asked.

"The women's correctional facility in Hanadi."

I'd been hoping for that intel. Now that we knew where MJ was, I'd get the AJAX team working on a possible extraction plan, even though I didn't have much hope that we could do anything. Brad had practically forbidden it. Our team was too valuable to go on such a risky mission, he argued. The guys all reluctantly agreed.

We couldn't save everyone, so our focus today was on saving Amina. My guys had attacked Amina's extraction like a group of hungry pigs. Overkill really. Josh put together the plan to the last detail. The four of them were in a van across from the courthouse, out of sight but in close enough proximity to see what was happening. I had a radio in my ear and a microphone attached to my lapel so we could communicate with each other.

Even though everyone else was in place in the courtroom, Amina hadn't yet arrived. The four men who had attacked her kept looking my way. Glaring at me. I stared back. The one I injured when he stuck his hand in my car trying to grab my cell phone was sitting on the end, closest to me.

Fortunately, a guard was sitting right behind him. Fortunate for him. If I could, I'd wipe that smug smile off his face with one back-hand. I also had a knife hidden in my skirt. I could envision taking it and slashing his throat.

Vengeance is mine, says the Lord.

Curly said that's true and that what we did wasn't vengeance. Our job was as the facilitator of God's work. We killed the bad guys to get them before God as soon as possible. So he could extract his vengeance. Also, so they couldn't hurt anyone else. That's how I justified carrying my anger for these lowlifes. Righteous anger. Like the kind Jesus had when he drove out the moneychangers in the temple.

The radio in my ear crackled.

"Vehicle approaching," Josh said.

I didn't respond. We'd already tested the mikes so I knew they could hear me. The last thing I wanted was a guard to see me talking to my lapel and become suspicious.

"I've got eyes on your girl."

"One guard."

"Belly hanging over his belt."

"Easiest job you've ever given us."

I couldn't help but smile. We all knew when weapons were involved, there were no easy jobs. Murphy's law had a way of rearing his ugly head at the most inopportune times. The guys did have enough weapons and ammunition to fight off a small army.

In the courtroom were two guards. Counting the one with Amina, I could take out all three guards with just the knife in the hem of my skirt or the gun in the console of my car. With a van full of trained lethal killers sitting right across the street, these guards were nothing more than target practice. Like a skeet shooter mowing down one fake bird after another. Having them nearby made me even more confident than I already was that this mission would be successful.

"Your girl has some new injuries to her face," Josh said. "Somebody has roughed her up again."

The words stirred around the anger inside of me like a cook stirring a pot of boiling water. When Amina was led into the room, one or two tears almost escaped my eyes. Her face was bruised and battered again. She walked with a noticeable limp. This time, it was her right eye nearly swollen shut. I could only imagine what someone had done to her. Probably a guard in the prison.

I took a deep breath to calm myself down. Her ordeal would be over soon. I'd be able to protect her from her father. We'd get her out of there and on our plane. Out of the country. Away from these horrendous, godless people.

The judge entered the courtroom. My understanding was that the trial of the four men would begin first.

As expected, the judge's first words were, "This is the trial of four men, Tarek Quadri, Lukman Mir, Rasul Siddique, and Waseem Akbar. Are the four defendants present and represented by counsel?"

Malak leaned over and whispered, "The first guy is the one who is married."

That meant he was facing the more serious charge of adultery.

A weaselly looking man stood and said, "I am counsel for all four defendants."

"Thank you, sir," the judge said. "The prosecutor will read the charges."

"Your Honor, I will begin with the charges against three men. Lukman Mir, Rasu Siddique, and Waseem Akbar are charged with sexual indignities. My understanding is that they intend to plead guilty to the charge of having sexual relations with a woman, Amina Noorani, outside of marriage."

"Counsel, do your clients plead guilty?"

"Yes, Your Honor."

Malak leaned over and said, "They pleaded guilty, so they'd have evidence against Amina."

I didn't fully understand the system of the tribal laws but was rapidly becoming familiar with it. Enough to know it was written by men and heavily skewed for their benefit. Women were victimized twice. Once by the men and then again by the judge. Hopefully, Amina would be able to get off on a technicality. Maybe, there were pockets of justice occasionally for women in these settings. Malak said that most of the UAE wasn't like this. These were the fundamentalists. Like the people in America who blew up abortion clinics in the name of God.

"Since the three men plead guilty, I'll go direct to sentencing," the judge said.

The three men stood next to their attorney.

"Don't let the judge see a reaction out of you," Malak said.

I didn't know why he said that. I expected the men to get lashes and prison time. It would be satisfying to see them taken into the yard and beaten with a cane.

"I find you guilty as evidenced by your plea. You'll each pay a fine of 600 dirham and six months in jail. The jail sentence is reduced to time served. As soon as you pay the fine, you're free to go."

What?

No jail time. No lashes. The fine was equivalent to $160 American dollars. I'd gotten speeding tickets with bigger fines. Now I knew why

Malak had warned me to watch my reaction. I wanted to stand and scream at the judge at the top of my lungs.

When the men sat back down, the one whose wrist I injured, looked my way and started laughing at me. Almost mocking me. I bit my lip to prevent a reaction. Malak was right. I didn't want to do anything to get the attention of the judge. My head was covered with a scarf, but my face was in full view.

I only wished I had the opportunity to get that man before God today, so he could sentence him to hell.

I had to focus. Amina was why I was there. She was the one who needed me. Someday, God would make things right with the world. Atrocities and injustices were allowed in this world so that we could have free will. A just God would eventually punish the wicked. That wasn't my job. I couldn't solve all the world's injustices.

"Prosecutor, please read the charges for the fourth defendant."

"Your Honor, Tarek Quadri is accused of adultery."

"Does Mr. Quadri intend to plead guilty as well?" the judge asked.

"No, Your Honor," his counsel stood and said. "My client pleads not guilty."

"Mr. Prosecutor, please present your evidence."

Barney was sitting next to the prosecutor with his little black book in his hand. I presumed that he'd speak next.

"We have no evidence to present, Your Honor," the prosecutor said.

I almost fell out of my chair.

"Then why was he charged?" the judge asked.

"The woman is the one who brought the charge against him. She claims she was raped."

"Malak, do you care to respond as to why your client brought this accusation?"

Malak stood to his feet. I could see his hand shaking. Even as an experienced lawyer, I could see why anyone defending a woman in these circumstances would feel intimidated.

"On the night in question, these four men attacked and raped my client on the side of the road as she was walking home. As Your Honor has already heard, three of the men pled guilty to the crime and admitted that they raped her."

"I believe they admitted to having sex with her," the judge said.

"My client did not consent to the sexual encounter," Malak argued.

Malak paused like he was waiting for the judge to respond. When he didn't, he continued. "The fourth defendant was present at the rape, and my client will offer testimony that Mr. Quadri also raped her multiple times. I might add that the men brutally beat her as well, putting her in the hospital."

"They weren't charged with assault," the judge said.

"They should've been," Malak said. "I have the medical records to prove her injuries."

"I can only consider the charges before me."

"Understood. The charges before the court are serious in and of themselves. While Mr. Quadri has pleaded not guilty to rape and adultery, Your Honor does have the guilty verdict of the three men and the testimony of my client. That should be more than enough evidence for the court to find the defendant guilty of adultery."

The judge rubbed his beard.

Malak sat back down.

"Does the counsel for the defendant have a response?" the judge asked.

"Yes, Your Honor. As you know, the law requires that for a man to be accused of adultery, there must be four male witnesses of good reputation who will testify to that effect. In this instance, there are only three male witnesses. The testimony of the woman doesn't count."

Malak stood to his feet. His hand was no longer shaking and was formed into a fist.

"Your Honor, this has been a controversy for some time in our law. As you know, men don't generally forcibly rape women in front of other witnesses. Especially four of them. Therefore, rape is almost impossible to prove unless there is a videotape, or the woman becomes pregnant. In this case, however, there actually are four male witnesses. These four men were present for the attack. This is obviously a defense ploy. Three of the men pled guilty. One pled not guilty. Why? That way, the court lacks four male witnesses. The court shouldn't let the defense get away with such a travesty of justice."

The defense counsel stood. "Your Honor, my client has the right to plead not guilty. Innocent until proven guilty is not a travesty of justice. If the counsel cannot produce four male witnesses as the law requires, then I would ask Your Honor to charge the woman with slander."

It's possible the judge saw my reaction. If he didn't see it, he heard it.

"I don't believe this," I said. I'm sure my face registered my utter contempt for what I was hearing. Malak motioned with his hand for me to keep quiet.

"Stay cool, Jamie," Alex said in my ear. They could hear everything going on in the courtroom. "None of this matters. We're going to get her out of there as soon as it's over."

"Mr. Malak? Do you have a response?" the judge asked.

"The facts before the court are clear. We all know what happened that night. These men brutally raped my client and then beat her mercilessly. Putting her in the hospital for nearly a week with a severe concussion and damage to her eye."

The counsel for the married man was still standing and said, "Your Honor, I ask that you sanction counsel. He continues to slander my client with no evidence. I suggest that he either produce four male witnesses as the law requires or that he sit down and shut up."

I could add this attorney to the growing list of men in this country who I wanted to kill.

The judge paused. Probably for dramatic effect.

"The laws of this jurisdiction are clear," he said. "The prosecutor has failed to produce four male witnesses of good reputation. Three men pled guilty to a sexual relationship with the girl. That's true. I've found them guilty of that offense. Therefore, I must dismiss them as reputable witnesses. By nature of their guilty verdict, they are not men of good reputation. The testimony of the woman is not admissible without four male witnesses, so I must discard her testimony as well. Therefore, I find that there is not a single witness present who witnessed the defendant commit adultery. Therefore, I find the defendant not guilty!"

I couldn't believe what I was hearing. The four men were clapping and slapping each other on the back.

"Further, the woman brought the charge of adultery against the man without four male witnesses to support her testimony. Counsel's argument is well taken. I find Amina Noorani guilty of slander. I withhold punishment until I hear the other evidence against her."

"Unbelievable!" Alex said in my ear.

"Just say the word, and I'll take out that judge," Josh said.

Depending on what happens in Amina's trial, I might just let them. Actually, depending on how the judge treated Amina in her trial, I might not be able to stop them.

27

The guys were fired up.

After hearing firsthand what I'd been dealing with for the last few weeks, Alex, Bond, Josh, and A-Rad were ready to storm the courthouse. My ear was filled with their chatter. Amina had just sat down at the defendant's table with Malak, her attorney, and we were waiting on the judge to begin the next phase of the trial.

"Scorched earth, Private?" Bond asked Josh. We never used real names over the radio. He was asking if they should just go in and kill everyone associated with the travesty. I wished we could.

"Not yet, seven," Josh replied. Bond's nickname. "Let's let it play out. Either way, we're getting that poor girl out of here today. From the looks of her, I bet Amina was raped and beaten by a guard. Makes me sick."

"If we kill everyone in the courthouse, they can't convict us of murder," Alex said jokingly. "They need four male witnesses. We won't leave any."

The law of four witnesses only applied to women, I wanted to tell them but couldn't. If a man brought a charge, he only needed one witness. His testimony counted as one. A woman's testimony was only admissible if combined with the testimony of four men.

Absurd!

I couldn't join in the conversation over the earpiece because the courtroom was dead silent as we were all waiting on the judge to begin again. The four men who had just gotten off were practically giddy. They kept looking my way, taunting me with their eyes. The prudent thing for me to do was to ignore them, but I stared back. Squinted my eyes at them in disgust. I may have even raised my fist at one of them. I don't remember.

Truthfully, I mainly wanted to get this trial over with and Amina out of there. If this was hard on me, I'm sure it was torture for her. Especially since she didn't know what I knew. She wasn't going back to jail. The fear inside of her must've been unbearable.

The judge finally began speaking. "We will begin the trial of Amina Noorani. Prosecutor, please read the charges."

The prosecutor stood and began reading from his notes. "Amina Noorani is charged with three counts of zina. She had a sexual relationship with three men who were not her husband. The court should know that a husband has already been chosen for Amina by her father who is a tribal elder and is also present today. Her tribe has voted and unanimously asks this court to sentence Amina Noorani to death by stoning."

"Let's not get ahead of ourselves," the judge said. "I haven't found her guilty of anything."

"I think the court can proceed to sentencing, Your Honor," the prosecutor argued. "You've already found the three men guilty of having a sexual relationship with Amina. They aren't married. Neither is Amina. She is guilty simply by their testimony."

"Nevertheless, fairness would dictate that the defense has an opportunity to answer the charges."

"Fairness!" Alex scoffed through my headset. "These people wouldn't know fairness if it slapped them upside their heads."

"Does the prosecutor have any further evidence to present to the court?" the judge asked.

"Yes. Your Honor. I would also remind the court that you did already find the defendant guilty of slander."

"So, noted," the judge said. "Present your other evidence."

"We'll hear from the detective who investigated this case," the prosecutor said.

Barney stood to his feet and began reading out of his black book. "When the woman, Amina Noorani, was brought to the hospital, she told the nurse that she'd been raped by four men. That is an admission of sexual intercourse. I have the notes from the hospital. The doctor who examined her confirmed recent sexual contact. The girl is not a virgin and is unmarried."

Barney sat back down.

"There you have it, Your Honor. The woman's own words condemn her. As does the doctor's testimony. You have no choice but to find her guilty."

"Malak, how does your client plead?" the judge asked.

"Your Honor, the hospital records confirm Amina's story that she was raped by the four men. She never admitted to consensual sexual contact. She was walking along the road. The four men stopped their car. They dragged her into a ditch and forced themselves on her. Multiple times. That is not zina. That's called rape."

"Your Honor, I must object," the prosecutor said. "I would urge the court to instruct Malak to watch his language. Once again, he slanders the good name of these men. The court has already found that the defendant is unable to present the testimony of four male witnesses to confirm a rape. The law states that if a charge of rape is made by a woman without four male witnesses, then the court is to assume that the encounter was consensual."

Malak countered. "While that may be the law, common sense dictates otherwise. The doctor who examined Amina said in his report, and I quote, 'the internal injuries sustained by patient are consistent with violent and multiple forced entry.' In addition, the physician documented numerous physical injuries to Amina's head and neck where she had been struck multiple times by their fists. To the point that she had a concussion and a bruised eye socket. Does that sound like consensual sex to you, Your Honor?"

"Malak. I didn't ask you to make your case. I asked how your client wishes to plead. Does she plead not guilty or guilty to the charges before this court?"

"The evidence supports a not guilty verdict," Malak said.

I knew what he was trying to do. Malak was trying to keep from getting her on the record as having pled not guilty. If the judge found her guilty, which he might very well do, that was a crime in and of itself. Smart lawyering on Malak's part, but I doubted the judge was going to let him get away with it.

"So, your client pleads not guilty. Is that correct?" the judge asked.

"Yes. Your Honor."

"Thank you. I'm ready to make a ruling."

"Your Honor, I have more evidence for the court to consider," Malak said with urgency in his voice.

"Make it quick."

"Amina Noorani was seventeen at the time of the attack. She was a juvenile."

A murmur went through the crowd. Even the prosecutor seemed stunned by the news. He bolted out of his seat.

"I don't believe that's the case, Your Honor," the prosecutor said. "The father said to me that she was over eighteen."

"That S.O.B," I whispered in my headset. "He lied so they could charge her."

"I have a copy of her birth certificate," Malak said.

Samitah stood to her feet. "Your Honor. I'm her mother. I can tell you that she just turned eighteen last week."

"You are only to speak when spoken to," the judge said to Samitah sternly.

Samitah's husband pushed her down with such force that she fell back into her seat. He raised his hand to backhand her but must've thought better of it. At least four male witnesses were present. According to the law of the tribe, a husband was allowed to strike his wife for insubordination, but only if he didn't leave any marks. A woman didn't need four male witnesses to testify to an assault as long as she had physical bruises to prove the abuse happened.

Fortunately, Amina's father sat back down. It took a lot of courage for Samitah to defy her husband. I was sure she'd pay a price for it later. I also wondered why that principal didn't apply to rape laws as well. Amina clearly had physical injuries to support the rape claim. As Malak argued, common sense would demand that a woman wouldn't voluntarily submit herself to the physical abuse that Amina went through.

Malak handed the prosecutor and the judge a copy of the birth certificate. After looking it over, the judge said, "This looks to be a legitimate stamped copy of the defendant's birth certificate. She was clearly a minor at the time of the incident."

"You can still find her guilty, Your Honor," the prosecutor said.

"I can and I do find her guilty of the charges of zina."

"Your Honor!" Malak said in protest.

The judge held up his hand.

"But... the law doesn't allow me to impose any punishment on a minor. So, while the defendant is guilty of having sex outside of marriage, the court will not impose any jail time or lashes."

"Thank you, Your Honor," Malak said.

I had a hard time controlling my jubilation.

The guys were disappointed.

"Damn!" Bond said. "I wanted to kill that bloody judge." Bond was from England and had a heavy British accent.

"Give me five minutes alone with the four guys. They'll wish they were dead," Alex said.

I let them vent.

The prosecutor stood to his feet. I shushed the guys through my microphone so I could hear what he was about to say.

"Your Honor, the defendant is not a minor today. May I remind the court that you have already found the defendant guilty of slander. Bringing a charge of adultery against a man without four male witnesses to support it is slander and punishable."

Malak stood to his feet. "Even that so-called slander was before her eighteenth birthday. The rape charge was made at the time she was brought into the hospital."

"The court has heard the defendant make claims of rape against the four men today, Your Honor," the prosecutor said. "She has slandered the four male defendants right in front of you. You heard it yourself."

"My client has yet to speak in this courtroom today, Your Honor," Malak countered.

"She has spoken through you, Malak," the judge said. "You're her attorney, advocating on her behalf. Whatever claims you make are her claims. The prosecutor makes a good point. She has claimed that the three defendants raped her and that the married man committed adultery with her."

"This court has already found otherwise," the prosecutor said. "You found no evidence of rape by the three defendants, and you found Tarek Quadri not guilty of adultery. Therefore, the defendant has slandered all four men in this courtroom today. The court has proof in front of you that she is over eighteen. The court should find her guilty of actions from today and sentence her to lashes and prison based on those offenses."

"Get your guns ready," Josh said. "We're going to put a stop to this."

I wanted to tell him to stand down, but I felt the same way.

"Further, Your Honor, the defendant pled not guilty to the charges of zina. You found her guilty. May I remind the court, that pleading not guilty to a crime you actually did commit is a crime in and of itself."

"I object to this whole ridiculous prosecutorial argument," Malak said. "The defendant was a minor. She should be found not guilty and released. All she did today was profess her innocence on the basis that she was a juvenile at the time of the attack. The prosecutor lost his case, and now he's trying to find some way to punish a woman who has already been punished enough by the actions of the defendants."

"I'm ready to rule," the judge said.

"Better rule the right way if you want to live, you scumbag," Alex said.

"I previously found the defendant guilty of slander. I also found the defendant guilty of zina as a minor. I've ruled that the offenses occurred before her eighteenth birthday and won't result in any punishment. For the slander and perjury committed by the defendant today, I find her guilty. I sentence her to six months in prison. If she takes sixty lashes today, I will reduce the sentence to time served."

"Arsehole," Bond said. "Let me take out the judge."

"I'll take the prosecutor," Josh said.

"The four lowlifes are mine," Alex said.

"You lay a hand on that girl, and I'll shoot you in the head," A-Rad said, speaking out for the first time. He rarely spoke on the radio.

We did have a dilemma. If we let her take the sixty lashes, then she was free to go. We could also rescue her, but it had its risks.

"Does the tribe wish to impose a further sentence?" the judge asked.

The father stood. "I am the tribal elder. We wish to impose a sentence of two hundred lashes and death by stoning."

"The father is dead meat," Josh said angrily.

The judge was silent for a good thirty seconds. He was rubbing his beard again. Something I was beginning to think he did for show.

"I sentence Amina Noorani to one hundred lashes and death by stoning!"

"Thank you, Your Honor," the father said.

Malak stood to object.

"Sit back down, Malak," the judge said. "I order that since the tribal elders have imposed the sentence, that they be the ones to carry it out. The lashes and the stoning shall all be at the same time. This court will not order the lashes today. The defendant also has the right to appeal."

"Let's roll," Josh said. I could hear the van doors open.

"Hold on," I whispered. "I have an idea."

I stood from my seat and walked over to Malak and told him my idea.

"Who are you?" the judge asked me.

"She's a friend of the defendant, Your Honor," Malak said.

"She needs to sit back down," the judge said.

I sat down right behind Malak. Not before I had a chance to touch Amina's shoulder in a weak attempt to comfort her.

"I have a request of the court," Malak said.

"Make it brief," the judge replied.

"What are we doing?" Josh said. "We're ready to infiltrate."

"Dolly said to wait! Don't move until she gives us the word to go," Alex said. Dolly was my handle for the radio.

Malak began. "Three days ago, the court sentenced Majahammaddan Tabithe to stoning as well. That ruling is on appeal to the Supreme Court. We intend to appeal the court's ruling today."

"As is your right."

"Should the Supreme Court reject the appeals for both girls, we request that the court order that the two sentences of stoning be carried out together. At the same time. The girls are friends."

The prosecutor stood. "We don't have any objection to that, Your Honor."

"Neither do we," the father stood and said.

"If there's no objection, then so ordered," the judge said. "The court's adjourned."

The judge hit his table with the gavel and stood and left the room.

"Do you want us to grab Amina or not?" Alex asked me.

I put my hand over my mouth pretending to cough, so I could speak without anyone noticing. "This is a chance for us to get MJ out as well. We'll make our move at the stoning."

"Do you really want to take that chance?" Alex said. "Amina is right here. We could lose her, too."

"You're also sending her back to that prison, where she was abused by a guard," Josh said. "Are you sure that's what you want to do?"

The arguments confused me. Before I was sure. Now I wasn't.

"Dolly?" Alex said. "We need an answer."

"I have eyes on the girl," Josh said. "The guard is leading her to the van. Running out of time here."

"Stand down," I said.

"Are you sure?" Josh asked.

"No. But that's what we're going to do."

"Everyone back to the van," Josh ordered.

I hope I didn't just make a big mistake.

28

Malak and I stayed at the courthouse for a good half hour after Amina's trial was over, discussing the events of the day. He was clearly distressed that both Amina and MJ had gotten the death penalty, and he was unable to prevent it. To me, things might still work out.

"We have a better shot at getting Amina's case overturned by the Supreme Court," Malak said, understandably angry.

"She was a juvenile. We don't kill minors in this country. The judge was wrong in letting the tribe punish her. Hopefully, the Supreme Court will do the right thing and reverse the sentence."

I couldn't say why, but I hoped that wasn't true. If my plan worked, MJ and Amina would be taken to the center of the village square to be stoned to death by the tribal men. Our team would be there to rescue them. If the Supreme Court freed Amina, we'd be back in the same predicament. We had no way to save MJ from stoning. Amina might also be released into the custody of her father without our knowledge. I was sure he'd kill her if given the chance. Preventing both of those scenarios created all kinds of problems.

We had to rescue the girls but also protect our cover. Brad had gone to great lengths to set up AJAX. Things were going well. We couldn't risk blowing our cover just to save a couple girls. With the girls together in the square, the team could sweep in wearing masks, rescue the girls, and the authorities would have no way to stop it. The girls would be on our plane in no time and out of the country to safety.

"Keep me posted," I said, as we walked out of the courthouse. Malak had my cell phone and would notify me as soon as he heard anything. Especially if a date was set for the execution.

I got in my car and sat there for a couple minutes, staring off into space. Thinking. My mind started to turn toward the Sheikh. We'd have at least ten days before we could do anything about MJ and Amina. I was anxious to start working on finding Odille.

I saw a flash out of the corner of my eye.

Then screeching tires.

A car pulled in right behind mine. Like the driver was trying to block me in.

I could still get out if I wanted. Curly trained us to always park our cars in such a way that no one could completely block us in. Fortunately, I had done so. Something that was now a habit for me.

In the center console was my gun. I opened it and slipped the gun into my skirt pocket. Then opened the door and stepped out of the car.

Four men were already out of the vehicle.

The four men who attacked Amina!

I closed the door to my car but kept my back to it so they wouldn't have the chance to circle around me. Adrenaline now pulsed through my veins. Not from fear. From elation and anticipation. I couldn't believe my luck. These men intended to attack me. Clearly. This was my chance to kill them. A chance I thought might come at the stoning. Even then, the guys were the ones who were going to carry out that mission. I'd have to be a bystander to protect our cover. Never in my wildest dreams did I think I'd get an opportunity or the satisfaction of disposing of these men myself.

"Vanhan fe taregana lagayam beck ma falnah lamina!" the married guy said to me in Arabic.

I think he said, *we're going to do to you what we did to Amina.*

I didn't think they'd do it right in front of the courthouse. The road was right there. I preferred more privacy as well. They hadn't made a move yet. Probably for that reason. So, I surprised them. Curly always said in a fight to make your first move a surprise. Throw your opponent off guard.

"Let's go around back," I said as I pointed to the back of the court-house.

A big smile came on their faces. They pointed for me to go first.

I assessed my options. The four men were not imposing in the least. Skinny. Unskilled, more than likely. That's why they preyed on women. I wasn't at all concerned about them hurting me. Even with four against one.

The question was, *how am I going to hurt them?*

They had to die, for sure. That much was certain. If I left them alive, they could testify that I did this to them. The easiest thing to do was pull out my gun and shoot them as soon as we went around the corner of the backside of the courthouse.

No witnesses. Clean kills. Unsolved murders. They'd never suspect that I did the killings. Amina's father might even get the blame.

But... that was too easy.

The men needed to suffer.

I had a knife in my pocket that would do the trick. It'd kill them, but not until they felt some pain. I could think of a half a dozen places to strike them with a knife that resulted in a slow and painful death.

We were nearing the corner of the courthouse. While we were walk-ing, I took the knife out of my skirt. Hidden from view, but sharp and ready to inflict damage. The men were surprisingly silent. When we rounded the corner, I stayed close to the building. The configuration I wanted was the four of them to be in a half moon, crescent shape so that my back was to the wall and no one was behind me.

Me in the middle of a circle was the only situation where a lucky blow from a blind spot might incapacitate me to the point where the men could win the fight. Not likely, but I didn't want to give them that chance.

Normally, I warned people before they fought me. I usually gave them a chance to walk away. Not this time. This was an opportunity that I'd been dreaming of. The anger inside me was on the verge of erupting, even though I was calm and cool on the outside. The men had to wonder why I was so calm. I suspected that Amina wasn't the first girl they had attacked. I'm sure they'd never seen a victim act like I was acting.

"Al-dhay wahid munkim yered an yamout ola?" I asked. *Which one of you wants to die first?*

Their smug grins turned to anger mixed with confusion. I didn't give them a chance to answer. Curly always said when faced with more than one combatant, I should dictate who I would attack first. After that, I couldn't necessarily control the order. That depended on the men. Once the first blow was struck, I had to rely on instincts. Until then, I could make my first move a well-thought-out lethal blow.

Married guy was on my left. For some reason, I held the most animosity for him. I took a step his way, then turned toward him. My back was to the guy to the right, but that was by design.

With one motion, I stepped my right foot across my left so that my right hand which held the knife was across my body. With speed and force, I brought my right hand back in an arc, as married guy started toward me.

His eyes widened when he saw the knife. Right before I slashed him across the throat. Cutting his jugular. I purposefully lessened the angle so that the cut wasn't deep. Deep enough to cut the vein, but not deep enough to kill him instantly.

He collapsed to the ground clutching his throat. The guy behind me was already moving. I expected that. Without even looking, I set my feet and brought my right heel backward. I'd either hit him in the groin or in his stomach. The shot was a direct hit to his groin, because when I turned back toward him, he was doubled over clutching his private parts. His head was about at my waist level.

Perfect.

I brought the knife high in the air and then down in a slashing motion. From right to left at a slight angle. It made contact at his temple just above his eyebrow and continued down his face. Penetrating his eye. Then cutting off half his nose. Finally, splitting his lip in two.

He screamed in horror.

I didn't have time to admire my handiwork.

The other two men were already on me. The one to my right reared back to hit me with his left hand. Somehow, in fights, I always got lucky. His left hand was high in the air. Perfect target for my knife which was still in my right hand.

I slipped the punch by stepping into it and thrust the knife into his chest. Between the ribs. It penetrated his heart. He collapsed to the ground. Probably dead before he hit it.

Oh well.

In a fight, you can't have everything you want.

The last guy took one look at the two men flailing away on the ground and the one dead, and he turned to take off running. I left the knife in the third victim and gave chase. I tackled him before he was ten feet away. I flipped him over from his back to his stomach and then pinned his arms down with my legs. He struggled to get away, but I am surprisingly strong.

His eyes were darting side to side in fear.

"Please don't kill me," he said.

"Don't speak to me," I said angrily. Then I took the palm of my left hand and smashed it into his right eye. For Amina. That was the same eye they'd damaged on her. I balled my right fist raising the knuckle on my middle finger slightly above the others. Then I smashed the knuckle into his throat, crushing his larynx and windpipe.

Of the four, he probably had it the worst. He lay on the ground writhing in pain. His hands clutching his throat. Trying to catch a breath that he'd never be able to get. It'd take about three minutes, but he'd die.

I stood and assessed the others.

One was dead. The other two would bleed out in a matter of minutes. I took their watches and wallets, so it'd look like a possible robbery. I retrieved the knife and cleaned the blade on one of their shirts.

Not bad.

I wish Curly could see my handiwork. He always quipped that I was better with my hands than with a knife. Now, I wasn't so sure. I'd worked on my knife skills for hours to prove him wrong.

I couldn't wait to tell him what I'd done. Four guys. Twenty seconds. All dead. Perfect kills. Efficient.

Curly would find something wrong with it.

I let the one guy get a punch off. The fourth guy could've gotten away. I should've used my gun. I acted out of emotions rather than mission expediency. Curly always argued to end a fight as soon as possible. Use the most lethal weapon at your disposal.

Maybe I wouldn't tell him about it. Now that I'd thought about it, Curly was right. I did too many things wrong.

Oh well.

The only thing that mattered was the outcome. The four guys were dead. I looked around and didn't see any witnesses.

Those four men didn't face judgment for their crimes here on earth because of a corrupt system of laws and judges and prosecutors who used the system to abuse women.

They were now before God. I was the facilitator. Whatever vengeance God wanted to mete out, was up to him.

I was satisfied.

29

Abu Dhabi International Airport
Eleven days later

"I don't like the plan," Josh said.

"It's your plan!" I responded.

"I know, Jamie. And I don't like it."

"I don't like it either," Brad said on a secured video conference line.

The rest of us were sitting in the plane discussing our plan to infiltrate the Sheikh's yacht to see if any girls were being held captive there.

Josh was in charge of developing the plan and was having doubts.

We would've acted sooner, but Brad insisted we take our time, gather intel, and put together an MSO. Mission Success Odds. If they weren't high, then we'd call off the mission. High MSO meaning in the ninety percent range, which was next to impossible given the mission involved twenty-to-thirty armed guards surrounding the Sheikh's house.

We didn't even have the element of surprise going for us. While no one was expecting us to launch an attack, the Sheikh was expecting the White Wolves to try something which was the reason for the heavy security presence.

"We've looked at all the other alternatives, and this was the best plan," I said.

"If it goes to hell, you and A-Rad will be sitting ducks," Brad said.

"That's why I think I should be the one to go with Jamie," Josh replied.

I let out a sigh. One of the things I hated most was rehashing the same arguments over and over again. We'd been through these various options a dozen times.

"A-Rad is the most proficient at hot wiring the boat," I said. "If we make it to the boat without anyone spotting us, he's going to have to get the engine running quickly."

"How are you going to get across the beach unnoticed?" Brad asked. "Can't you come in from the water?"

The Sheikh had a boat at his dock. We determined that was the best way to get to the yacht. A-Rad would hot wire the boat, we'd drive it out to the yacht, kill the three guards, search the yacht for the girls, and then drive the boat up the coast where we'd ditch it on the beach. From there, we'd hike to a rendezvous point on the road where they'd pick us up and we'd come back to the plane. Hopefully, with one or more rescued girls.

We discussed the water option and dismissed it, but Brad wasn't in on those discussions, so Josh filled him in on why. "I don't want them in the water because of the stonefish," Josh answered, "and the sea snakes."

Stonefish were the most venomous fish in the world, and a sea snake bite was ten times more lethal than that of a king cobra. They're all over the muddy bottom of the Persian Gulf and liked to live in shallow water.

"We need to keep Jamie and A-Rad out of the water," Josh added.

"I agree with that," A-Rad said, shuddering his shoulders.

I did too. I'd go in the water to save the girls if I had to, but I wouldn't like it.

"You don't even know if the girls are on the yacht," Brad argued.

I let out a groan. We'd had that argument with Brad before. I was losing patience.

"There are three guards on the yacht," I said for the umpteenth time. "They're guarding something."

"The boat is worth five-hundred-million dollars. If it were mine, I think I'd have a guard as well."

"Maybe," I said.

"Have you actually laid eyes on any of the girls?" Brad asked.

He already knew the answer to that question but clearly asked it to cement his point. We hadn't seen any sign of the girls. None of the satellite images picked up anyone but the guards. I assumed the girls were being kept below deck. If they were there at all.

Alex was surprisingly quiet. Probably because this was my mission, so he was letting me take the lead. Something I appreciated. Rarely, if ever, did Alex play the *I'm the man, you're the woman* card. He treated me as his equal in every way. What I say goes—a sharp contrast to what I'd witnessed in the tribal court.

"You need to get more intel," Brad said.

I shook my head no. So did Josh.

"Tonight is a moonless night," Josh said. "I mean... it's not moonless. It's cloudy out. If we're going to go, we need to go when there's no moon illuminating the beach."

Another reason we'd waited so long to act. Every night, the moon had been clear and bright. There's no way we could've gotten across the beach unnoticed. Even with the clouds, we might not be able to make it unseen. The biggest risk to the plan was running across the beach in plain sight of the guards. If they spotted us, we would be sitting ducks. At that point, we'd have to shoot our way out of the situation.

Not ideal, but if this was the plan, then we needed to go when we had the best opportunity for success. When there was no moon visible.

I added, "Also, MJ and Amina are scheduled to be executed two days from now. As soon as we snatch them, we all need to get out of the country right away. If we're going to rescue Odille then we need to do it before we rescue MJ and Amina."

Malak let me know he heard from the Supreme Court, and they rejected both of the girl's appeals. He was despondent, but I was thrilled.

That meant we could rescue them. He gave me the place and time, and Josh was already working on an extraction plan.

"You don't even know if Odille is on the yacht," Brad said.

"We've been over that ground several times," Alex spoke up. "I agree with Jamie. The guards are there for a reason. You only need one guard to watch a yacht. You don't need three. We need to find out if Odille is there. For Jamie's peace of mind, if for nothing else. We don't want to leave any girls behind."

I touched Alex's hand to let him know I appreciated the support.

"Then it's settled," Josh said. "We'll go tonight. But I'm in charge of the mission. If I see something I don't like, we'll abort. Agreed?"

Everyone nodded in agreement.

"Are you on board with that, Brad?" Josh asked.

"I am. I trust your judgment, Josh. Don't let those two do something stupid."

He meant Alex and me. I wasn't offended. Brad was right. Since I had the AJAX team around me, I took less risks. A couple days before, I had the idea to go to Dubai, rent a boat, and get to the yacht from the water. That took the guards at the Sheikh's house out of play.

If I hadn't had the team around, that's what I might've done. Josh looked at the suggestion and dismissed it out of hand. He showed me why on a map.

"These are Iranian waters. The Gulf is patrolled by Iranian warships and submarines. They'd track your every move from the moment you left the marina. You stray too far from the shore, and they'd be on you in a second."

Not a good plan.

We said goodbye to Brad, signed off the secured line, and then took a vote. One no and we wouldn't go.

Everyone voted yes.

"Great!" Josh said. "Let's go over the plan again."

My mind was elsewhere. On a girl I'd never met. I'd never even seen her face. I couldn't pick her out if she walked right by me on the street. But I was risking my life for her. She didn't even know it. Didn't matter. My heart was already beating out of my chest. This was what I lived for. Rescuing girls.

Odille was on the yacht. I could feel it. I had a sixth sense about these things. It might be stupid. Brad might be right.

If I were Odille, I'd want someone to come and rescue me.

Stupid or not, that's exactly what I intended to do.

* * *

The Sheikh's house

Everyone was in position.

A-Rad and I hid behind some trees to the east of the dock. Near the beach. About fifty yards away from the pier that led to the twenty-five-foot speed boat. Bond was to the west, situated behind a sand berm. He would have our back if a threat came from that direction.

Alex and Josh were strategically situated higher up, looking down on the Sheikh's estate. From their vantage point, they could see the entire area, except for a blind spot directly behind the house. Bond had eyes on that location. Josh had done a good job situating everyone.

The three of them had assault rifles. A-Rad and I carried small arms and a couple explosive devices in case we needed a diversion. And a FOG. Fast Obscurant Grenade. To provide instant cover if necessary by creating a smoke screen around us.

The beach was dark. The only light was from the reflection of the lamplights around the swimming pool and the ground lights leading from the house to the dock. Our path was clear until we got to the pier. The guards were primarily situated on the front and side of the house. They clearly didn't expect a threat to come from the Gulf.

"How does it look, Private?" I asked through our radios.

"All clear here," Josh said. "You've got a clear path. Seven? Are we a go?"

"All clear," Bond said. 007 was Bond's nickname, but they called him seven for radio expediency.

"On the move," I said, as A-Rad and I sprinted for the boat. We slowed as we got to the dock and into the lighted area. I prayed the guards weren't paying attention. I bolted onto the pier with A-Rad right behind me. We slowed our pace once we got on the wood so we wouldn't make any noise.

After a few steps, the darkness engulfed us again all the way down the pier to the location of the boat. An eerie feeling came over me as we ran down the deck, wondering if someone was going to shoot us in the back.

I flung my backpack over the side of the boat and slipped into the center of it, keeping my head down. A-Rad followed me.

"We're in," I said.

"We saw you," Bond said. "I can't believe you let a girl outrun you, Willy."

"Shut up," A-Rad said as he pulled out his tools to begin hotwiring the boat. He estimated that it'd take him about ten minutes.

Willy was A-Rad's nickname. The antithesis of A-Rad on purpose. William Shoemaker was a professional jockey. He stood four feet ten inches tall and weighed ninety-one pounds. A-Rad was a huge man. Not overweight. Just bulky. I forgot how much he said he could bench press, but it was a lot. He also loved shoes for some reason. Sneakers actually. He was always on the lookout for a new pair of high-end sneakers. A-Rad hated the nickname, which was why it stuck.

Mine was Dolly, as in Dolly Parton. Because my boobs weren't that big. I barely filled out an A cup. I'd always been lean and thin. I hated the nickname, but pretended to like it, so the guys would search for a new one. So far, they hadn't come up with one. If I were to suggest one, they'd dismiss it out of hand. The whole point of a nickname was for it to be funny. At some point, the right nickname would come along.

Alex was Whiskers for the longest time because he couldn't grow a beard if his life depended on it. By noon, Bond had a five o'clock shadow. Something he continually teased Alex about and held over him.

"You should be with a real man, Jamie," Bond would say. "Someone who can actually grow a beard."

A few times, I thought the two of them were going to come to blows. Probably would at some point if Bond kept it up. That's why I made them change it. Now they call Alex, Bama, which was not any better than Whiskers. Alex was the starting quarterback for the Stanford Cardinals. They lost in the national championship game to Alabama. Alex played a great game, but the defense gave up a touchdown on the last play. Alex was a good sport and played along, but I could tell that the nickname Bama hit him where it hurt.

I allowed myself to stick my head up long enough to look out at the yacht. It looked huge even from a distance. Majestic. The lighting around it illuminated the sea, creating almost an aura, except from below not from above.

Lights were on below deck. I was certain it had to be the girls. One guard was on the stern and one on the aft. I couldn't see them from that distance, but every time we took a picture from a satellite, they were in the same location. A third guard rotated with them. Once a week, the Sheikh changed out the guards.

The boat we were on took supplies to the yacht once a week. Bond thought the supplies were more than what would be needed for three guards. Another circumstantial piece of evidence that the yacht had more than three people on it.

A-Rad cursed under his breath as he struggled with something. I knew enough to leave him alone so he wouldn't be distracted.

Then something caught my eye. Nothing more than a glisten in the Gulf.

A flash of light.

I heard what sounded like a small engine. Maybe two.

And a wake. I strained to see if I heard it again.

Before I could send it across the radio, gunfire erupted.

I ducked my head down.

The radio exploded with noise.

"Who's shooting?" Josh asked with urgency in his voice.

"Not me!" Bond said. "Sounds like it's coming from the water."

I peered over the side of the boat.

Then ducked down again as a barrage of gunfire rained down around us.

30

"Keep your head down, Dolly," Josh said.

He didn't have to tell me. It felt like we were in the middle of a major firefight. We were cowered down behind the engine block. Just in case a stray bullet came our way.

Josh started giving us a blow-by-blow account of the action. Like a ring announcer for a boxing match.

Bond filled in what Josh couldn't see.

"Two amphibian vehicles landed on the beach," Josh said.

"Twelve to fifteen hostiles piled out of each," Bond added. "They opened fire on the guards."

"The Sheikh's guards are engaging them back," Josh said. "But they're outmanned."

"Sounds like tracer fire," I said.

"It is. The hostiles are mowing them down," Bond reported.

"That's what we're seeing as well," Josh said. "These guys on the boat are good. Who the hell are they?"

I think I knew. They were the White Wolves. Coming to exact revenge. Not perfect timing, but something we could use to our advantage. As long as they didn't know we were there.

"Hostiles just breached the house," Bond said.

"Two guards are fleeing. Bama, take them out. No witnesses."

"I'm on it," Alex said.

"Two more coming your way, Bama," Bond said.

"I see them."

I heard eight distant shots. I suspected Alex killed them. Two shots each. Efficient.

"Four tangos down," Alex confirmed.

The action was fast and furious. As soon as one guy stopped to take a breath, another was filling up the radio with more urgent information.

"I got a dozen or more dead in the back," Bond said. "A bloody massacre."

"More dead on the side of the house. What are the hostiles doing now?" Josh asked.

"A dozen or so are in the back, guarding the perimeter. Don't look up, Dolly. They might see you."

I didn't intend to, even though the curiosity was eating away at me.

"I have eyes on the Sheikh," Bond suddenly said excitedly. "Hostiles are dragging him out of the house."

Up to that point, Bond had been speaking in a mostly monotone voice. His words suddenly reached a fever pitch.

"The Sheikh's in one of the boats!" Bond said. "I repeat. The Sheikh has been kidnapped!"

"Confirmed. I can see him," Josh said.

All of that was happening near us. I could hear the shouting. I had to look up. Twenty feet or so to the right side was the boat Josh had described. To the left was the other one. Some hostiles were gathering up their wounded and putting them in the boat to the left. The boat to my right shoved off to sea. The Sheikh was sitting in it. Half dressed. A stunned and vacant look had taken control of his face. His head was down, and shoulders slumped. Like he was resolved to his fate. Blood was coming from his nose and upper lip.

The boats sped away. Full throttle. This time they didn't try to disguise their engines. I ducked back down. I could hear the bottom of the boats pounding the waves until they were away from the shoreline.

I looked up again and my gaze followed them out to sea. The boats made no move toward the yacht which was my next concern.

"Anybody left alive?" Josh asked.

"I don't think so," Bond replied.

"We're coming down. Approach carefully," Josh said. "Dolly, you can come up for air now."

A-Rad and I stood up. I stretched my arms and legs and then assessed the situation. Feeling safe, we got out of the boat and walked down the pier back toward the house. I had my gun drawn though, just in case.

The smoke from the machine guns still hung as a haze over the scene. The back of the house looked like something you'd see in a movie. Bodies were strewn everywhere. Bullets had busted the large panoramic windows along the back. Bullet holes had peppered the stucco and siding. The swimming pool had blood in it from where one of the guards fell in.

I approached the house with my gun still drawn. A-Rad followed right behind me, sweeping his gun from left to right and back again. Down when we came across a casualty. He made sure they were dead.

"Bama and I are going to clear the house," Josh said. "Seven, keep your eyes peeled."

"I'm coming in too," I said. "There may be two girls still here. You guys clear the downstairs. I'm going upstairs to where the Sheikh kept the girls."

I had both hands on my raised weapon. I checked before going around every corner. My shoulders were taut, and my finger tense as I eased up the stairs. Not bothering to look behind me. A-Rad still had my back covered.

At the top of the stairs was a long and wide hallway. Rooms were on each side, and I remembered from the floor plans a large kitchen and living room area at the end of the hall. I cleared the first two rooms. They didn't seem like they had been lived in recently.

I didn't find anything after searching the entire upstairs.

The girls were gone.

* * *

Clearing the house took a while since it was over sixty thousand square feet.

Alex was going through the Sheikh's office and bedroom.

A-Rad found the keys to the boat, so he didn't need to hotwire it. He also found the keys to the yacht.

Josh was doing what Josh was good at. As a Colonel, he'd seen many battlefields after the fog of war dissipated. He was assessing the situation to decide what to do with the dead. He decided to leave them where they lay. The White Wolves left a note, so they'd get the blame for the carnage. Josh made sure the note was in clear view for the authorities to see once they arrived. Which hopefully, wouldn't be for a few days.

Alex made sure the security footage was erased.

They were each telling us what they were doing over the radio.

Bond was still outside and kept his eyes on the yacht to make sure there was no movement. He also watched the road to make sure no one approached. Through his binoculars, he could see the guards on the yacht standing on the edge, looking our way. They'd clearly heard the gunfire but couldn't know what had happened.

The men on the yacht kept calling the house over a radio wondering what was going on.

That gave me an idea.

I said to A-Rad, "Tell the guys on the yacht that we're going to come and pick them up. Tell them there was an attack, but the Sheikh survived it. Ask them how many girls are still on the boat."

A-Rad took a deep breath, picked up the microphone and said in Arabic, "We're okay. The Sheikh is alive. Inshallah."

That made me smile. A-Rad wasn't known for his intellect. I thought he was smarter than most people gave him credit. He was playing the part perfectly. Down to exactly what a Muslim would say.

"We will send the boat for you soon," A-Rad continued. "The Sheikh wants the girls brought to the house."

"Okay."

"How many girls are there?"

"Five."

My heart did several somersaults.

Five more to fit on the plane.

Including Bianca and Anya, we were nearing the numbers to where Brad might even think this was a valuable mission.

Alex came out of the Sheikh's office. "Not much intel in there that Brad would be interested in."

"Did you see a file for the yacht?" I asked.

"I did."

"Is the title in it?"

"It is."

I could feel a huge smile come over my face. Then Alex's eyes widened.

"Are you thinking what I think you're thinking?" Alex asked.

"Why not? The Sheikh's not going to be using it ever again."

"We stole the jet from Omer. Why couldn't we steal the Sheikh's yacht?" Alex asked.

"Can you change the transponder ID?"

Alex had changed the transponder ID on the airplane, so it identified as an AJAX plane so we could get it out of Belarus undetected.

"It's called an AIS. Automatic Identification System. I'm sure the yacht has one. All I have to do is turn it off, then it can't be tracked by satellite. But I should wait until we're out of the Persian Gulf. I'm sure the Iranians recognize the Sheikh's yacht, and it comes and goes all the time. No one knows he's been kidnapped. If I turn it off beforehand, it might draw scrutiny."

"Can you drive it?"

"I don't see why not. You don't drive a yacht though. You captain it. Or skipper it."

"What direction will you go?"

"After I get out of the Persian Gulf, I can go around the tip of Africa and then home. That would take too long. I can go through the Suez Canal. That's a lot shorter route. That's probably how I'll go. Once we get home, we'll give the yacht a new name, and no one will ever know it belonged to the Sheikh. It'll belong to AJAX."

"This is great. I wondered how we were going to get all the girls out of the country. You can take the five girls on the yacht. We'll sneak MJ and Amina on the plane."

"So, we're really going to do this?" Alex said.

"One thing we've got to do first," I said.

"What's that?"

"We've got to kill the guards on the yacht."

31

Odille

"How do you want to play this, Josh?" I asked.

We were discussing a plan to attack the guards on the yacht and rescue the five girls. The White Wolves had done all the fighting for us at the house. So far, we'd captured the Sheikh's house without firing a shot. Actually, Alex fired eight shots to prevent four guards from escaping. That hardly counted as a firefight. They never got a shot off at him. Probably never even knew what hit them.

"It won't be so easy to do if they know we're coming," Josh said.

"And they'll see us coming as soon as we leave the pier," Alex said.

"It's dark enough that they won't know *who's* coming. They'll think it's one of their own," I said.

"They'll be on high alert, though," Josh retorted. "They saw the fire-fight. They can probably see all the dead guards laying on the ground. I know A-Rad told them everything's okay. But I have to believe they'll still be on edge."

"We have a long-range rifle in the SUV," Alex said.

"That'll help. We still need to get close. You've got the wind and the bouncing waves. It won't be easy to hit them from a distance. We also have only one rifle. As soon as they hear the first shot, the other two will scatter. If they get to high ground, in this instance, the upper deck of the yacht, they can hold us off for a long time."

"I also don't want to fill the yacht with bullet holes," Alex said, looking over at me.

We smiled at each other. Josh didn't know about our plan to steal the yacht. We didn't want to ruin our new toy with a firefight.

"I have an idea," I said motioning for Alex and Josh to follow me.

A-Rad was still monitoring the radio so I explained my plan to him and then to Josh and Alex. Everyone liked it.

A-Rad picked up the microphone and radioed the men on the yacht. "We're going to come out and get you. Keep the girls below deck. Have all three guards come to the back of the ship and help us dock with you. Don't worry about the girls. We'll take care of them."

"Okay," the man on the other end said.

A-Rad signed off.

"Good job," I said. "That sounded believable."

A-Rad made it easier for us. The guards would be in perfect position for us to kill them if they followed his instructions. The yacht had a lower platform, water level, where passengers got on and off. The area was well lit, but they wouldn't see us until the last minute.

"I'll go get the rifle and meet you at the pier," Josh said. "Jamie, you should stay here."

"Not going to happen. I want to be there when we rescue the girls. I'm hoping and praying Odille is there. I'll be worried the entire time if I'm not with you."

"All right," Josh said. "Bond and A-Rad can stay here in case there's any trouble."

Josh was down at the pier in no time. The boat started right up with the key, and we were on our way. Once we were on the water, an eerie feeling came over me. I could see the lights from the house behind us and the lights from the yacht ahead of us. Other than that, everything was pitch black. A slight warm breeze combined with the salt spray from the warm Persian Gulf water was refreshing, but the lights reminded me of the danger ahead.

Alex steered the boat, and we were soon at the yacht. He circled around and approached from the back, careful to keep us out of the lights of the yacht which illuminated a radius of several hundred feet around the perimeter. The yacht was even bigger up close. Other than a cruise ship, I'd never seen anything that big before on the water.

The three guards were on the platform as A-Rad had instructed. They had their assault rifles around their shoulders, so they didn't act like they were anticipating any trouble.

Alex idled the boat.

Josh raised the rifle and aimed. He didn't shoot right away. It appeared he was judging the up and down motion of the boat, so he could time his shot. I had a handgun, but we were too far away for me to hit a second target.

The sound of the first shot pierced the calmness of the night. One of the guards fell right where he'd been standing. Josh reloaded the rifle and aimed to fire again.

Just as he fired the second shot, a wave hit the boat, rocking it slightly. Our own wake had reached us. Josh lost his balance, and the shot flew harmlessly into the ocean, missing the yacht entirely.

The two remaining guards bolted off the platform and onto the middle level of the yacht before I could get off a shot. Alex pulled up to the platform and Josh jumped out and tied us down.

One of the guards stuck his head up from behind the railing. I warned Josh and he dove for the back wall of the lower decking a moment before the guard got a shot off. I fired a warning shot in the direction of the guard, and he ducked back down.

It looked as though he retreated because I could no longer see him. Alex and I exited the boat and put our backs against the wall, cutting off any shooting angle from above.

Josh gave us the okay sign that he wasn't hit. He held up three fingers meaning he was going up the stairs when the fingers were countdown to zero.

3. 2. 1.

Josh rushed up the stairs in a flash. No shots were fired, so Alex and I followed. We didn't bring radios which I now realized was a mistake. Everything had to be done by hand signals.

We split up. Josh motioned for me to go to the left and Alex to the right. Josh continued up the stairs to the upper deck. He needed to secure the highest level. I went along a walkway, with the ocean directly to my left and the inside of the yacht to my right.

I raised my handgun with both hands. Ahead was a corner, and I slowly glanced around it and then returned to my position with my back against the wall. I didn't see anyone. In this circumstance, I had to be careful not to hastily pull the trigger even if I did see a person. I didn't know exactly where Alex and Josh were.

When I looked around the corner again, I saw a flash of movement. Definitely one of the guards. I didn't see him clearly enough to get off a shot. He was on the move. I ran after him. We went through the kitchen galley. Then out the other side. Toward the front of the ship. I was cautious in exiting the galley which gave him the advantage. He had thrown caution to the wind and was running away as fast as he could.

The other way now. Sprinting down the walkway, back toward the boat we came in on.

I knew his plan. If he got on the boat, he'd get away and we'd be stranded. I could clearly see him, but I didn't have a good shot, so I sprinted after him. He made it to the platform before I bridged the gap. When I got there, he was untying the boat. I tackled him and rolled him over.

The yacht rose ever so slowly from the sea, but enough to cause me to lose my grip on him. He dove into the water. It looked like he was going to swim to the back of the boat and board it that way. Without thinking, I dove in after him.

He got around to the back and started to climb up the back steps. I reached up and grabbed him by the belt buckle and pulled him back into the water with me.

The salt water burned my eyes from the splash, and I swallowed water when I took a big gulp of air as he dragged me underwater with him. I fought my way back to the surface, still trying to maintain my grip on him. He was kicking and trying to get away. Flailing away at my head and neck. It took all my strength to keep my head above water.

I felt something brush my leg and released my grip on the man as a bolt of fear shot through me like a dart.

A Sea Snake.

Had to be.

The man let out a scream of horror as he must've felt or seen the same thing. Josh had warned us about the sea snakes. Their venom was lethal, and I could die within minutes if one bit me.

The current had pulled us away from the boat. I began swimming toward it, no longer concerned about the man. He'd never survive in the Gulf. We'd drifted further away than I thought. I was a strong swimmer but wasn't going nearly as fast as I would've liked. At any moment, I expected one of the deadly creatures to rear its ugly head and bite me.

I could hear the man behind me fighting for his life but didn't dare look.

I heard a gunshot.

Coming from the yacht.

I could only assume that either Josh or Alex had engaged the third guard.

By the time I made it to the platform, Alex was there. It must've been Josh who fired the shot. Alex reached out and pulled me up like I was a rag doll and set me on the platform.

Then he pointed to the water.

I could see a sea snake slithering away. It looked to be four feet long.

I bent over from the exertion and tried to catch my breath. We couldn't see the guard but could hear him in the water. Screaming for help. "I've been bit," he kept saying. Eventually, we didn't hear him anymore.

I heard a splash come from the other side of the boat. Alex and I bolted up the stairs to look to see what made it.

Josh came running down the walkway toward us from the front of the boat.

"We heard a splash," I said.

"That was one of the guards. I threw him overboard. He's dead."

Josh scrutinized my wet hair and clothes. "You went in the water?" he asked.

"I went after one of the guards. He's dead as well. I think a sea snake got him. Almost got me, too."

Josh put his arm around my shoulder and squeezed it.

"We made this harder than it had to be," Josh said.

"At least they're dead. Let's go find the girls," Alex said. We'd do a mission critique later.

I was right behind him. Josh followed. By instinct, he still had his gun raised. I'd lost mine in the water during the tussle with the guard. Alex had holstered his.

The yacht was more luxurious than I'd imagined it to be. Alex led us through room after room of sheer extravagance. I couldn't wait until Alex and I could be alone on it. Relaxing somewhere warm and tropical. While the Persian Gulf qualified as warm and tropical, this was far from relaxing. I'd be glad when this nightmare was over. We'd made a big step in that direction tonight.

It wasn't over, though. In two days, we had to save Amina and MJ. That'd be another pulse-pounding, nerve-wracking experience, as I had no idea what to expect at the execution. All I knew was that I was going to bring a lot of firepower to the situation. And the element of surprise.

We found the five girls in the lower cabins. They appeared to all be in the same room with the door locked. We tried to forcibly open the door and heard a couple screams from inside.

I always kept a small pin hidden on me for that reason. I pulled it out and picked the lock.

"How did you do that so fast?" Josh asked. "It'd take me ten minutes to pick that lock."

"I robbed houses in my former life," I said jokingly.

I entered first. Five beautiful girls in shorts and tee shirts were standing together on one side of the room. Not cowering, but they backed up when we entered the room. I recognized two of them from the art gallery. Their eyes widened in surprise making me think they recognized me as well.

"Don't be afraid," I said. "We're here to rescue you."

"Oh. Thank God," one of them said. "I remember you from the gallery."

"Are one of you Odille?" I asked.

One of the girls raised her hand halfway and put it back down right away.

"A lot of people are looking for you," I said.

Odille introduced us to the other four girls. I quizzed them on what had happened to them. They all had horrifying stories of how they were trapped in the same way Bianca and Anya were. None of them had believed they were signing up to become high-end prostitutes. They almost seemed apologetic. Like this whole mess was their fault. I tried to be reassuring.

"The Sheikh was going to kill us," Odille said. "I'm sure of it."

"The guards said as much," one of the other girls said. "He said that one day they'd sail out into the Persian Gulf, tie a weight to our legs, and throw us overboard. Never to be heard from again. I believe them."

The girls were opening up. Talking faster. All of them adding to the story.

"They kept us locked in this room and wouldn't let us out," Odille said. "They brought us food and water a couple times a day, but that was it."

"The Sheikh is dead," I said. "We'll take you home. Or wherever you want to go."

"Anywhere but here," Odille said as the other girls voiced their agreement.

"I'm going to go check out the yacht and learn how to captain it," Alex said, then left the room.

I led the girls to the deck. They were practically overwhelmed with excitement to be out in the fresh air. Finally, able to get out of their dungeon. Even though their room would be considered luxury accommodations in most instances, when being held captive, it certainly wouldn't feel like it.

The joy on their faces was heartwarming. These were the moments I lived for. That's what made the danger worth it. There's something incredibly fulfilling about seeing these girls' faces when they're finally out of danger. Although the thought occurred to me that they were not completely out of danger. I wouldn't feel comfortable until Alex had them out of the Persian Gulf and away from Iranian waters.

"We've got to go back to the house to get a few things," I said to them. "Do you girls want to come with us? Get your feet on land for a few minutes. Alex is going to drive you out of here on the yacht as soon as possible. He wants to be out of the Persian Gulf before first light."

Alex wasn't around to correct me for saying drive the yacht.

"No way!" one of the girls said. "I don't ever want to step foot in that house again."

"I don't blame you."

"Can you get my passport from the house?" Odille asked.

"Mine, too," one of the other girls said.

"I'll look. It won't matter, though. We'll take care of everything you need and get you another one."

"I can't believe the Sheikh's dead," Odille said. "I guess that means we'll never get paid either."

That gave me an idea. Alex had seized almost a billion dollars of the Sheikh's money.

"You're all going to get paid. Three hundred thousand euros. Just like your contract says. The only thing is that you have to sign a confidentiality agreement."

"What's that?" one of them said.

"It means that you won't tell anyone what happened here tonight. You forget you ever saw me or the two guys with me. How you escaped is our little secret? Can you do that?"

"Yes!"

"Great. Once you get to land, we'll get all your information, and wire you the money to whatever account you want."

The girls all gave me a hug and kept effusively thanking me.

"I'm so sorry you all had to go through this," I said. "Promise me you'll never fall for something like this again."

"We promise."

Alex was back with a captain's hat and shirt on. I laughed out loud. The shirt was two sizes too small. He wore it anyway, even though he was only able to get one button latched. His six pack abs were showing. I had to admit he looked sexy in that outfit.

"This is my husband, Bama," I said to the girls.

"You can call me Skipper," Alex quipped.

That might have to be Alex's new nickname.

He pulled me aside to talk privately.

"I'm torn," he said.

"Why's that?" I answered.

"If I bring Bond with me, then these girls are going to have to endure his constant flirtations for four or five days. I'll also have to put up with his nonsense. Imagine Bond and me alone in the ocean for that many days. But... if I leave him with you, then you'll have to put up with him constantly hitting on you. What should I do?"

"Definitely, take him with you," I said, laughing. Releasing a lot of tension that had built up over the day.

"Okay. I can do that."

"Just don't throw him overboard," I said.

"I'm not making any promises."

I laughed again, releasing even more tension. The first time in several days I didn't feel the weight of the world on my shoulders. Then I thought of MJ and Amina and the weight returned.

Heavier than before.

32

Amina and MJ

Day of the stoning

The village square had the feel of a carnival show. Excitement. Anticipation. A flurry of activity. Shop owners moved some of their wares to the outside and were vending items on the sidewalk. The men had a bounce in their steps and walked around with their chests out and heads held high like they were about to do something that made them feel important.

The contrast with the women couldn't have been starker. They walked around in slow motion. Like someone had drugged them with tranquilizers. Their faces were vacant. Numb even. At least those who weren't completely covered by burqas. Even they had their heads down, and their sagging shoulders indicated a collective state of resignation. Probably just glad it wasn't them being stoned in the village square by their oppressors. Namely the husbands, fathers, brothers, and sons of the village tribes. Ironic, considering these women gave birth and raised the very men who turned around and abused them.

The lowest of the low in my opinion. MJ and Amina were eighteen years old. Innocent of any crime if common sense and fairness were applied. Not even guilty of bucking the heavy-handed system. Just a victim of a depraved tyranny where a man can commit a crime against a woman, and *she's* punished for it.

I was confused.

Three holes were dug in the center of the village square. There must be three girls who were going to be stoned.

Malak had explained to me the process. The girls would be brought from the jail in a van and paraded in front of the mob of men who were congregated on one side of the square. The women of the village were forced to stand together on the other side to watch. Supposedly as a deterrent to make them think twice before they defied the men.

The sentences would be read by a tribal elder. Amina still had to endure a hundred lashes. MJ would be spared lashes since she still hadn't recovered from the hundred administered at her trial and had only been sentenced to a hundred per year. A man had in his hand the cane that would be used to administer the so-called justice. After the lashes, the girls would be placed in the holes and buried up to their necks, with only their heads sticking up out of the ground.

The men would pick up stones that were piled in front of them. One by one they'd take turns throwing them. The tribal elders would cast the first stones. Not so much stones as small rocks. The rocks couldn't be too big or too small. Too big, and the blow to the head could kill the girls too quickly. Too small, and they wouldn't inflict enough pain. A doctor would periodically stop the process to see if the girls were dead. If they weren't, the carnage would continue until they were. The bodies would then be left in place for several days for the townspeople to view.

Something I knew wasn't going to happen.

The crowd was getting restless. The girls should've already arrived. I knew they were never coming.

Josh had come up with a brilliant plan. He didn't think rescuing the girls in the square was a good idea. There'd only be a couple of guards with guns, but that wasn't what Josh was worried about. Hundreds of men would be armed with stones which could become weapons if thrown their way.

The last thing we wanted to do was open fire on the men and have mass casualties. Not that I cared what happened to them. I just feared that the airports would be locked down, road checkpoints would be set up, and getting the girls out of the country would be more difficult.

Josh decided to stop the van right after they left the prison. They'd force the vehicle off the road, hogtie the guards, or kill them if they resisted, and then take the girls back to the plane. There, they'd hide them in the vault until I got back and then we'd leave the country for good.

I already had confirmation that the plan worked. Josh and A-Rad safely captured the girls.

Packages are wrapped, Josh's text to me read.

That meant the girls were safe. He didn't mention a third girl, but I was certain they would rescue her as well if she was indeed in the van.

About fifteen minutes from now, they'd arrive at the airport and load the girls onto the plane. The security guard at the gate was paid a handsome sum to let them through without inspecting the vehicle.

So, why was I there?

Brad would say it was on account of my stubbornness. Curly would say my emotions were getting the best of me again. I had my reasons. One, I wanted to convince Aunt Shule and Samitah to come with us. That hadn't gone well.

"I'm too old to start over again in another country," Aunt Shule said. "I'm comfortable in my home. I'll be okay. God will watch over me."

"I have five other kids," Samitah said. "Two girls. I'll have grand-daughters soon. Someone has to stay here and protect them. I'm so happy for Amina, though. Please take good care of my baby."

Samitah shot down my second reason for being there.

"Please don't kill my husband," she said. "He's our financial provider. If he's dead, I'll have to marry his brother. He's even worse if you can imagine."

I couldn't imagine it, but I had to trust her judgment. The two guns in each of my pockets would have to stay there.

That left the third and final reason why I was still there.

Barney.

He came right up to me as soon as he saw me.

"Do you know anything about four murders behind the courthouse?" Barney asked accusingly.

He stared at me intently. Like he was trying to ascertain if I had a reaction. See if I was lying. It took all of my self-control not to laugh in his face. I was a trained liar. I could beat a lie detector. Was trained to never give away a "tell" even under extreme torture. Barney was a buffoon. He couldn't tell anything from my expression, even if I did make a mistake, which I didn't.

"Four people were murdered at the courthouse? My word! Who were they?"

"The four men on trial."

"Really. Do you know who did it?"

"I think it was you."

"It wasn't me. How did he kill them?"

"I never said it was a he."

"It'd have to be. A girl is no match for four, big, strong men." My words dripped with sarcasm. The closest I'd come to giving anything away.

"Where were you at the time of the murders?"

I had to give Barney a little credit. He was setting me up. He hadn't said when the murders occurred. If I answered with an alibi, he'd know I was lying. This wasn't my first rodeo, as the saying goes.

"When were the murders?" I asked.

"The day of Amina Noorani's trial."

Barney looked at his watch. He must be wondering why the van hadn't arrived for the stoning. They were more than fifteen minutes late by that point.

"You saw me at the trial," I said. "I left afterward."

"No, you didn't. I saw you there talking to Amina's attorney. After everyone else left."

"I think the father would be the primary suspect, don't you?"

"Why's that?"

"If somebody raped my daughter, I'd want to kill them."

"Do you want to get arrested for slander? The men were found not guilty of rape."

"Oh yeah. I forgot."

"Don't leave," he said sternly. "I'm not through with you. After the stoning, I want to question you further."

Barney walked away and began talking to the tribal elders. The sense of urgency was ratcheting up with every passing minute that the girls didn't show.

I had no intention of leaving.

I know.

I was stubborn that way.

Barney took out his phone and dialed a number. Probably checking to see if the guards had left the prison.

He hung up the phone and started walking briskly toward his car. I made a beeline for my black SUV.

Barney sped away. I followed at a distance.

Twenty minutes later we came upon the van that had been holding the girls. Barney pulled to the side of the road and got out of his car with his gun drawn.

I parked a distance away and walked over carefully, so he wouldn't see me.

Barney looked in the van. What he saw caused him to spring into action. He holstered his weapon and opened the door. I wasn't going to let him free the guards.

Within seconds, I was ten feet away from him with one of my guns pointed directly at him.

"Close the van door and then step away from it," I said.

He did as he was told.

"Put your hands in the air," I said roughly.

Barney lifted his hands. I took several steps forward, so I was about eight feet away.

"I do have a confession to make," I said softly. I didn't want the guards to hear my voice.

"What's that?" Barney said.

"I did kill those four guys. It wasn't murder though. Self-defense. They attacked me first."

"The judge will decide if you're guilty of murder."

"Oh, I'm guilty of murder," I said.

"So, you admit it," he said.

"I admit that I'm guilty of murdering you," I said.

His eyes widened as soon as the words registered.

I fired one shot. Right between his eyes. A red dot appeared in the lower part of his forehead.

Barney stood there like a statue for several seconds. His eyes stared straight ahead. Fixed right on me.

Then he fell forward. Like a tree that'd been felled by a logger.

His head smacked against the ground with a crack and his body with a thud.

I checked for a pulse.

A wave of satisfaction came over me when I didn't feel one.

I could leave the country now. My work was done.

Ten girls rescued.

The four men who raped Amina, dead.

Barney dead.

MJ and Christopher soon to be reunited in America.

AJAX got a new yacht, a forty-million-dollar painting, and nearly a billion dollars in cash from the Sheikh.

The wealth of the sinner is stored up for the righteous.

Justice. To the extent that we can find justice on this earth for the heinous acts of some evil men.

The only thing I wondered was—what happened to the Sheikh?

33

Kayapinar, Turkey

B aha Dalman, the leader of the White Wolves, entered the prison where Sheikh Saad Shakir was being held. He covered his nose and mouth from the vileness and stench coming from the cells that held prisoners condemned to die.

The Sheikh was in the last prison cell on the right, deep in the bowels of the prison. Baha stood outside the ten-by-ten cage looking through the bars. He'd ordered the Sheikh tortured almost nonstop for five days. Waterboarded dozens of times. Electric shock to various parts of his body. Physical beatings to within an inch of his life. The Sheikh almost died several times but was resuscitated per his instructions.

"Keep him alive until I can question him," Baha had ordered the guards.

He had to know why the Sheikh started the war with the White Wolves. He'd been warned that the Sheikh was practically incoherent.

"Salam," Baha said to the shell of a man cowering in the corner of the cell.

The Sheikh mumbled something. Maybe the Muslim greeting. He couldn't be sure.

"Why have you done this, my friend?" Baha asked. "You killed Rafiq and bombed my building. Killed my men. Why?"

Strange calling his enemy his friend except that the teachings of his religion commanded him to love his enemies.

The Sheikh mumbled something. Baha could barely make out what he said.

"Speak up," Baha ordered. "I can't understand you."

The Sheikh said something about stolen money and a painting.

"I don't know anything about a painting," he said to him. "What money?"

The Sheikh was sobbing in the corner. Huddled like a baby.

Baha walked away.

He said to the guard, "Kill him. Then burn the body. I have no further use of him."

I guess I'll never know why he decided to attack us.

Not The End

GET YOUR FREE GIFT

As a thank you for finishing my book, I want to give you a free gift. Go to terrytoler.com and sign up for my mailing list and I'll give you the first three chapters of *The Launch*, a Jamie Austen novella free of charge.

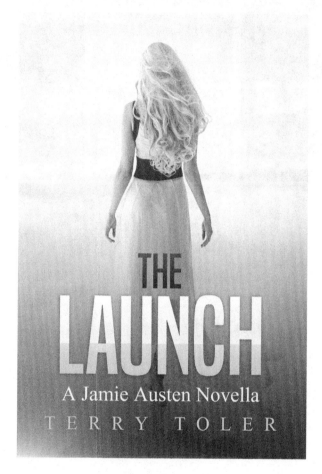

Terrytoler.com

SPY STORIES

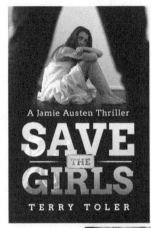

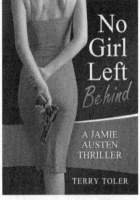
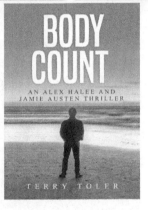

Thank you for purchasing this novel from best selling author, Terry Toler. As an additional thank you, Terry wants to give you a free gift.

Sign up for:

Updates
New Releases
Announcements

At terrytoler.com.

We'll send you the first three chapters of The Launch, a Jamie Austen novella, free of charge. The one that started the Spy Stories and Eden Stories Franchises.

BeHoldings Publishing

Made in the USA
Las Vegas, NV
09 November 2023

80518500R00152